THE WOMAN WHO MET HERSELF

LAURA PEARSON

B
Boldwood

First published in Great Britain in 2025 by Boldwood Books Ltd.

Copyright © Laura Pearson, 2025

Cover Design by Lizzie Gardiner

Cover Images: Shutterstock and Adobe Stock

The moral right of Lizzie Gardiner to be identified as the author of this work has been asserted in accordance with the Copyright, Designs and Patents Act 1988.

All rights reserved. No part of this book may be reproduced in any form or by any electronic or mechanical means, including information storage and retrieval systems, without written permission from the author, except for the use of brief quotations in a book review. This book is a work of fiction and, except in the case of historical fact, any resemblance to actual persons, living or dead, is purely coincidental.

Every effort has been made to obtain the necessary permissions with reference to copyright material, both illustrative and quoted. We apologise for any omissions in this respect and will be pleased to make the appropriate acknowledgements in any future edition.

A CIP catalogue record for this book is available from the British Library.

Paperback ISBN 978-1-83603-465-0

Large Print ISBN 978-1-83603-466-7

Hardback ISBN 978-1-83603-464-3

Ebook ISBN 978-1-83603-467-4

Kindle ISBN 978-1-83603-468-1

Audio CD ISBN 978-1-83603-459-9

MP3 CD ISBN 978-1-83603-460-5

Digital audio download ISBN 978-1-83603-461-2

This book is printed on certified sustainable paper. Boldwood Books is dedicated to putting sustainability at the heart of our business. For more information please visit https://www.boldwoodbooks.com/about-us/sustainability/

Boldwood Books Ltd, 23 Bowerdean Street, London, SW6 3TN

www.boldwoodbooks.com

For my editor, Isobel. I can't thank you enough.

PROLOGUE

When two cars are involved in a head-on collision, you know the impact on both will be huge. That afterwards, whether they're written off or patched up, those cars will bear the imprint of one another. And it's the same with people.

Ruth Waverley is sixty-two when it happens. She lives with her husband Nigel in a spacious house on the edge of Loughborough, and she has twin sons who have grown up and moved out. One has started a family of his own. She has a small business, making cakes for birthdays and weddings in her large, light-filled kitchen. You might think she has it easy. But you'd be wrong.

Debbie Jones is also sixty-two. She lives alone. Her husband Richie died from a sudden heart attack a year ago. They hadn't had children. Debbie had moved to Loughborough on a whim, for a new start. She'd taken a job going door to door, cajoling people into signing up to make regular donations to a mental health charity. You might think her life is a bit empty. But you'd be wrong about that, too.

1

Ruth stands back, wipes her hands on her striped apron, and admires her work. The spring sun is streaming through the window as if it's been specifically asked to highlight the wedding cake she's just finished decorating. It has four tiers, each a different flavour, with icing that has the barest hint of pink, raspberry macarons cascading down one side, and figures in the likeness of the bride, the groom and their dog standing on the top. She blows air out of her cheeks and then lurches forward to rescue a macaron that is sliding, sticking it firmly back in its place. She's learned the hard way that it is essential to let a cake settle for a while before announcing that it's ready for collection. Last-minute adjustments are common. Once she is happy, she'll go through her emails on the iPad, make a shopping list for ingredients. Tomorrow, she is doing a cake for a divorce party – her first – and the customer has said Ruth can do what she likes, as long as it features the band Queen, vodka and stilettos. Ruth had raised her eyebrows at that.

There is no doubt that the requests are getting more and more outlandish. When she'd started doing this – God, was it thirty years ago? – people had always just asked for a three-tier wedding cake with white ribbon around each tier and a floral decoration on the top. Or for kids' birthdays, mums had asked for a swimming cake or a football cake or a teddy bear cake, and it had been pretty much up to her how she interpreted that. Now a swimming cake is expected to be a pool complete with swimmers, a lifeguard, rubber rings and diving boards. If a kid likes Maltesers, it is no longer enough to make a chocolate cake and decorate it with them. No, you have to suspend a Maltesers bag several inches above the cake and have the little balls pouring out and onto the cake's surface.

She can't really complain. She likes what she does, and the increasingly challenging requests certainly stop her from getting bored. She likes the fact that she can work from her own kitchen, that she isn't answerable to anyone. It's just the attitude of some of the customers she finds hard to take. The expectations. Ruth never meant to go into the baking business. Before she had her boys, she worked as a secretary, and after... Well, women didn't really work after, back then. Not for the early years, at least. But baking was something she'd always enjoyed and when she invited mum friends to celebrate the birthdays of her two sons, they heaped praise on the candle-filled cakes she swept out of the kitchen with. One day, someone asked if she would make one for their child. Said she would, of course, pay. And it grew from there. Now, she has a Facebook page, a rudimentary website, and she spends most of her evenings fielding WhatsApp messages from people who have mostly left it too late and want to pay a pittance.

Ruth puts the kettle on and sends a message to Nigel.

> Cup of tea?

She waits for the ticks to appear to show it's been delivered, but they don't turn blue, meaning he hasn't read the message. She'll just make him one anyway. Despite them having a good-sized house with four bedrooms and only the two of them living in it, Nigel had one of those garden office pods delivered during the first Covid lockdown and now he works from the bottom of the garden three days a week. Sometimes, Ruth forgets he's there. Sometimes, when he's in the actual office, she forgets he isn't in the garden. She's been known to take him a mug of tea, being careful not to slip on the wet slabs, only to find the pod locked up. On those occasions, she would cast her mind back to the morning, trying to remember him leaving the house. But she had an endless memory of mornings in which he did and didn't leave the house, and she found it hard to pinpoint which one was the latest. Ruth's sister, Kate, says that Ruth and Nigel have stopped seeing each other. That they are like wallpaper to one another at this point. And Ruth doesn't disagree.

She makes the tea and puts some biscuits on a plate. She never used to buy biscuits, would always make them. Cookies and shortbread and, when the boys were small, gingerbread men. But there isn't time now, with all these outlandish cakes to be made. She is pretty sure there's a request in her inbox waiting to be dealt with that involves making a pair of sponge roller skates. Ruth leaves her tea on the side and goes down to the end of the garden, where she is pretty sure she'll find Nigel frowning at his computer. She does. He looks up with an expression of confusion when she opens the door. As if he has no idea what tea and biscuits are, or that he has a wife, for that matter.

'Thanks,' he says, reaching to take her offerings from her.

'It's fish pie for tea,' she says. 'Is six o'clock okay?'

'Better make it seven.' He turns back to the screen.

Ruth stands there for a moment, thinking the exchange isn't

quite finished, but it becomes apparent that it is, so she shuffles out and back up to the house for her own cup of tea.

While she is waiting for it to cool, she fires off messages to both of her sons.

To Max:

> Hey love, how are you all? Hope you're getting some sleep. Send more photos of gorgeous Grace when you have a minute.

To Chris:

> How did the big meeting go? Will we see you at the weekend?

She checks her phone a few times, but neither of them replies. There were times, when they were little, that she would have given anything for this. To sit, alone in a quiet house, with a cup of tea. It seemed like an impossible dream when they clung to her legs and her arms and followed her into the toilet and often crawled into her bed in the early hours. And now that she has all the peace and time alone she could possibly want, she finds that she misses them terribly. She misses them as chubby, mischievous toddlers, the way they planted their hands on her chest when they fell asleep on her. She misses them as awkward pre-teens, with front teeth that were too big for their mouths and appetites she could never satisfy. She even misses them as sullen teenagers who wouldn't keep their rooms tidy and sometimes went days barely speaking to her, before seeking her out and telling her all the ins and outs of their latest dilemmas.

Now, they are halfway through their thirties and caught up in their busy lives, and she suspects they rarely give her a thought. Chris is in London with an impressive-sounding job in finance that she doesn't understand, and Max is closer to home,

The Woman Who Met Herself 7

in Leicester, with a wife and new baby and a business and no spare time.

Ruth opens up her iPad and starts scrolling through the latest baking messages – enquiries, confirmations, and the occasional change to a request (a couple of years ago, she got a message that read 'Sorry, asked for Peppa Pig but as of this morning the pig is out and the Paw Patrol are in. Is it too late to switch?' and had answered through gritted teeth that it was fine before taking the cake from the fridge and doing a reshaping job, using Peppa's nose to make Marshall's ears). And when she's convinced that she's as up to date as she needs to be, she goes into the lounge and turns on Netflix. She likes to watch reality TV shows about people falling in love. When things start to fall apart for the couples, she loses interest, abandons the series partway through. It is the beginning that she craves, when they have just met and they are full of wonder and hope.

Every now and then, Nigel suggests she retires. Some of their friends have taken the plunge, and they could afford to join them in their endless leisure. Nigel claims he's working until he's sixty-five and not a day more, but the thought of all those empty days scares Ruth a bit. She worries that she would fall down a reality TV rabbit hole and never come out. No, she will keep going as long as her hands are steady enough to decorate. She's been perfecting a brownie recipe, testing various iterations out on Nigel and her sister. She's thinking about expanding, if anything.

There's a ping from her phone and her heart lifts, wondering which of her boys has been in touch. But it's her sister, Kate.

> With Mum. She says she hasn't seen you in weeks. Do you think we could just stop going, and she wouldn't know the difference?

Ruth visits their mum every Tuesday, Kate goes every Thursday. On Sundays, they take it in turns to drive and they go together, before dropping the car back and heading to the pub, where they talk about how shit it all is and encourage each other to drink more wine. She considers Kate's message. Would their mum know, if they didn't go at all? She knows Kate's at least half joking but there's temptation in it. The care home is nice enough, but it always smells faintly of urine and bleach, and if you turn your head when walking past other residents' rooms, you always wish you hadn't.

When their dad died, their mum said to both of them that she would stay at home as long as she could, but she didn't expect either of them to move her into their homes. She was clear that she might have to go into a facility at some point, if she survived longer than she was able to look after herself. Ruth and Kate had discussed it at length. Was it a double bluff? Was she angling for them to say that of course she could move in with them and they wouldn't hear of her going to a home? Silently, Ruth acknowledged that if their mother was going to live with one of them, it would have to be her. Kate's house was smaller and fuller – her son James was still at home and her daughter Connie was back and forth with her own two daughters in tow, depending on the current status of her marriage. They decided, between them, to take it at face value. And so when their mum started showing signs of confusion, started thinking she was a young girl and the war wasn't long over, started occasionally wandering around the neighbourhood in her nightdress at all hours, they found the nicest place they could and moved her in. That was three years ago, and now it's hit and miss whether she knows who they are. Sometimes, Ruth will hold her hand and tell her that she's her daughter, and her mum will look so baffled for a moment or two, before relaxing and saying either her name or her sister's. They've agreed between them that as long as she thinks it's one of them, that's good enough, so they don't correct her.

Ruth sends Kate a reply.

> Could we still go to the pub on Sundays if we stopped visiting Mum?

This is how they cope. They pretend, both of them, that it doesn't tear them apart that their mother is reduced to this shell of a person with a rapidly deteriorating brain. They make jokes, and drink wine, and help each other through it.

By the time Ruth gets replies from her sons, she's stopped expecting them. Max's comes on the Saturday, two days after her message.

> Are you free to have Grace next Saturday? I have to work and Layla's hoping to see her uni friends.

She doesn't reply immediately. She knows she's doing it as a sort of punishment and she knows, too, that he won't notice. Grace is seven months old and crawling. She's harder work than when she just slept and ate. And Nigel's bound to be useless, claiming he doesn't know what to do with babies, as if that's something that is inherent in women. There were long days with the boys when she had no idea what to do, when she sang every nursery rhyme she could think of before looking at the clock and seeing that a mere seven minutes had passed. But Ruth knows she'll say yes. Eventually. She ends up holding out for almost an hour.

She doesn't hear from Chris until Monday, which makes her question about whether they'll see him at the weekend rather redundant. He's single and lives alone and comes home for the weekend (for a good dinner, Ruth often thinks) about once a month.

> Work manic. Maybe next wknd.

She types out a reply saying that it would be lovely to see him whenever he has the time. And then she deletes it without sending.

2

Less than a mile away, Debbie is leaving her rented terraced house and stepping out into the spring sun. It's the first day of her new job, and she is wearing a lanyard to prove she isn't a scammer and has a bundle of sign-up forms and leaflets in her bag. As she makes her way on foot to the area she's been asked to cover today to meet her new colleagues, she goes over the initial script in her head. *Of course, we've all had times when we've struggled in life. We all deal with grief, and stress, and change, but some people find it harder to cope than others. What we're doing, at Hopeful Horizons, is trying to reach out to those people who are in trouble and give them a helping hand, or be there at the end of the phone when they come to us for help.* She's personalised it, like they said to at the induction session. She knows she'll get a lot of doors slammed in her face, but hopefully she'll get some people signed up too.

Debbie feels sure that this is the ideal job for her. She'll be out walking, getting a bit of exercise, and she'll be talking to people, which is her favourite thing to do. Obviously the weather will play a part. It won't be quite so appealing to get out there on a blustery or rainy day, but she knows how to wrap herself up. What's that saying Richie used sometimes? *No such thing as bad weather, just the wrong clothes.* Something like that. She has a good raincoat and a hat and gloves for winter. She'll be fine. The only thing she's worried about is someone breaking down and telling her they've lost someone to suicide. But if that happens, she will handle it in the same way she handled tears when she was working at the Citizens Advice Bureau. Sympathy and smiles.

The street she's starting on is just another couple of minutes away when she sees a tree in full pink blossom and is struck by a memory of her and Richie on one of their walks. Him, reaching up to pick a flower from the tree and tucking it into her hair. After she lost him, she found these memories hard. They were so vivid. She's always had them, but it's different now he's gone. But she's learned, over the past year, to embrace them. To feel lucky to have had him, to have these lovely memories to draw on. Under her breath, she speaks to him.

'I'm doing okay, Richie. Don't you worry about me.'

And then she's at the corner of Queen's Road where she's due to meet her teammates in – she checks her watch – two minutes. Not bad at all. Debbie prides herself on never being too early or too late. She doesn't want to waste her own time and she doesn't want to waste anyone else's either. She looks down at her walking boots. No blisters for her. And when she looks up again, there are two men approaching from different directions. Both considerably taller than her, neither of them more than about twenty. She can see their lanyards swinging as they walk. When they get close enough, she offers a cheery hello, and they nod in response.

It turns out they know each other, Matty and Jitu. They're both students at the university. Different courses, but they've seen each other in passing. They had a seminar together last term and they know some of the same people. Debbie watches as they do a complicated-looking handshake and hopes they won't try to do it with her. They don't.

'Right then,' she says. 'How shall we divide up the streets we've been given?'

Jitu looks at her a bit blankly and Matty puffs on one of those vape things. Has she got this wrong? Have they been told something different to her?

'I mean,' she goes on, pulling her phone out of her pocket to show them. 'I've been sent this map with streets highlighted in a different colour for each day. We have to cover this area between us today.' She points, and Jitu looks at her phone screen before moving slightly away and shrugging.

'I'll take Queen's Road,' he says.

Matty comes closer and points to her screen, and Debbie notices that the smoke he's exhaling smells like pineapple, but artificial and sickly sweet. How strange. 'I'll do these streets and the roads that go off them. Okay? Leaves you with the ones on the far side.'

Debbie's about to agree when she has another idea. 'Or,' she says, 'we could just stick together, splitting the houses up as we go.'

Matty and Jitu look at each other and shrug. And that seems to be it, decided. They start on Queen's Road. It's a long, straight road with 1930s semis all along it. Debbie's surprised by how many people are home. Mums with young kids, retired people and some who are clearly working from home (one man comes to the door in a shirt and tie paired with jogging bottoms). They take three houses at a time, then whoever finishes first goes to the next one up, and so on. Debbie knows she's working harder than the boys, but she doesn't really mind. They're surprisingly good company, opening up about their social lives and their studies.

It's all going pretty well until late morning, when they've decided they'll break for lunch after the next twenty or so houses. They've signed up a few people, perhaps not as many as Debbie might have hoped, so she decides she'll really go for it on these last few before lunch. She marches up another paved path and raps confidently on the door, which is opened by a harassed-looking man in his forties.

'Hello,' she says, 'do you have a minute to talk about mental health?'

She knows from the way he folds his arms against his chest and tilts his head to one side that what follows isn't going to be good.

'Do I have a minute to talk about mental health?' he repeats.

Debbie nods and swallows. 'That's right.'

'What would you like to talk about? My daughter's eating disorder or my son's self-harm?'

Debbie feels her face fall. 'I'm so sorry,' she says. She knew this would happen sooner or later. But she'd expected sadness, possibly weeping. This guy is furious.

'The thing is, it doesn't matter how sorry you are, it's not going to make any difference.'

'No,' Debbie says, and she thinks about launching into her speech about how Hopeful Horizons makes a huge difference to people like his children, but thinks better of it.

He's closing the door when a woman appears behind him. She puts a hand on his shoulder and Debbie feels like she's watching the most intimate of moments. She bows her head, prepares to walk away.

'It's not her fault,' she hears the woman say, and then Debbie looks up and they make eye contact. Her and this mother, who doesn't know how to help her children. 'Sorry, it's just all quite raw.'

Debbie holds her hands up. 'No, I'm sorry. I'm sorry to have disturbed you. I wish you all the best.'

She feels shaky when she gets to the end of the path. Thinking of that woman, saying sorry for her husband's bluntness. Having the capacity to care about that, in the middle of her own personal nightmare. When she sees Matty and Jitu coming down the paths either side of her at the same time, she turns from one to the other.

'Could we break for lunch now? I just had a tough one and I feel a bit shaken.'

Jitu asks whether she's okay, and Debbie is warmed by the compassion of this near stranger. They agree to meet again in an hour, and Debbie makes her way to the park. She finds a bench and pulls out the packed lunch she made herself this morning. A cheese and pickle sandwich, an apple, a packet of Hula Hoops, and a bottle of water. She runs back through the morning in her head. The people who were kind, the ones who were rude, the ones who were dismissive. That last couple, who were broken. And in between, snippets of conversation with Matty and Jitu. She has signed some people up for regular donations, and that makes her feel that she's doing something good, something worthy.

Debbie's lost in her thoughts and doesn't notice the man approaching the bench until his dog is straining at the lead to greet her. She laughs.

'Hello! Who are you?' She looks up at the man, who looks to be in his thirties and has thick blonde hair and a good jawline.

'Bonnie. Cockerpoo. Mind if I sit here for a minute?'

Debbie shakes her head and gives Bonnie a bit of a fuss. She's finished her lunch and is wondering what to do with the remaining half an hour of her break. The man beside her makes a phone call and Bonnie races around as far as she can go on her lead while he tries to control her. When he's finished, Debbie clears her throat.

'You seem busy,' she says, 'and she seems like she wants a walk. And I'm not. Busy, that is. So I wondered whether I might take her for you, for twenty minutes or so.'

The man looks at her with a furrowed brow, as if he's trying to work out why she would offer this. He holds a hand out. 'Pete.'

'Debbie,' she says. 'I'm not a dog owner now, but I have been in the past. I'd take good care of her.'

He must decide that she's harmless because he hands over the lead and pulls poo bags from his pocket, and before she knows it Debbie is up and walking around, smiling at the way Bonnie stops to sniff everything and to greet every other dog. She has missed having a dog more than she realised.

By the time she gets back to the bench, Bonnie's owner is on another call. She makes to hand the lead over but he holds up a hand for her to wait, so she stands there for a minute while he wraps up his conversation.

'Thanks,' he says. 'That was good of you. I come home from work at lunch to take her out but' – he gestures at his mobile – 'the calls don't stop.'

'No,' she says, pretending she understands that kind of work. What kind of work is it, even?

'She likes you,' he says.

'I like her.'

'Would you be interested in walking her sometimes? I'd pay you, of course. It's just, when we first got her, my boyfriend and I were both working from home because of Covid and she got used to having us around. Now we're both back in the office.'

Debbie crouches down and puts her hands on either side of Bonnie's head. Bonnie licks her face. 'Could I have a think about it? I could take your number and...'

'Yes, of course. Thank you. Debbie, was it?'

'Debbie,' she confirms.

He takes her phone from her hand and inputs his number under Pete and Bonnie. And then his phone rings again and he grimaces at her, and she smiles and waves and walks away.

When she gets back to Matty and Jitu, Debbie feels lighter. Ready to go again. Matty uses his phone to direct them to a street that opens up into a warren of cul-de-sacs, telling them on the way about a lecturer who he accidentally poured coffee over in the uni café and how he's been avoiding his seminars ever since.

'Bro,' Jitu says. 'I'd have transferred to a different uni by now.'

'It's not like I slept with his wife,' Matty says.

Debbie laughs, and it's only when she does that she realises there hasn't been much laughter in her life for a while. Since this move. Since she sold the house in Southampton she'd shared with Richie for twenty years and picked up her life and moved it over one hundred and fifty miles to a place she'd never even visited, because her mum lived there before she was born, had met Debbie's dad there. What was she looking for? Her mother was long dead, and she'd never known her father. And still, she felt this pull, to the place they'd both come from. But since she made the move, she's been wondering whether it was the right thing. Things have felt bleak, unmanageable. But now she's got this job, and these boys are making her laugh, and she might have a dog to walk. It adds up. It's a start.

Later, when she's eating a microwaved lasagne in front of the TV, she looks back over the day and concludes it's the best one she's had in a while. She reaches for her phone, sends Pete a text to say she'd love to walk Bonnie, letting him know her availability.

3

'Hello, dear.'

Ruth steps into the room, takes her mum's hand. 'Hi, Mum.'

Joan tilts her head, her expression one of bewilderment. 'I don't have a daughter,' she says. 'You must be confused.'

In the early days of this illness, which came in deceptively gently but soon showed its true colours and is now the cruellest thing Ruth has ever known, she argued endlessly with her mother about the things she got wrong. She would have told her, in this instance, that she did have a daughter; that she had two, in fact. She would have pulled out her phone and shown her mum photos, and it would all have been in vain. So now, she goes along with her mum's beliefs about the world as best she can. She agrees, tries to gauge where in her life her mum is on this particular day, and she makes it work. Her mum never asks who she is, why she's there. She has never asked her to leave. Sometimes, Ruth wishes she would. It would feel like a saving grace, in a way, if she had made the effort to do the visit but her mum didn't want her there. She could spend a couple of hours looking around the shops, or having coffee, or going for a swim, without feeling guilty, because it would be the hours that she'd already accounted for with a visit.

Ruth goes to the window, pushes the curtains open wider. The room feels closed in, a bit stuffy. Her mum is sitting in the armchair, and Ruth perches on the edge of the bed.

'How are you?'

'Oh, you don't need to worry about me. It's everyone else that's the problem.'

Ruth forces a smile, reaches for her bag. 'I've brought you some fruit, and some flowers. Shall I take them through to the kitchen and find a vase?'

'I'll do it; you don't know your way around. I've got six coming for dinner later, there's so much to do.'

'Who's coming?'

'Oh, colleagues of my husband's. He's in sales at a chocolate company, making quite an impression, I can tell you. He's invited his boss and someone from marketing and their wives. I'm making a souffle.'

Not for the first time, Ruth wonders whether her mum's caught in a particular day, whether this dinner party ever happened. She thinks it probably did. Her dad did indeed work in sales for a chocolate company for many years. That's where they met, and he stayed there through most of Ruth and Kate's childhoods.

'I've never made a souffle,' Ruth says. It's a lie, but she's learned that her mum likes to feel that she is helping, that she is imparting knowledge.

'The trick is to never open the oven while it's cooking.'

Ruth nods. It's true. She remembers times they spent together in the kitchen, when she was a child, or when one of them catered at Christmas and the other helped out. Oven gloves and red cheeks, darting around each other, Kate observing. As a child, with her arms folded across her chest, and as an adult, with a large glass of red wine in her hand.

'What's for pudding?' Ruth asks.

Her mum's eyes widen, and she reaches out and clutches Ruth's wrist. 'Pudding! I've forgotten all about it. I'll have to go to the shops again.'

Ruth curses herself. But how could she have known? 'You could do your bread and butter pudding. Everyone loves that.'

'Everyone does love that,' Joan says, and then she closes her eyes and almost instantaneously, she is asleep.

Ruth waits a couple of minutes and then gets up and goes in search of one of the carers. She finds a young woman with a name badge that reads Tala. Has Ruth seen her before? She isn't sure. They change so frequently, some of them employed by the home and others from an agency. It isn't easy work, and many of them don't last.

'Do you have a minute?' Ruth asks. 'I'm Joan's daughter.'

Tala breaks out into a broad smile. 'Joan! She's such a character.'

English isn't her first language and there's something sweet and charming about her pronunciation of 'character'. Ruth imagines her hearing that phrase for the first time, then putting it into use. 'Yes. I was wondering, is she eating well? She just looks so thin.'

Tala frowns. 'I'm afraid I don't know that, but I can find out and send you an email if you leave an address with the office.'

Ruth nods and watches Tala hurry away. And it isn't Tala's fault, but she wants to scream. Because she could probably wallpaper a small room with the notes she's left in the office, and no one ever comes back to her. They're overworked, underpaid. It isn't – she reminds herself – that they don't care. She goes back along the corridor and stands in her mum's doorway. She is still asleep in the chair, her mouth hanging open. Ruth feels a rush of affection. She goes over and gently presses a finger against her mum's chin to close her mouth. It falls open again almost immediately.

A thought comes. She could just leave. Usually, she spends two hours here and comes away feeling drained and emotional. But there's no knowing how long her mum will sleep for, and she hasn't brought a book. She stands, picks up her bag and jacket, and she's at the door when the voice comes.

'Could you get me a cup of tea?'

Ruth spins as if caught, and her mum is looking wide-eyed, as if she's been awake the whole time. 'Tea,' she says, putting her bag down and hanging her jacket on the bedframe. 'Of course.'

* * *

Later, Ruth makes three batches of cookies – Oreo, chocolate orange and salted caramel – for a party order and then a lasagne she's not looking forward to eating. She finds pasta stodgy, would rather have a salad and a piece of fish, but it's a favourite of Nigel's and although he never comments on what she makes for them, she can tell when he's not happy about it. As a compromise, she puts together a mixed salad to serve it with. Nigel comes in from the garden office just as she's opening the oven door to check on it. He rubs his arms.

'Bit nippy down there.'

He often says this, but she's suggested getting a little heater and he always dismisses the idea, so she's at a loss. 'This will be ready in five minutes,' she says.

'Great, I'll wash my hands.'

They sit opposite one another, the way they've sat for meals throughout their marriage, and Ruth tries to conjure up something to say while she serves them both salad and he pours the wine.

'Did you see your mum?' he asks.

'Yes.'

'She okay?'

'So-so. She didn't know who I was and she kept falling asleep.'

Nigel flashes her a look of sympathy. He understands. They went through this with his dad. That's how Ruth knows just how it's all going to go. She's exhausted by it. She has never said out loud that sometimes she wishes they would get the dreaded call to say that her mother has passed away. It's not the kind of thing you can say out loud, is it? He certainly never said it, when it was his dad. But sometimes she thinks perhaps she could, she might. And then she backs out. Every single time.

'Do you think we're doing the best we can for her?' she asks.

Nigel puts down his fork, which is loaded with layers of pasta and meat. 'I don't think we can have her here, if that's what you mean.'

'It isn't.' But good to know, she thinks. 'I just... It breaks my heart every time I go there. The staff turnover, the shabby furniture, the sad little dining room.'

'I think all care homes are like that, though. Unless you pay an absolute fortune.'

The plan is that Joan will pay for her own care herself. Her savings are dwindling at an astonishing rate but they will sell her house when they need to, and that will cover her for a few more years. And Ruth prays she won't live with this disease for longer than that. But she knows she and Nigel could chip in, if they wanted. They could make the difference, get her into a nicer place. Does Kate wonder why they don't? She can't afford to, but they can. Something holds her back from mentioning it.

She knows Nigel will say that he wants all the money tied up in investments for the boys. But do the boys really need it? They both have good jobs. Whereas her mum is the one who's living out her final years in a place that smells of boiled fish and cheap cleaning products. Ruth doesn't even have a sense of how much money they have. Not really. Nigel's always been the main earner, and he's always looked after the finances, too. She's involved in the day-to-day stuff, the bills and the food shopping and all of that, but it's him who looks after the bulk of it.

What she doesn't say, but what is hanging in the air between them, is that both of his parents went to a much nicer care home than the one her mum is currently in. They didn't contribute to that either, though. His parents had a bigger house in a nicer area, and that was it. For a moment, Ruth wonders what kind of care home she and Nigel might end up in. What their boys would choose for them, how often they would visit. She would rather go the way her own dad did. Fast, without warning. A stroke, or a heart attack, or even an accident of some kind. Anything but the slow waiting, her children having to estimate how many years she might last in order to make financial decisions.

'I might have a look around,' she says, pushing the unwanted food around her plate.

'You look, but I don't think you'll find anything significantly better at the same sort of price.'

But when did they agree that they had to stick with the same sort of price? And also, what if she just found something that was slightly better? Isn't her mum worth that?

The house phone rings and Nigel gets up to answer it. Ruth knows it will be a cold caller or one of their sons. For some reason, despite using their mobiles for everything, they always still call on the landline. She listens to what Nigel is saying, trying to work it out. But there is something wrong with Nigel's voice. Whatever this is, it isn't a run-of-the-mill sort of phone call. She feels a cold shiver of dread, the way she used to when they were in a playground and one of the boys climbed too high and was standing on a ledge, looking down at her. Or when they started to go out until all hours and she would check and find one of their bedrooms empty at three in the morning.

Nigel reappears, thrusts the phone at her, mouths 'Chris'.

'Hello, love,' Ruth says.

And he is crying. Ruth cannot remember the last time she heard him cry, with the possible exception of family funerals. When he was little, he cried freely, about not wanting to go home from the park, about not being able to keep one of the monkeys at the zoo, about missing his friend when he was away on holiday. When did that stop? She didn't notice it stop. And now he's this stoic man who gives very little away, and so why is he crying down the phone line from London?

'What is it?' she asks. 'What can I do?'

That's the crux of being a mother, she thinks. *What can I do?*

'I need to come home,' he manages to get out.

'Come,' she says. 'Come right now. Do you need us to pick you up?'

She avoids Nigel's eyes, knows that he will be glaring at her suggestion that he – because let's face it, it would be him – might get in the car at this time and drive to London to rescue their adult child.

'No,' he says. 'I'll get a train. Tomorrow. But are you sure it's okay? I might need to stay for a while.'

Ruth is surprised by this. She'd thought he was talking about a visit. He might need to stay 'for a while'. As far as she's concerned, he can stay forever. But she can already imagine the ways in which Nigel and Chris will rub each other up the wrong way, the ways Chris will regress to his teenage years and start leaving mugs and plates and clothes all over his bedroom floor.

'Of course it's okay,' she says. 'Don't be silly. This is your home. Will you be all right, tonight? Can you tell me what's happened?'

Chris takes a deep, shaky breath, and Ruth wishes more than anything that she could pull him through the phone and into her arms. There was a time when she could fix anything for them, her boys. When she was the centre of their worlds.

'It's complicated. I'll tell you when I'm home.'

And he's gone. Nigel's eating his lasagne again and Ruth wonders how he can. How it is that he isn't affected by their sons' emotions in the same way she is. She remembers that phrase about only ever being as happy as your unhappiest child. Is that only mothers?

'He's coming home,' she says.

'I gathered that.'

'It sounds like it might be for a while, though.'

'What do you mean, a while?'

'I don't know, Nigel. He just said a while. Did he tell you anything about what's happened?'

'He couldn't get his words out.' There's a look of slight distaste on Nigel's face, and Ruth knows that he thinks men shouldn't cry. He's old-fashioned like that. Out of nowhere, she wonders what made her fall in love with him. What made her choose him, out of everyone, to have a family with. But if it hadn't been him, she wouldn't have Chris or Max, of course. 'I suppose we'll find out tomorrow.'

Ruth stands to take the plates through to the kitchen, finds herself leaning against the kitchen counter with great sobs heaving in her chest, threatening to break out.

'Anything for pudding?' Nigel calls from the dining room.

4

When Jitu asked Debbie to come and meet them for some drinks at the Students Union, she laughed at first. But he kept asking, and eventually she said yes. She liked to say yes to things, when she could. And it was fun.

Now, a week later, Jitu is telling her that the doorman thought he recognised her.

'So then I said to him, "That was my good friend Debbie",' Jitu says, slinging one arm around her. 'And then "Do you have a problem with that?"'

'And did he?' Debbie asks. 'Have a problem, I mean?'

'He thought you were someone else. We don't get many women of your...'

'Age?'

'Pedigree. In the Students Union. Anyway, what happened to you that night?' Jitu turns to Matty, who's vaping. He blows the smoke away from them, but Debbie can still smell that it's some kind of citrus. Lemon, perhaps. Or lime.

'Oh,' Matty says, 'I got held up. There was a party.'

Debbie has learned that their lives are filled with nights like this. Bars and parties and dancing.

The conversation moves on, to their workloads. Matty is studying Maths, and Debbie has intuited that he's under a lot of pressure from his parents. When she asked him what he wanted to do with the degree at the end of it, he shrugged and said, 'I don't know, go back in time and take something interesting instead?' Debbie knows how much it costs to go to university these days. It seems such an awful shame that he's studying something he doesn't want to, that might lead him to a career he won't enjoy.

Jitu is more laidback. His degree is in Business and Economics and he doesn't seem to take it very seriously or know what he's aiming to do with it. Debbie doesn't think there's anything wrong with that. He's just a kid. They both are.

They've reached the street where they're starting work today, and Matty points to the house he's going to go to first. Jitu slaps him on the back and heads for the next house, and Debbie walks towards the one after that. This is a different kind of street to most of the ones they've covered so far. There are trees planted at regular intervals along the pavement, and the houses are all detached and have three storeys. Debbie imagines that inside they're all sleek, minimalist kitchens and shiny tiled floors. She's never fancied a house like that, not that it's ever been on the cards. But walking up the path, seeing the bay trees on either side of the matt-grey front door and the big porch, Debbie can see the appeal. She reaches forward, rings the bell.

Almost immediately, she hears footsteps but the door doesn't open for a while. Debbie imagines the person on the other side is looking for the keys. She goes over her opening lines in her head, though she knows them so well by now she doesn't need to. It's something she does when she's a bit nervous. Why is she nervous about this one? Is it intimidation, about the big house? She doesn't think so. She doesn't get envious of things like this, things other people have that she doesn't. Because life just goes different ways for different people, and she is more or less happy with how hers has turned out so far. At last, the click of the key, and the door swings open and Debbie opens her mouth to speak but no words come out.

Because the woman standing in front of her is... well, it's her.

* * *

She's slimmer, in more expensive clothes, with a better haircut. But the face. It's *Debbie's* face. She meets the woman's eyes and sees a bewilderment and panic that she suspects is reflected in her own. This can't be happening. It doesn't make any sense. As if in slow motion, Debbie notices that this woman – her double – is wearing a blue and white striped apron with a dusting of flour on it. Ankle-length navy trousers and a white shirt. Her feet are bare. The woman's feet, Debbie notices, are her feet. The second toe is slightly longer than the big toe. But this woman's toenails are painted coral. No chips. And Debbie knows that hers are bare.

'What is this?' the woman asks, in Debbie's voice. 'Who are you?'

'I...' Where to begin? With her name? 'Erm—'

Debbie has never been lost for words, has always thought that was a strange phrase. If anything, when she's upset or confused or surprised, she talks more. But nothing like this has ever happened in all of her sixty-two years, and besides, it's impossible. Why on earth would there be a woman living in Loughborough with her face and her body and her voice? How *could* there be?

There's a cough, a cleared throat, and Debbie turns to see Jitu standing at the end of the path, by the gate. She'd forgotten about Jitu. It's like her whole life has fallen away, and she is stranded.

'I'm heading on up to the next one,' he says. 'Matty's still chatting away.' Jitu makes a chatty mouth sign with one hand. 'Is everything... okay here?'

He hasn't looked at the woman, Debbie thinks. If he looks, he'll see. And then he must do it, because a hand flies to his mouth.

'Oh! I didn't realise you had... family here.'

'I don't,' Debbie says, and she turns back to look at the woman, but she is backing away, slowly closing the door. 'No! Please!'

'I can't... I don't understand,' the woman says. And then she is gone, the door shut, Debbie on one side of it and a woman who can only be her – what? Sister? No, sisters don't have the exact same face. This woman is her identical twin. She knows it, in her bones, even though she knows she's an only child. And it doesn't make sense, but it doesn't have to, because it just is.

'What the fuck?' Jitu whispers.

Debbie is back down the path, and she is shaking.

'Debbie, did you... not know?' Jitu asks. He takes off his jacket and puts it over her shoulders, over her own jacket, and there's something so sweet and kind in this that Debbie finds herself on the edge of tears.

'I had no idea,' she says.

They are standing there, silent, Jitu's jacket on Debbie's shoulders, when Matty bounds up to them. 'Signed one up! I knew these minted families would be good for a bit of commission.'

His face changes when he realises there is something wrong.

That something has happened. Debbie thinks about when they were walking here, before she knocked on that door. When she was a different person, with a steady sort of life.

'What?' Matty asks, throwing his arms wide. 'What's happened?' He's looking from Jitu to her and back again, like he's watching a fast-paced table tennis game. And Debbie has never been a secret keeper, but she doesn't know how to say this, because she isn't sure herself. She gives Jitu a pleading look.

'There's a woman in there,' Jitu says, gesturing to the house, which they're still standing close by. 'She's, like, Debbie's double.'

'Is she family?' Matty asks, fixing his gaze on Debbie.

Perhaps they think that's all it is, that she knows she has family but they are estranged and she wasn't expecting to see this woman today. How can she explain that it's more than that? That she grew up with her mother, just the two of them, her father never on the scene. That this woman simply cannot exist. She glances back at the house and she sees her, standing in an upstairs window looking down, but she is gone before Debbie can tell the boys.

'I don't have any family,' she says, and she feels as if she's swallowed a rock and it's making its way through her body. Down her windpipe and into her intestines. She needs to sit down. 'Is there... somewhere I could sit?' she asks.

The boys lurch into action, leading her back the way they came and onto a road nearby that has a bench. And they sit down, them on either side of her, waiting for her to be ready to speak.

'I don't want you to miss out, or get in trouble,' Debbie says, because they should be halfway up the road by now, and she can't do it, but they can.

'Fuck it,' Jitu says. 'This is big stuff. We're not going to leave you on your own.'

Debbie is touched, because when they don't knock on doors, they don't earn, and she knows Jitu worries about money. That they both do.

'Go,' Debbie says, looking from Jitu to Matty. 'Please. Both of you, go. I need a bit of time. I'll go home. I'll call them and explain, later.'

'We'll cover you,' Jitu says. 'Don't worry about it.'

'Yeah, no worries,' Matty says.

They stand up, stretching their long legs, and Debbie thinks about what good people they are, how she wasn't sure about working with such young lads at the start, but how quickly she's come to see them as friends. It's only after they've been gone for a few minutes that she realises she still has Jitu's coat hanging on her shoulders. She looks up the road but she can't spot him. They're probably working fast, trying to catch up. She could follow him up the road, but she isn't sure she can go past that house again so soon. She'll have to return it to him tomorrow. She hopes he isn't too cold.

Slowly, slowly, Debbie walks back to her house. Slips her key in the lock and lets herself in. Picks up the post from the mat. Puts the kettle on. It's all autopilot, and when she's run out of things to do, she sinks down into the armchair she favours in the living room, the one that's almost threadbare but so comfortable, and she picks back over what she knows, trying to find a way to make it make sense.

5

'Who was that?' Chris calls out.

Ruth hears him but she doesn't know how to answer, doesn't know if she can speak, even. More than anything, she wants to walk away from her son, with his heavy problems, and let this sink in. But that's not what mothers do. So she calls that she'll be back in a minute and goes up the stairs, watches the woman – the stranger – and two young men who are huddled on the street outside her house. Did this woman know about her, somehow? Did she come looking?

No, she reasons. They had both been as shocked as each other. Just then, the woman looks up and their eyes meet for a second. Ruth retreats into the shadows of her house, shaken. Desperately trying to come up with a reason for it not to mean what it seems, on the surface, like it must mean. She hits on it. Doppelgangers. There was a documentary about it, or a *Telegraph* article. How everyone had one out there somewhere, how most people never met theirs. A coincidence, a twist of fate. She tells herself that will be it. After all, there are only so many ways for human faces to be arranged. Is it any wonder, in a world of more than eight billion people, that some faces look exactly the same? Besides, the other option is too hard to contemplate.

Downstairs, Chris is sitting at the breakfast bar, his shoulders slumped. He's eating a bagel. Ruth wants to wrap him in her arms and ask him how she can make it better, the way she would have done when he was a child. But he is not a child. He is a man edging ever closer to forty. Her firstborn, by three minutes. The one who put his career first, so she didn't worry too much about the fact that he never seemed to have anyone to love. And now look.

'Who was that?' Chris asks again.

Everything about him is defeated. His slump, his voice.

'Nobody,' Ruth says, and it's then that she realises she doesn't know what the woman was actually doing there. Assuming she didn't know, hadn't come looking. She must have had a reason to knock on the door. Her and those boys. Were they selling something? She walks through to the dining room and shoots a quick look out at the street, but they are gone. It surprises her to feel a small kernel of disappointment about that. She goes back to the kitchen, pulls out the bar stool next to her son. 'So, what's the plan?'

He looks at her, confused. Bewildered. Did he really not think beyond coming home? Beyond sitting at this breakfast bar and asking her to buy the kinds of sugary cereal he used to eat – bowl after bowl – when he lived at home? 'What do you mean?'

'Well, you said you were made redundant. So I assume you'll be job-hunting. And you said something, the day you came, about a breakup?'

Chris has never brought anyone home to meet them, and if he was in a relationship, it wasn't one he'd told them about. Ruth is sure he's gay, but he's never said. And is it her place to ask?

She's always come down on the side of no. Chris swipes at his eyes as if his tears are a betrayal.

'I'm getting a good payout,' he says, as if that answers her questions.

'Right, but...'

'Christ, Mum, please don't go on. I'm getting a good payout. I'm going to weigh up my options for a while.'

Ruth wants to say that he could always weigh them up while doing something to earn money. That he can't exactly weigh them up here, in her kitchen, where she runs her business. 'Was there a breakup?' she asks gently.

Chris nods, and it's barely perceptible.

'Well,' she says, covering his big hand with her own. 'I'm sorry to hear that.'

He looks at her then, and she wonders whether this will be the moment. Whether he'll finally say, 'You know I'm gay, right?' She has never given him reason to suspect she wouldn't be okay with such a revelation. So why doesn't he tell her? There's a heaviness to his look, and she suspects it's caused by sadness. She wants to know who this man is, who has broken her boy's heart.

'Have you been in touch with Max?' she asks, because she's never been good at silence, at letting it settle. 'I'm sure he'd love to see you while you're home.'

Chris shakes his head. She thinks about the way the brothers had fought when they were little. The way they'd loved. Begging her to let them have sleepovers in each other's rooms, wriggling down into sleeping bags like worms. Everyone said they would always be close, what with them being twins and both boys. But you couldn't tell with that stuff. Since they've become adults, Chris and Max have less to do with each other, as you'd expect.

But they still have a closeness that awes her, even when they go weeks and sometimes months without seeing each other.

'We'll get him over for dinner,' she says, as if someone has suggested this might be a good idea. 'Layla and Grace too, of course.'

Without warning, Chris stands up and pushes back his stool. Leaves the room. Ruth listens to his heavy tread on the stairs and wonders, as she often did when he was a teenager, what he does for long hours in his room with the door closed.

Thoughts of the woman at the door start to return, but Ruth resists. She has baking to do. A batch of brownies and fifty Minecraft cupcakes. She gets her antibacterial spray out, wipes the tops down. Starts assembling ingredients. And all the time she is making them, she keeps the questions at bay.

But later, when she's having dinner with Nigel and Chris, they pile up and she realises it's no good. She can't pretend this didn't happen.

'Funny thing, earlier...' she says, and even as she's doing it, she's not sure why she's positioning it this way. Light. An anecdote. Nothing that would tilt their world. 'This woman came to the door, and she looked exactly like me.'

Nigel puts his fork down, looks up at her. 'What do you mean?'

'I mean, she could have been my twin.' She feels a slight shiver at the word. It's an expression, isn't it? But what if it's true?

'A lot of women your age have the same sort of hair and dress the same way, I've noticed,' Nigel says.

Ruth isn't sure what to make of that. 'We didn't have the same sort of hair, though.'

'Well, then how did she look exactly like you?'

Ruth pauses, questions how to make herself clear. 'We had the same face. The exact same face.'

Nigel laughs. 'But that's ridiculous.'

'I know that.'

'Neither of your parents had any children before they had you and Kate, right?'

'No,' Ruth answers, but it strikes her that she doesn't actually know that for sure. If they did, they certainly didn't advertise the fact. Didn't see the other child. But what if she wasn't theirs at all? What if she and this stranger belonged to someone else, at first? No, it's ridiculous. Why is she even contemplating it?

But the answer comes, unbidden. She is contemplating it because she has to. Because she has to find a way to make sense of this.

'There were these two guys at work,' Chris says, and Ruth realises she'd almost forgotten he was there. 'Clive and Dean, I think. Everyone was always getting them mixed up. Even I did, and Dean was on our team for a while. Funny thing was, when you saw them together, they weren't all that alike, but if I saw one of them, I was never totally sure which one it was.'

Ruth wants to say that's not the same. That's not what she's trying to tell them. It's her own fault, for waiting hours and then bringing it up like this, over dinner, her face composed. A story from her day. If she had told them immediately, shown them how shaken she was, it might have been different.

'What did she want, anyway?' Nigel asks.

'I don't know.'

'Well, didn't she say?'

Ruth runs through the encounter again. She remembers it in vivid detail, as if it's a film she watched. 'She didn't say anything.'

Nigel makes a noise that sounds like a scoff. Reaches for a piece of garlic bread. They are having spaghetti bolognese, because it's Chris's favourite, despite Ruth having made lasagne so recently. Sometimes, Ruth imagines them turning into blocks of mince. You are what you eat, and all that. Both Nigel and Chris have tomato sauce around their lips. 'So you're telling us that this woman, who looks like you, came to the door and said absolutely nothing?'

Ruth sees a look pass between her husband and her son, and it's one she recognises. As the only female in a household, you can be sidelined, laughed at, not taken seriously.

'She didn't say anything because she was shocked,' Ruth says, her voice pulled taut like clingfilm over a bowl of leftovers. 'And I was, too. It was really quite... disturbing.'

Nobody says anything, and Ruth stops eating. She is sick of eating meals that are other people's favourites. Tomorrow she will do something with those mushrooms in the fridge, and she will ignore any comments Nigel makes about it not being a proper meal if there's no meat in it.

'Sounds like quite a day,' Nigel says.

And it's impossible to tell what he means by it, but Ruth thinks she catches that look between the two of them again, the shadow of a smirk, and she has had enough. She takes her bowl through to the kitchen and scrapes what's left of her dinner into the bin.

'Mum,' Chris says from the dining room.

'What?'

'Are you all right?'

Is she? She puts her bowl in the dishwasher and then leans back against the counter. 'Fine,' she says.

She stays where she is, listening to the low grumble of their talk. Should she have invited the woman in? At least asked her some questions? Who she was and where she had sprung from, and why Ruth's life felt sort of torn in two. Into before, and after. What if she never sees her again? She wasn't ready, this morning, isn't sure she's ready now, but she might be one day. And this woman has the upper hand, because she knows where Ruth lives, and Ruth knows nothing.

When Nigel appears in the kitchen, Chris closely behind him, she forces a smile.

'You seem rattled, love,' Nigel says. He puts an arm around her and squeezes her into him.

She remembers when they were first together, how every touch felt so intense it was almost painful. And now, he can squeeze her like this and she is numb to it. Has she become numb to everything? She thinks of the people she's watching on her latest reality show, *Finding Paradise*, the way they look at one another like they've found the answer to all their questions.

'I am, a bit.'

She is more than rattled. She is lost at sea, holding up a hand to ask for rescue. And her husband and her son are waving at her from the beach, unaware of how far out she's drifted.

'I bet you've exaggerated the likeness,' he says.

'Exaggerated? Why would I?'

'Oh, I don't mean in telling us about it. I don't mean on purpose. I mean in your mind. I bet there was a resemblance, something about the eyes or the mouth, and over the course of the day you've built it into something bigger.'

She doesn't know how to say that that's not it. So she smiles and nods as if accepting that it is. Chris has already disappeared back up the stairs, and Nigel turns his focus to their son.

'What do you think is going on with him, then? I know there's the job thing, and obviously that's a shock, but I think it's more about the personal side, myself. I think some girl's broken his heart.'

How can he not know, that Chris is gay? How can it be that she and Nigel have never discussed it? 'More likely a boy,' she says. 'A man.'

Nigel does a double take, and she sees that it really is a surprise to him. 'What, you think...?'

She nods again. 'I do.'

'For how long?'

Is he asking how long she's thought it or how long Chris has been gay? And does the answer to either of those questions matter? If Chris is gay, he always has been. Surely Nigel knows that.

'He hasn't told me,' she says, and saying it is like an admission of failure. Why hasn't he told her? 'I just think it's sort of obvious.'

Nigel is standing at the breakfast bar now, both hands on it, as if to steady himself. And her story is forgotten, swept aside. Easy as that.

6

To Debbie, it isn't so much about the how of it all. It is about the indisputable fact of it. You don't get two people who are entirely unrelated to each other but look exactly the same. You just don't. Every time she pictures the moment when that door swung back, she catches her breath. The woman's eyes, the slope of her nose, the point of her chin. There is no denying it.

She doesn't tell anyone other than Matty and Jitu about it at first. She wants to tell Richie. Richie might have marched her back round there, knocked on the door and refused to be shooed away the way she'd been. He would have said something like 'Let's get to the bottom of this' and folded his arms across his chest and asked her and the woman to tell their stories, looking for the lie or the part that could cross over. For a day or so, she finds herself talking to Richie aloud again, like she had in the early days after losing him.

'The thing is...' she starts, standing by the kettle. But by the time those words are out, she's already forgotten what the thing was.

'Why did she close the door?' She knows what Richie would

have said to that. He would have said that not everyone was as brave and sure as her. That some people needed time to adjust to things.

'What should I do?' That is the one that stumps her. Would Richie have told her to leave it be, like the time she saw a work friend's husband kissing another woman outside a Spanish restaurant? Then, he had said that everyone's lives were more complicated than you ever knew. That it wasn't her place. Or would he have said that she owed it to herself – to the girl who grew up with just a mother who wasn't really equipped to be a mother – to find out? She can imagine it going either way. And that fact unnerves her, because she is so used to feeling sure about what Richie would think, or say, or do.

The day after it happens, Debbie calls in sick to work, and when she isn't thinking about the woman, she is thinking about Matty and Jitu, how they'll be talking about her, wondering whether she is okay. In the late afternoon, there is a knock on the door and she opens it expecting the postman, but it's Jitu, his hands clasped in front of him, an unsure look on his young face.

'I wanted to see if you're all right,' he says.

'How do you know where I live?'

'We came past the end of the road once, and you said. You pointed, said "That one with the burgundy front door".'

Debbie remembers that now, but it is strange, how it feels like a hundred years ago. How long has she known Jitu? Three weeks? Her life has been cleaved in two by the sight of a woman's face, and everything from before feels distant. 'Come in. I still have your jacket. I hope you weren't cold today.'

Jitu shrugs. 'It's fine.'

He refuses tea and coffee but takes a biscuit, so she brings the packet of bourbons into the living room with them, in case he wants more.

'So are you? Okay?' he asks, perching on the edge of her sofa.

Debbie wants to tell him to sit back and relax for a minute, but perhaps he doesn't feel able to, here. 'I don't know,' she says, and it is at least honest.

'So really no idea? No knowledge of a sister at all?'

That word, sister. How she had hated the girls she grew up with who tossed it around so casually. One girl had three sisters, and she seemed to hate them all. And there was Debbie, with no siblings to her name, wishing on every birthday candle for someone to play with, even once she was a bit older and knew that there would have to be a man on the scene for it to come true.

'Nothing,' she says, and her voice sounds a bit echoey.

It's clear that he wants to ask her about the facts, about how and where she grew up, all of that, but he doesn't. Perhaps he thinks he doesn't know her well enough. And she's glad. Because she doesn't want to start digging around in the past. Not yet. She wants to look to the future.

'I want to write her a note,' she says, the words tumbling out. 'Just to say I'm sorry I shocked her, and that I was shocked too, and to give her my number in case she wants to reach out. Otherwise, she doesn't know where to find me, if she wants to.'

Jitu nods. 'Are you sure?'

Debbie didn't expect this. She's never been the type to worry about being sure, more of a dive in and see what happens type. And where has it got her? Well, it got her into a happy marriage, a variety of friendships, a host of interesting jobs. She looks at him, offers the biscuits again, and he takes two, makes a plate with his hand.

'When I was a kid, about eight or nine, I found out that my dad had had a kid with another woman before he met my mum. I knew her, too. I just... thought she was a cousin, or a cousin's cousin. Our family was like that. Big and messy. But once I knew she was my sister, it changed things between us. I resented her, blamed her for what Dad had done. It was stupid, I know, but things were never the same after.'

Debbie takes this in. Tries to imagine this sprawling family that Jitu has described. Family doesn't mean that, for her. In her childhood, it meant awkward silences and dry roast dinners and love that felt forced. And as an adult, with Richie, it had felt powerful and intimate. The two of them against the world. If she can find out that there is more, that she is linked to more people in this world than her dead mother, wouldn't that be the most wonderful thing?

'It was just me and Mum,' she finds herself saying. 'She wasn't well. Mentally. When she had to go into hospital, I stayed with her mum. She didn't really like children. It wasn't a happy time.'

Debbie finds herself thinking the thing she's been trying to avoid. What if her mum wasn't her mum? What if she had a mum somewhere else, could have had an entirely different life? But how? Adoption? She tries to picture her mum's face, tries to spot similarities to her own, but both the faces in question are too familiar to her. It's impossible.

Jitu looks pained. There are crumbs in his hand and he is keeping it cupped to contain them. Debbie knows that they are both trying to imagine the other's childhood. Her, picturing all those people, all that love. Him, trying to get his head around loneliness when he probably wished for a bit of peace on many an occasion.

'What would you do?' she asks.

Debbie likes hearing from other people. She doesn't believe in wisdom coming with age, just in different perspectives. New ways of seeing.

Jitu shrugs. 'I like to think I'd leave it, but I probably wouldn't. I'd probably do what you're suggesting, write a note. Because if you knock on the door again, and she sends you away... that would be... tough. But with a note, you're leaving the ball in her court. Giving her the option.'

He leaves soon after that, and she promises she'll see him tomorrow. She just needed a day, to get her head straight. Her thoughts return to her mother, to the past. There's a photo in her purse and she goes to fetch it. Their colouring was different, her mum much darker than her. But didn't they have similar features? Debbie peers at the photo, then at herself in the mirror above the fireplace. They both have small, slim noses. Is that enough? She remembers, then, that people sometimes remarked on them having similar mannerisms. They both moved their hands a lot when they talked, and they screwed up their faces when anything was slightly uncomfortable. But what was that, really? Were those things you were born with, or things you learned?

Debbie gets out a notepad and pen, tears a sheet out and then worries that it looks untidy, torn like that. She fetches scissors and cuts a new, neat edge. All of it is procrastination, of course. She can feel the words bubbling up in her, but they won't get in order. And how do you start a letter, when you don't know the recipient's name? A cheery hello? Or nothing at all, a launch straight into the heart of things. After an hour, she has nothing, and she screws up the paper, frustrated, and goes into the kitchen to make herself something to eat.

It's not until she's on the edge of sleep, poised to tip into unconsciousness, that the words come. She forces herself to sit up, turns on her bedside lamp. Sleep is still nipping at her ankles, but she makes her way downstairs, where the notepad and pen are still on the table, waiting.

Hi, I'm Debbie Jones. I came the other day and I think we both had a shock. I wondered – can we talk? I've put my number at the bottom of this note. If I don't hear from you, I won't bother you again. But I hope you'll consider getting in touch. Debbie.

Once it's written, sleep comes easily, and Debbie doesn't wake again until almost seven. That morning, she sets off earlier than she needs to, goes to the woman's house. The closer she gets to it, the more her heart races. She holds the note in the pocket of her fleece. It is folded, and there is no name on it. It is addressed to no one. Debbie thinks about what the woman's name might be. Michelle. Katherine. Linda. Nothing quite fits. How do you guess a name for a person who has your face but a completely different life?

It's when she's walking up the front path, the note in her hand, that the woman's door opens. Debbie never imagined this possibility. It isn't her, coming out. It's a man of around the same age, wearing chinos and a casual shirt. Her husband. Nothing like Richie. But then, why would he be? Debbie freezes. She isn't prepared for this. She could turn around, undo it. But no, it's too late. He's seen her, and his jaw has dropped. He's holding a stack of books, and she thinks for a moment that he's going to drop them, but he is just changing his grip.

'Ruth said...' he says.

Ruth. Debbie has known a couple of Ruths. One at school, who was unkind and unintelligent. One in a job she had at a pizza restaurant, who was always laughing. Now this one. The man doesn't finish his sentence, and they just look at one another, and Debbie thinks, fleetingly, how funny they would look to anyone passing.

'Is she here?' she asks. And straightaway she isn't sure why.

Because she hadn't planned a meeting, had she? And she's on her way to work.

'No, she's at the supermarket.'

Debbie nods, relieved. She remembers the note in her hand. 'I brought this. Could you give it to her, or I could just put it through the door?'

He holds out a hand and the note is passed, like they're at school, hiding what they're doing from a teacher.

'I don't understand,' he says. 'How...? She has a sister, but no one else.'

Debbie turns that over in her mind. Ruth has a sister already. This woman has the thing she wanted most for herself. 'I don't know,' she says. 'Truly, I don't.' She turns and starts to walk away, and when he calls out for her to stop, she just steps up her pace. She calls back, over her shoulder. 'My number's on the note. I have to go.'

She doesn't look back, and he doesn't come after her. All day, while she is knocking on doors and chatting to Matty and Jitu, she is saying the woman's name in her head, over and over. Ruth. Trying to feel some kind of connection to it, some kind of recognition where there is only a blank space.

7

The second the doctor said the word 'twins', I knew. I didn't tell you, that day. You were excited, saw it as a blessing. So I hid my dread and fear at the thought of looking after two babies at once. I still remember lying on that bed, the feel of the doctor's hands on my belly. The way he said 'two heads' and the shiver of dread it sent through me.

You'd been pushing for children since the day we got married. Had made no secret of the fact that you'd like three or four. Twins were just a head start, as far as you were concerned. I didn't want to trample all over that with my reluctance. I swallowed it down, hoped that if I pretended it wasn't there, it would go away.

But it got bigger as I did. Do you remember how I could hardly walk towards the end? Two almost fully grown babies turning, moving beneath my skin. Sometimes I lay awake in the night, watching the ripples and prods with awe. With alarm.

I knew they were girls. I told you I did. I let you choose the names for boys because I knew we wouldn't need them. We agreed on their names, after some discussion. Ruth and Deborah. I thought about which one I'd keep, how I'd tell you that we had to give the other one up. Every day I tried to bring it up, and every day the words died in my throat. And all the time, I was getting bigger, and more afraid.

8

Ruth and Nigel go over the facts of it, late at night when Chris is in his room.

'Could you both have been adopted?' Nigel asks.

Ruth has thought about this a lot. Has even thought about the thriller she read a few years back in which twins were stolen.

'It's possible, but what about Kate? We're too similar, aren't we? For me to be adopted and her to be theirs?'

Even as she's saying this, Ruth is wondering whether it's true or whether it's just that she's always believed they are sisters.

'But I suppose it's possible that she was adopted too,' Nigel goes on. 'I've read about adoption cases where the birth parents go on to have more children. If those children are taken away from them, they're sometimes offered to the adopting parents so the siblings can be together.'

Ruth shakes her head. It's too convoluted, surely.

'Okay then, how did your mum and dad meet?' Nigel asks. 'When?'

Ruth mentally flicks through the information she holds about life before she was born. 'They met at work. She was his secretary. I don't know how long they were together before they got married. I know I came along quickly. I've often thought she was probably pregnant when they married. You know how it was, back then.'

Nigel nods. Since he'd run into the woman outside their house, he's been worrying at it like it's a bone. 'Suppose they had twins, and gave one away? Had her adopted?'

'I just can't imagine it. Why would they?' Ruth asks. She has already asked herself this question so many times. 'People don't give up one child and keep another, do they?'

'I suppose they might, if they really couldn't cope with two.'

Ruth shakes her head. 'But if they thought they couldn't cope with two, for some reason, why would they then have Kate?'

Nigel shakes his head, and Ruth knows that this is him admitting he can't work it out. She can't, either. It's like trying to do a jigsaw when some of the pieces are missing and there's no picture on the box.

Her mind keeps returning to the idea of her parents giving Debbie away. Ruth pictures her boys as babies, the way they would lie in the same crib with their limbs entwined. The thought of separating them would have been heinous. And choosing which one to keep, and which to give away? But there's the fact of her own children being twins. People always asked, when she took them anywhere, whether there were other twins in the family, and she always shook her head and said a polite no. But what if she was wrong? What if she'd got it all wrong?

'Your birth certificate,' Nigel says.

And it's this that sets something inside Ruth churning. She remembers that her mother's name didn't match, remembers discovering it as a child. She'd always known her mother as Joan, but the birth certificate says Elizabeth. They told her that Joan was her mother's middle name, that her first name was

Betty. *Elizabeth*. Did she ever check Kate's? And if not, why didn't she? 'I'll get it.'

She goes up the stairs, to the filing cabinet in the corner of Max's old room, where they keep bills and documents. The deeds to the house, the car's MOT certificate, the vaccination records of several deceased pets. Ruth knows where to look and less than a minute later the piece of paper is in her hand, and it's just as she remembers it. Mother: Elizabeth Simpson. Father: Frank Thomas Simpson.

Back in the kitchen, Nigel has poured them both a whisky, and Ruth knocks hers back. It's a while since she's drunk anything stronger than wine, and she enjoys the burning feeling in her throat, the way she feels slightly fuzzy almost immediately. She hands the birth certificate to Nigel, explains about the name.

'Why isn't her middle name on here?' he asks.

How did she not see that? 'I don't know.'

Is that anything? Could it be? They look at one another, and Ruth isn't sure what Nigel is thinking. She barely knows what she's thinking. There's an unspoken agreement that they'll leave it there for tonight, and Ruth's pleased that he senses her need for this. She cannot do this swiftly. It's too complicated, too layered. Nigel goes to the living room and turns the TV on, and Ruth stays in the kitchen and calls her sister.

'Ruth. Bit late, isn't it?' Kate's voice is always soothing. Ruth feels her breathing and her heart rate slow.

'Sorry. Quick question. On my birth certificate, Mum's listed as Elizabeth Simpson.'

'Elizabeth?'

'Yes. She told me once that her first name is Betty but she's always gone by Joan.'

'Okay?'

'But it doesn't say Joan at all. On the birth certificate. It just says Elizabeth Simpson. Do you know what it says on yours?'

Kate doesn't speak for a moment. 'No, I... Ruth, why are you thinking about all this? And what exactly *are* you thinking? What's this about?' She sounds worried but there's a hint of amusement, too.

Ruth hasn't told her, hasn't wanted to. Because Kate likes to 'bottom things out', as she calls it. She's a journalist. She never lets anything lie. But now Ruth feels scared and the person she goes to when she's scared, at least since they lost their dad and their mum started forgetting who they were, is her sister. So she tells the story, about the first encounter with Debbie on the doorstep and about Nigel running into her and the note with her phone number. Kate lets her speak on and on without interrupting and when Ruth stutters to a halt, when it's all out, she remains quiet.

'Kate?'

'I'm here. Just, give me a second. You're saying you think you have a twin? Seriously?'

'Kate, if you'd seen her...'

'Call her! She might have the answers to all of this.'

Ruth doesn't know how to say she's frightened. That she is beginning to think she's been lied to her whole life and she's terrified of having it confirmed. Even as Kate talks, she can feel herself retreating like a snail who's popped its head out, had second thoughts and is now going back into its safe and cosy shell.

'Have you asked Mum?' Kate asks.

And Ruth's thoughts turn to their mother. For some reason, whenever Kate says 'Mum', Ruth pictures the mum they had as children. Not the one they have now, who isn't quite a full person. She imagines having this conversation with a younger version of their mum, the one who was always busy, who very rarely sat down, and if she ever did, she perched on the edge of the chair and did something useful, like knitting, at the same time as chatting or watching TV. What would *that* mum say?

'No, I don't know whether it's a good idea, when she's so confused anyway.'

'You could wait for a clear day,' Kate says.

This is what they call the days when their mum is herself. They message one another. *Clear day today.* The clear days are getting further and further apart. Despite making this call, despite starting this conversation, Ruth wants to talk about something else. She asks Kate about a job interview her daughter Connie had, and Kate plays along, doesn't push it. But when they are about to hang up, Kate returns to the subject.

'I'll see if I can find my birth certificate, okay, and I'll check it. And if you want to talk to Mum, or this woman, I can be with you, if you want me to. Okay?'

Ruth nods, knowing her sister can't see her. She feels exhausted. There are footsteps behind her and she says a hasty goodbye and ends the call, assuming it's Nigel looking for a late-night snack. But when she turns around, it's Chris behind her, wearing checked pyjama bottoms and a tatty old T-shirt. When the boys first left home, within a few months of each other, Ruth missed them so acutely that she would lock herself in the bathroom and stuff a towel in her mouth and sob silently. She knew Nigel missed them too, but he never really showed it outwardly and she didn't feel able to share her grief with him. Because that's what it felt like – pure grief. She was thrust back into those days after her father died, when she couldn't function properly and kept forgetting why she was in rooms.

But now, she's found a rhythm. Baking, yoga, visits to her mum, reality shows about strangers finding love, Sunday evenings with Kate. And she would never have described herself as lonely, or pining, but Chris being back has brought something to life in her. She makes them tea, and he puts crumpets in the toaster. They sit at the breakfast bar. Ruth suspects Nigel has gone to bed. They used to tell each other, when they were going up, but now it's more and more like they are separate entities who happen to share a bed. Will that stop, at some point? If one of them is ill, they go to the spare room to avoid disturbing the other. One day, will one of them just stay there?

'Do you want to talk about it?' Ruth asks her son.

She's keen to talk about something other than her family, because thinking about the woman with her face makes her feel like she is walking straight off the top of a tall building and into air. Like those cartoon characters who keep running for a while before realising they've gone off a cliff.

'The job?'

'Any of it,' she says.

Chris was always the more open one, when they were teenagers. If he was upset, it showed on his face and he'd always tell her over a cup of tea. Max was more likely to go to his room and shut them all out. Chris would often tell her what was wrong with Max, too. She rests her face against his arm, breathes him in. He smells of a washing powder that is not the one she uses, but underneath that, of him. She could tell them apart, when they were babies, by their smell. Chris's slightly less sweet, slightly earthier than Max.

'I knew there were redundancies coming but I thought I'd be safe,' he says.

Ruth senses that this is the start of the story, not the whole of it, so she remains quiet.

'I was seeing someone. My boss. I thought I'd be safe because of our... relationship.'

She is barely breathing, because here is the moment she has waited all these years for. Surely he will say the boss's name and she will know, once and for all.

'It was... a man. My boss. Matthew. I... Christ.' He runs his hands roughly over his face, and Ruth sees that he can't quite look at her.

'You know it's okay—' she says.

'With you, maybe. But I'm not sure about Dad.'

Ruth takes a sharp breath in. Is he right? Would Nigel struggle with this news? She thinks back to the conversation they had, when she said she suspected it. But she can't picture his face. Since menopause, her memory has been like this. Temperamental. Broken.

'I'll talk to Dad,' she says, and it's the kind of thing she would say when Nigel had said they couldn't go to a party and she thought he was being too strict. But this? Having to talk him round when Chris is finally coming to them to tell them who he loves. No, she won't do it. If Nigel has a problem with this, she'll walk away from him. It's a shock to her, the realisation.

'Will you tell me about him?' she asks.

Chris bites his first crumpet in half, and Ruth is reminded of the food they got through, in those last few years that they lived at home. A loaf of bread every twenty-four hours or so. Endless apples and packets of crisps. Sometimes she would roast a chicken for sandwiches and find the carcass picked clean before she'd had a chance to make any. She makes a mental note to buy more crumpets. To buy more of everything. Does he still drink Diet Coke?

'He's older than me, late forties. And he's...'

Chris breaks off, but Ruth knows what he's going to say, in that moment. Married.

'Oh, love,' she says, because Chris is crying now, tears dropping into his tea. He lets her hold him and she feels grateful for this moment, their bodies pressed together, despite the heartache that has caused it, and then she feels selfish for thinking that way.

'He's married,' Chris confirms. 'To a woman.'

'Children?'

'Two. But he doesn't love her, Mum. He loves me.'

It's the oldest story in the book, isn't it? Ruth has had friends over the years who've fallen into these traps, who've held these beliefs. That he'll leave her. That she is really the one, that their love is different.

'And the job?'

'An easy way to get rid of me, I suppose. He can't accept it. I'm the first man he's been with. Mum, did you know?'

The change of topic is swift but Ruth doesn't veer off course. 'I thought I did,' she says.

'Always?'

Ruth thinks of her two little boys, the way they played with trucks and diggers, dug in the mud, kicked balls. When did she notice a difference? Secondary school, she thinks. Max was into football and brushed off friendship issues and Chris was far more sensitive, and that's when she started to wonder.

'Not always. But for a long time. I was hoping you'd tell me.'

'I don't know why I couldn't.'

'Well,' she says. 'It doesn't matter now. I'm just sorry you're feeling like this.'

He looks at her, eyes red-rimmed. 'What am I going to do?'

'I don't know.' And she doesn't. But then, a moment later, she does. She's switched back into thinking like a mum. 'You'll stay here, and I'll look after you, and we'll sort everything out.'

He goes up to bed soon after that, but Ruth stays in the kitchen for another half an hour, looking for something to do.

There are a couple of things to wash up, and she tidies up the cupboard with tins and packets in it. The two things are competing for space in her brain. Chris's problems and Debbie. The mystery of her existence. How strange, for something like your own existence to become a mystery after decades of ordinary life. When she eventually goes up to bed, Nigel is fast asleep and she lies beside him on her back for what feels like hours before dropping off herself.

9

If Ruth was going to call, she would have done it by now. Debbie knows that, if it were the other way around, she would have called immediately, without stopping to think about what she wanted to say or even what she wanted to come of this contact. She is impulsive like that. Always has been. But it appears that either Ruth is not, or she is and she's decided it's a no. That she doesn't need the complications this will bring to her life. Debbie thinks about what she knows of Ruth's life. Big house, living husband. Chances are she has children and all that entails. Maybe grandchildren. Debbie remembers her apron, her hands dusted with flour. Imagines, idly, that Ruth was baking a cake for a grandchild's birthday. Who would want to stir up trouble in a life like that?

Debbie cannot go there a third time. She won't. The last thing she'd want is for this woman to think of her as a nuisance. As a person who doesn't know when to leave something alone. But she'll always be curious about it. She knows that for a fact.

When she gets to the street corner where she's meeting

Matty and Jitu for today's door-knocking, it's only Jitu there. He tells her Matty has messaged him. He's sick.

'Hungover is my guess. I saw him last night when I was on my way home and he looked like he was just getting started.'

Debbie feels a flash of irritation. They are a team, and if one of them is absent, the other two have to work harder. Still, there's the opportunity to earn more commission, she supposes. The thing is, Debbie isn't really motivated by money. She needs to earn enough to cover her rent and bills, enough to buy the odd new piece of clothing and an occasional cup of tea and piece of cake in a café, but her needs are quite basic. It's different for the boys, with their tuition fees and rent and social lives to be funded. If it has to be just one of them, though, she is glad it's Jitu. She likes Matty well enough but Jitu feels like he's becoming a real friend. She hadn't expected it, but it's nice, the way they make each other laugh and teach each other things.

'Let's get going,' she says.

And they start up a hill on the edge of a new-looking estate, peeling off to the first two doorsteps when they reach them. It's slick, now, the way they work. It's only been a few weeks but they have it down pat. Debbie rings the doorbell and waits. She can hear Jitu start his spiel and there is no answer at hers, so she goes on to the next one. This time, a man answers almost immediately. He is about her age, dressed in navy-blue cords and a polo shirt. He smiles at her before she speaks in a way that she's learned is unusual. People are much more likely to start off sceptical.

'Good morning, I'm Debbie from Hopeful Horizons. Have you heard of us?'

The man's face falls, and Debbie knows at once that he is bereaved. She's learned to recognise this, and she usually takes it as a sign to wrap up and move on.

'I have,' he says. 'My wife, Gail. Late wife, I should say. I lost her to cancer eight months ago, but she lived with depression for most of her life.'

Debbie remembers when she counted the time since she'd lost Richie in months. First days, then weeks, then months. It strikes her that she doesn't know exactly how long it's been now. And that saddens her, but she thinks it's probably a good thing, too. Debbie notices that the man has a button hanging by a thread from his polo shirt, and she wishes she could offer to fix it for him. His button, his life.

'I'm so sorry,' Debbie says.

She's vaguely aware of Jitu passing behind her on the street, going on to the next house. She should be telling this man she'll leave him in peace, but something is keeping her here.

'Listen, would you like to come in? I've just put the kettle on.'

Going in is the cardinal sin. It's dangerous, for one thing, and it's a waste of time. She can't spend half an hour drinking tea with this man when she already knows he's unlikely to sign up to donate. But she's surprised to find that she wants to. There's something about him – something comforting and calming.

'I can't do that, I'm afraid.' She gestures to her paperwork and hopes he understands what she means – that she has a lot of ground to cover.

'Of course not. What am I thinking?'

'It's okay,' she says, hoping to reassure. 'We're going door to door today, looking for people to sign up for a regular donation or buy tickets for our one-off lottery.' Debbie hates herself for making him listen to this, when grief has so recently ripped his life apart, but she can't just leave, the way she did at Ruth's house. She has to at least appear to be doing her job.

'I'll buy some tickets for the lottery. How much are they?'

'A pound,' Debbie says, and he disappears for a moment, comes back with a debit card.

While he's filling in the form, Debbie steals glances into his home. It's neat and tidy, the hallway walls painted a muted green, three pairs of men's shoes in a row beside the door. There is something moving about the way they are lined up, the neatness of it. Out of nowhere, Debbie wonders who this man has in his life.

When Debbie catches up with Jitu, he's done another three houses.

'Tell me you signed him up,' he says. 'You were ages.'

Debbie shakes her head. 'Lottery tickets,' she says. And it's only then that she looks down at the form he filled in and sees that he's bought one thousand tickets. She presses her finger to the number, as if expecting it to change. But it's clear as clean glass.

'My God,' she says, 'look at this.'

Debbie holds up the form and Jitu's eyes widen. 'No freaking way.'

One day, Jitu sold ten lottery tickets to a young mum and Matty went on all day about how she must have fancied him.

'Shall I go back?' Debbie asks. 'Check whether it was a mistake?'

'No!' Jitu stops walking and holds both hands up. 'If the guy spent a grand by accident, that's his problem.'

They go on, split off to knock on the next two doors. And the day carries on like any other.

10

Ruth waits until she has the house to herself, which feels like weeks but is actually about three days. How is it that she so often feels alone but never actually is? Nigel's mostly in his office pod at the bottom of the garden, but now Chris is back and doesn't have a job to go to, he's rarely out of the house. There've been visits from Max, too. She's looked after Grace twice. But now, it's an ordinary Tuesday afternoon and Nigel and Chris have gone fishing, which is something they used to do when the boys were young, and all she has on her physical to do list is making a Christening cake, and all she has on her mental to do list is phoning Debbie.

Debbie. Short for Deborah, she assumes. The night they first met, Ruth had spent half an hour locked in her en suite bathroom, looking at her face in the mirror. Did that woman look like a Debbie? And does she look like a Ruth?

Before she can change her mind, she taps the number into her mobile and waits, her heart jumping as it rings.

'Hello?' It's her voice, too, Ruth thinks. The woman has Ruth's voice.

'Is that Debbie?' she asks, though she knows it is.

'Yes, is that...?'

'Ruth.' She hears a loud exhale.

'I'd told myself you weren't going to call.'

Ruth doesn't know what to say to that. It has been a while, but it was a lot to adjust to. She's still in the process. Isn't Debbie? She wonders for the first time what Debbie's home setup is. Does she have a husband, children? Does she live with a friend, or alone? It feels unfair that Debbie knows some of these things about her, and she is in the dark. But she can rectify it, get things back in balance.

'Would you like to meet for a coffee?' Ruth asks.

'Yes.' Debbie's answer is immediate, sure.

'Do you know Mildred's, on the High Street?'

'I'll find it.'

It makes Ruth wonder whether Debbie is new to this town, where she's lived her entire life other than her three years spent at university. If she'd always lived here, surely they would have come across each other before now. 'Tomorrow?'

There's a pause. And God, was it too soon? Has she scared her off? But no, Debbie was the one who said she'd given up on Ruth calling. Debbie was the one who brought the note in the first place. She is all in, and Ruth is the one who's been hanging back, refusing to leave the safety of the shore.

'I'm working,' Debbie says, 'but I could do afterwards. About six?'

Ruth is about to say it isn't convenient, because she's always home at that time, making dinner for her family. But she stops herself. It strikes her that she's been living a life that is small, confined. Saying no to things without thinking them through. This is more important than a Tuesday night dinner. Nigel and

Chris can fend for themselves while she drinks coffee and starts excavating the life she thought she knew.

'Six,' she repeats. 'Tomorrow. Mildred's. I'll see you there.'

Debbie says goodbye and then she's gone, and there's a ringing in Ruth's ears, as though something's happened with the line. She stands quite still for five minutes, until the post drops through the door and it's like it shatters something, breaks her out of her trance. She starts to gather the ingredients for the cake, pulls out a mixing bowl and begins sifting flour. The brief is fairly simple – lemon in flavour and colour, the baby's full name iced on the top, dolly mixtures to decorate. Ruth acts without thinking. Her brain and her body know how to do this. Cracking eggs, weighing out butter. The cake is in the oven before she realises that there are tears on her cheeks.

Upstairs, she opens the small cardboard box that she keeps under her bed. It's the things she keeps to remind her of her dad. Not that she needs a reminder. But her mum was all for getting rid of things. His clothes, his books. Ruth took the things that meant something to her. A Graham Greene paperback, a handful of letters from his parents, a scarf that still carries a hint of his scent when she holds it to her face. Did he lie to her, all these years? Did he keep the biggest kind of secret about her identity?

She's hit by a need to see her sister, the sister she has always had, always known about. She taps out a message to Kate, telling her she's coming, doesn't wait for a reply. And then she gets in her car and drives the two miles to Kate's house, her head chockfull of confusion.

'Are you okay?' Kate is at the door, waiting to let her in.

'Not really.' Ruth wants to fall into her sister's arms, but she has always taken the role of being the older one so seriously. Kate has so rarely seen her fall apart.

Kate ushers her in, has tea ready and waiting. Offers biscuits, which Ruth waves away.

'Has something happened?' Kate asks.

'I called her. Debbie. Kate, she has my voice. My exact voice. We're meeting tomorrow for a coffee. And I want to, but I don't. You know? What the hell am I going to find out?'

'I don't know,' Kate says simply.

Ruth doesn't know how Kate feels about all of this. She's good at keeping things inside, her expression neutral. But of course, this is big for her too, whatever the truth. Kate might find out that she has another sister, or that the sister she's always had isn't really hers. When Ruth first told her about Debbie, she asked a lot of questions, like she always does. Ever the journalist.

'Do you want to come with me?' Ruth asks.

Whatever this is, it doesn't only affect her. They might both be about to find out their lives have been built on lies.

'I do want to meet her, but I think you should go on your own this first time,' Kate says.

Ruth feels deflated. Not like a popped balloon, more like one with a tiny hole, slowly losing firmness. 'Okay, if that's what you want. Can we talk about something else?'

Kate nods, launches into a story about their mum. 'She was so lucid when I first arrived, calling me by my name, asking about you, and the boys. She even remembered about Grace. It reminded me of how quickly she's slipped. It was only about a year ago that a visit like that wasn't unusual, and now it feels like some kind of miracle.'

'It sounds like there's a but coming.' Ruth sips her tea, watches Kate. She thinks about how well she knows this woman, how connected they are. How alike. Or so she's always thought, but is it really just the fact that they are both blonde and blue-eyed? Kate is shorter, curvier, like their mum. Ruth always assumed she inherited her more masculine shape from their father. But what if there was more to it than that?

Kate was born when Ruth was three, and she can just about remember their mum being pregnant, being taken to the hospital to meet her sister for the first time. Is it possible that she already had a sister? She searches her memory but there is nothing, of course.

'It just all took a turn, after I'd been there about an hour. She called me Ruth, and then she asked who I was, what I was doing there. She was so agitated I thought I was going to have to leave. I hate seeing her like that.'

Ruth sighs.

'Sorry, when you asked to talk about something else, you probably didn't mean our rapidly deteriorating mother.'

'What if she isn't?'

'Isn't what?'

'Our mother. My mother.'

Kate bats this away. 'She's our mother.'

Ruth wants to ask her what she means. There's every chance that she's not, isn't there? Does Kate mean that Joan is their mother in every way that counts? That she raised them, in partnership with their dad? Ruth feels like everything she knew about her life is slipping. To ground herself, she reminds herself of things she knows. Nigel. Chris and Max. These men who are definitely hers.

'Tell me about Connie and James. How are they?'

It's Kate's turn to sigh. 'Connie's going back to her husband.'

'You don't sound too happy about that.'

'I just don't really trust him. They've broken up and got back together so many times. I feel like we're going to pack her up and get her settled just for him to break her heart. I know that when

I'm helping her pack I'm just going to be envisaging helping her unpack again in a few months.'

Ruth considers this, glad to have a problem that isn't her own to think about. 'You have to just let them do it, though, don't you?'

'But you know me, I like being in control.'

Ruth does know this. It's something she would have said about Kate, but not necessarily about herself. But look at her now, out of control and spinning. Struggling.

'Are the girls happy?'

'You know kids. They want their parents to be together.'

'And James?'

'James is good, as far as I know.'

Kate's son James got married young, had two daughters, split up with his wife. Ruth doesn't know what went on, exactly, but Kate has hinted at there being infidelity on both sides. Now, he lives with Kate and has his daughters at the weekends. There have been times, lately, when Kate has confessed that it's too much for her when all four granddaughters are there.

There are a few beats of silence, and when Ruth looks at her sister, she knows Kate is thinking about Debbie again.

'I'll let you know, when I find anything out,' Ruth says.

'You know, it would make a great story.'

Ruth is shocked. Would Kate really do that? Is this what she's been thinking about all along, while Ruth's been feeling all churned up inside? Ruth knows that Kate contacts people through Facebook groups when she gets a hint of a story. That she can be ruthless, prying and poking at people's wounds. You have to, to be a journalist, don't you? But would she treat Ruth that way?

'It's my life,' Ruth says. 'Our life. Our family.'

Kate puts a hand on her arm. 'I know, I know. I didn't mean it like that, Ruth. Nothing sensational. I just meant that I could do some digging, if I was reporting on it. In the name of research. I might be able to find out things that you can't.'

'I just don't know whether I want it all uncovered.'

'Well, I can understand that. Think about it.'

On the drive home, Ruth thinks about what Kate said, about digging. She feels as though her family life is a neat lawn and she's about to take a shovel to it, loosen the ground and see what's beneath. And she doesn't know whether it will make anything better, but she has to do it, because she can't live the rest of her life just not knowing.

11

Debbie arrives at the café at one minute to six and debates whether she should go in or stand outside. Ruth could already be here, of course. She looks in the window. And yes, there she is, at a table for two in the back corner, a mug in front of her. Will there ever be a time when it's not a shock to see Ruth's face? Perhaps, if they come to be in one another's lives. Debbie takes a deep breath and opens the door. It feels like she's transitioning from one life to another, more so than when she moved all her belongings from Southampton to Loughborough. That felt like a big change, but this feels seismic. She goes to the counter, gives Ruth a little wave to show she's seen her. Ruth is dressed smartly, and Debbie wonders what she might be doing afterwards, or what she's been doing before. Is this just a small part of her busy day? Debbie has nothing planned for afterwards other than going home and eating a microwave meal in front of the TV.

When she's got her cappuccino and a thick slice of carrot cake, Debbie carries them over to the table where Ruth sits. She's conscious of the woman behind the counter looking over, noticing the similarity.

'Hello,' she says, putting her mug and plate down with an unintentional clatter. 'I'm Debbie.'

Should they shake hands? It feels so formal, and Debbie would rather hug, but she doesn't want to frighten Ruth off. She thinks of Ruth as a sort of scared rabbit, one who could bolt at any moment.

'I'm Ruth,' Ruth says, and they both laugh a little nervously because they already knew each other's names, and because of how utterly bizarre this is.

Debbie is fascinated by everything Ruth does. The way she stirs her latte. The way she holds her body, more carefully than Debbie does. Ruth is slimmer than Debbie and looks like she's taken better care of her skin. But Debbie doesn't mind her lines and her bulges. They're all a reminder of the life she's lived. Ruth looks like she is careful with herself. Clothes in muted colours, hair neat and tidy, body taking up so little space.

'I don't really know where to start,' Debbie says. 'Do you?'

Ruth shakes her head. But then she speaks. 'I've been going over the possibilities. I'm sure you have, too. That we were both adopted, that we were taken.'

'Taken?' Debbie cuts in.

'Yes. It sounds so far-fetched, but this whole thing is far-fetched, isn't it?'

'I hadn't considered that. I was thinking along the lines of one of our mums being both of our mums.'

Ruth nods, takes a sip of her drink. 'Maybe you could tell me how you grew up. Where, and who with, and all that.'

'Okay.' It's as good a place to start as any. 'It was just me and my mum. Her name was Lizzie Cooper. She wasn't very well. Mentally. She was in and out of hospital when I was young.'

'And what happened to you, when she was in hospital?'

Debbie pulls the sleeves of her jumper down over her hands.

Remembering. She doesn't think about her childhood very often. Doesn't like to. 'I went to my granny's. But she was old and didn't really make a secret of the fact that she didn't want me there. She felt like her hands were tied, I think. Otherwise I would have had to go into care.'

Debbie looks at Ruth and sees compassion in her eyes. She has guessed that Ruth didn't have this kind of upbringing. That she is used to families being more stable, more present. 'What about you?'

'I had a mum and dad. Frank and Joan Simpson. And a sister, Kate. Three years younger than me.'

How is it possible? Debbie tries to work it out. Where is the crack that she can get her finger into, to loosen things?

'Do you know who your dad was?' Ruth asks.

Debbie is a child again, tugging on her mum's skirt, asking about her dad. Being pushed away, told to leave things alone. She asked her granny too, once. They were making scones. Her granny had her fingers in the flour and butter, rubbing. She didn't look at Debbie when she spoke. *He's dead.*

'He was never in my life, and my granny told me he was dead.'

Where to go from here? Debbie sees that Ruth is smiling, and she tilts her head. 'What?'

'I'm sorry,' Ruth says. 'You just told me your father is dead. I'm so sorry. It's just, I can't get over how strange this is. I can't stop looking at you.'

Debbie is glad Ruth has acknowledged it. It is strange. It's the strangest thing that's ever happened in her life. She goes back over what Ruth said about her family. A mum and dad. A sister. All those people to love, to be loved by. She feels a bubble of envy start to rise in her. It's something she's always avoided. She isn't materialistic, and has never envied anyone for the things they have or can buy. Houses, cars, holidays. But this is different. Ruth feels like an alternative version of her, and one who had a better chance.

'So what do you think about adoption?' Debbie asks.

'I have my birth certificate, and my parents' names are on it. Do you have yours?'

Debbie pictures the boxes of paperwork that she hasn't unpacked since moving. Richie used to handle the bills and all that, but neither of them were particularly organised. It's a jumble to be dealt with at some point. And she thinks her birth certificate is probably in there somewhere. She tries to picture it. Can't.

'Somewhere,' she says. 'I'll dig it out.'

There is a moment of quiet, and Debbie wonders whether Ruth is judging her, for not having sought it out already. They are each weighing up the differences between them, she thinks. Finding where the other is wanting.

'I don't know whether this sounds strange,' Debbie says, 'but what about we stop trying to work it out? For now, at least. What about we just have a go at getting to know each other?'

Ruth frowns, two distinct lines between her eyebrows. Debbie has seen those same lines a hundred times in the car's rearview mirror. Has she crossed a line, suggesting that something will continue between them beyond this meeting?

'When is your birthday?' Ruth asks.

Of course. Why didn't Debbie think of that? 'Eighth of February.'

'1962?'

'Yes.'

She doesn't need Ruth to confirm that hers is the same, but Ruth gives a tight little nod anyway. And that's their answer, isn't it? Debbie has heard of people finding people who look astonishingly like them, but the birthday thing seals it, she thinks. She doesn't believe in coincidences. Certainly not on that scale.

'Okay,' Ruth says, and Debbie isn't sure for a moment what she's referring to. 'Let's get to know each other.'

Debbie breaks into a smile. She likes this woman, she realises. She wants to understand her better, to know her history and be able to ask her casual questions about her family.

'When you came to my house, what were you doing?' Ruth asks.

Debbie sits back. Her coffee is finished. 'I work for a mental health charity, Hopeful Horizons. Trying to get people to sign up for regular donations.'

'So you do that every day, going door to door?'

Debbie nods. 'I haven't been doing it long, but I really like it. I love meeting people.'

Ruth looks bemused, like she can't imagine feeling that way.

'What do you do?' Debbie asks.

'I have a baking business. It's just small. Birthday cakes, trays of cookies and brownies, that kind of thing.'

Debbie remembers the floured apron, how she'd imagined Ruth was making a cake for a grandchild. 'Do you have children? Grandchildren?'

Ruth nods. 'Twin boys. Chris and Max. And Max has a baby daughter. Grace.'

Debbie's brain hooks onto the word twins. She knows that twins run in families. Of course she does. 'Do you want another?' she asks, gesturing towards Ruth's empty mug.

Ruth looks at her watch. 'I should get home,' she says.

Debbie remembers what it was like to have someone at home, waiting. And Ruth has so many people in her life. A husband, children, a grandchild. Debbie doesn't know whether it is just her husband who lives with her, but she wants to. She wants to know everything. Despite saying that she has to go, Ruth hasn't stood up, and Debbie wonders whether perhaps she's open to persuasion. But she reminds herself not to go too far, too fast. Not everyone is like her, keen to gather up people wherever she goes. In time, this might be the kind of thing she knows about Ruth, whether her no can sometimes be persuaded to change to a yes. But for now, she will go home and wait until next time.

Finally, she is the one to stand, and Ruth follows suit.

'Where do you live?' Ruth asks. 'Have you lived in Loughborough long?'

Debbie shakes her head. 'Not long. I'm renting a little place on Manor Road.'

Ruth nods and Debbie can't tell what she's thinking.

'You've got my number?'

Debbie feels like this is encouragement, and is pleased. 'Yes,' she says.

On the walk home, Debbie runs back over the conversation, searching for clues she might have missed at the time. She remembers the names of Ruth's sons, her twin sons. And her granddaughter. What must it be like, to have all those people to love? Debbie isn't lonely. She never has been. Her life has always been full of people, but other than her mum and then Richie, they haven't been hers. She suspects it's different when they are. That there are layers of duty and wonder and pure, pure love. She wishes Richie was waiting for her at home, that she could share this incredible development with him. Richie had family, and his mother treated Debbie like she was one of her own. But she is long gone, and now Richie is gone too, and Debbie isn't sure who to go to with her news.

Debbie's getting ready for bed when her phone beeps. She thinks it will be Matty or Jitu. They have a WhatsApp group where they let each other know if they're running late or ill or something like that. Sometimes the boys post gifs or memes that make her laugh. But the message is from Ruth.

> Debbie, it was good to meet you. I'd like to do it again, if you would. Take care, Ruth x

It's simple, giving little away, but it's enough to make Debbie feel warm and hopeful. She's okay with not knowing what the future will be like, but that it might just have this woman in it.

12

Ruth sits by her mother's bed, waiting for her to wake. There's a plate with toast crumbs on her mum's tray table, a few crumbs on her lips. Usually, when she's waiting like this, Ruth pulls out a book or her phone, but today, she just waits and thinks. Her mind is on Debbie, on the way she grew up, with what sounded like a paucity of love. Ruth can't quite imagine having had that experience, the moving around, the worry about her mum that Debbie had. She has that worry now, and she's a sixty-two-year-old woman and she still finds it hard to handle sometimes. Mental illness is scary. Was Debbie often scared as a child? Did her mum do things that were confusing and unpredictable? Did Debbie know when an episode was coming on? Was it up to her to call her grandmother, make sure her mum got the help she needed? Ruth hopes not. She hopes there were at least enough adults involved to shield Debbie from the worst of it.

Joan wakes with a start, and Ruth reaches out to touch her hand, hoping it will still her. 'Mum, are you okay?'

Joan looks back at her, clearly confused, but she doesn't pull her hand away from her daughter's touch. 'Where am I? This isn't my bed.'

Ruth doesn't know how to answer, but she forces herself to. 'You're at the care home, Mum. This is your room. Those are the curtains you chose, and the flowers Kate brought.'

Joan settles, and Ruth is relieved that she doesn't ask who Kate is. Perhaps she'll have a good visit, the kind she used to take for granted.

'How have you been?' she asks, though she calls every other day and comes in twice a week. Often, she finds that it is hard to make conversation with her mother, a problem she never could have foreseen ten or twenty years ago. Joan doesn't always have full access to the past, and her present is dull, her future unknown. Which leaves... what?

'Bored to tears,' Joan says. 'Can we go out somewhere?'

Ruth is taken aback. They never go anywhere. But then, she's not sure why not. When Joan first went into the home, Ruth and Kate used to take her out for a cup of tea or even to the cinema a couple of times, but it's been a while since they've done anything like that. It's just so much easier not to. She feels a twinge of guilt. If she was the one stuck in here, she'd give anything to go outside.

'Why not?'

Getting her mum up and dressed is a long process, but Ruth manages. At one point, when they're in Joan's en suite bathroom and Ruth is helping her to brush her teeth, she catches a glimpse of them in the mirror and is shocked by the two old ladies looking back. She used to stand like this with the boys, squeezing the toothpaste out for them because they inevitably either couldn't get any or squeezed out half the tube. How did she get from there to here, in what feels like a couple of years at most?

At last, they are ready to go. Joan insists on wearing a coat even though Ruth tells her that it's a gorgeous spring day. They link arms as they step outside and Ruth prays that nothing will go wrong. That her mum won't trip and fall, or suddenly turn and start telling everyone she doesn't know who Ruth is. They don't go far, just to a café a couple of streets away. Joan wants to pay, and Ruth has to bite her lip to keep from crying as she insists it's on her. She doesn't point out that Joan doesn't have a bag or a purse or a card with her. They order a pot of tea and toasted teacakes and sit at a little outside table that is in a small patch of sunlight, and Ruth thinks she must do this more often. It's such a little thing, but she can see how her mum has brightened.

If only she was always like this. Ruth knows from experience that she might not get another visit like this for a long time. She might never get one. And that's what prompts her to speak. She doesn't go to the heart of the matter, doesn't dare. She leaves Debbie out of it, for now.

'Mum, I came across my birth certificate the other day, and I noticed that your full name isn't on it.'

Joan looks wild-eyed. 'Your birth certificate?'

'Yes. Do you remember, it says Elizabeth Simpson, and you told me that your first name is Betty but you've always gone by Joan.'

'That's right.'

'But on the certificate, it doesn't say Joan at all. Just Elizabeth.'

Joan pours her tea. Is she stalling? It's impossible to say. 'I don't know why that would be.'

Ruth thinks about her meeting with Debbie, when Debbie said her mum's name. Lizzie. Lizzie Cooper. Another form of Elizabeth. She hadn't reacted at the time, hadn't been ready to share this nugget with Debbie. But now, here, she wishes she had some answers.

Should she push? Is it fair to? Her mum is an old woman, nearing the end of her life. If there is mess to be uncovered, should Ruth wait until she is gone, out of kindness? She imagines spilling the whole story, about Debbie at her door and their shocked, identical faces. Ruth leaves too much of a gap to respond and her mum changes the subject, saying that one of her favourite carers is going on maternity leave and she hates it when they fill in with agency staff who she only ever sees once or twice before they're gone. Ruth thinks of the carers she sees at the home – mostly young, all jaded. They do the work other people don't want to do for so little money. She reaches for her toasted teacake, and a cloud covers the sun and she feels chilly.

'Shall I get you back?' she asks.

'No.' Her mum is firm. 'There's more tea.'

'I don't want you to get cold.'

'There are worse things.'

Ruth doesn't respond to this, because it's true. Her phone beeps and she checks it. It's a message from Debbie.

> How are things?

Ruth feels herself flush as if she's been caught talking to a lover. She looks at her mum, who hasn't noticed. 'You know how twins run in families—' she says.

'So they say.'

'Were there any in our family, before my boys?' Ruth feels like she's stepping out onto a frozen lake with no idea how thick the ice is.

And then it's mayhem, because Joan has knocked over her mug and there is tea on the table, on her lap, dripping onto the floor. Ruth's out of her seat, going to the counter for paper towels, checking that her mum hasn't been burned. But the tea was lukewarm. She is fine, just damp. The decision is made, and they get up and leave once Ruth has cleared up as best she can. On the walk back to the home, they are mostly silent. But as they approach the door, Joan speaks.

'Don't take me back there.'

Ruth stops on the pavement, unsure what to do or say. 'Why?'

'It's not my home.'

She looks so sad, so defeated, that Ruth wants to bundle her into her car and drive away. But what would that solve? She reminds herself of the conversations she and Kate have had, about this being the best place for her now that she's so confused. If she was living with Ruth and Nigel, she might wander off at any time of the day or night. There are staff keeping watch twenty-four hours a day at the home. Ruth can't do that.

'I'm sorry, Mum,' Ruth says, and she enters the code to open the front door.

It's when they're back in Joan's room and Ruth is helping her take her coat off that the change comes. It's like a switch, flicked. With fear in her eyes, Joan pulls her coat out of Ruth's hands.

'Leave me alone!'

Ruth knows the drill. She steps back, holds her hands up to show she doesn't mean her mum any harm. A carer knocks on the door and brings in medicine, and Ruth decides it's time she went home. But as she's leaving, she hears Joan speaking to the carer, her voice full of agitation.

'I told him I didn't think it was the right thing. They should be together, shouldn't they?'

'Who, Joan?'

'The twins. They belong together.'

* * *

Ruth drives home, feeling like someone's pulled her feet out from under her. Was her mum just babbling, or was there something in those words? The twins. She couldn't have been talking about Chris and Max, could she? It doesn't make sense. But by the time she said it, she was confused again, so there is no way of knowing.

At home, she finds Nigel eating a cheese sandwich standing up in the kitchen. He's cut the cheese into thick, uneven slices, hasn't added any cucumber or tomato. He's perfectly capable of looking after himself, of sorting out his washing and his meals, but if she isn't there, he just doesn't really bother, which leaves her feeling guilty, and like she should make sure she is.

'Where's Chris?' she asks.

Nigel grunts. 'Up in his room.'

'Have you seen him today?' Ruth hasn't. When she left for the care home, he hadn't surfaced.

'No, but there are tea bags in the sink, so I know he's alive.' Nigel picks something out of his teeth, and Ruth looks away, wishing he would do that kind of thing in private. 'What should we do, do you think?'

'About Chris?'

'Yes. He can't go on like this indefinitely, can he?'

Ruth isn't sure what he means. Can't go on... what? Moping? Not working? Living in their house? 'I mean, I think he just needs a bit of time.'

'A bit of time? It's been nearly two weeks already and he's showing no signs of shifting. Or job-hunting for that matter.'

When the boys were young, Ruth was the good cop to Nigel's

bad. He doled out the punishments, most of the time, and she the love. Not that Nigel didn't love them, but he wasn't tactile. He didn't sweep their hair from their foreheads and kiss them, snuggle up next to them when they were upset or scared or lost.

'Do you know what happened, with the job?' Nigel asks.

Ruth hasn't told him about the conversation she had with Chris. Will Chris want to tell his dad himself, or would he rather she did it for him? She isn't sure. 'Redundancy, but I think it hit him hard because he wasn't expecting it. He was, um, close with his boss, and he thought he'd get special treatment.'

Nigel snorts. 'Good lesson to learn, that.'

Ruth shakes her head, as if it might change her husband's levels of compassion for their son. 'Have *you* tried talking to him?'

'What do you mean?'

She clasps her hands behind her back, because she's worried that she might try to choke him. 'You know what talking is. Ask him how he's feeling, where his head's at.'

'Where his head's at?' Nigel's voice is mocking, cruel. 'You watch too many of those awful American TV shows, Ruth.'

She wants to sink to the floor. To say that she feels like her life is coming apart at the seams. Her mother, fading. Her son, flailing. And this woman, Debbie, so likeable and full of spark, but such a mystery, too. Until Ruth knows where she fits in, she can't relax. Her marriage feels like a city she's never visited before, and she doesn't know where to turn.

'I'll talk to him, then,' she says.

'Give him a timeframe. A couple more weeks, should we say?'

Her mouth drops open. 'Are you asking me to give him notice? Our son?'

Nigel rolls his eyes. 'Come on, Ruth. He's not a kid. He's been fending for himself for years and now you're acting like he's not capable. Well, he is. Sometimes people need a bit of a push...'

'Sometimes they need compassion.'

Stalemate. Ruth looks at this man who she has loved and lived with, and she feels there is nothing left. Like a sponge wrung dry. And then she is aware of movement out of the corner of her eye, and she sees that Chris is in the doorway. How much did he hear? Nobody speaks, or moves. And then everyone does.

'Chris, love, can I get you...?' Ruth isn't sure what to offer.

'I'm going back to work.' Nigel stomps out of the room.

'I was just...' Chris doesn't say what he was just doing.

The air in the room is flat, Nigel gone but somehow still making himself felt.

'Tea?' Ruth asks, and Chris nods gratefully, slides onto one of the stools at the breakfast bar.

'Does he want me to go?' Chris asks.

Ruth looks at the kettle, at the floor, anywhere but at her son. 'It's not to do with you. It's this tough love thing he has. He thinks the best thing we can do for you is make you stand on your own two feet.'

Chris nods. 'You know, you always do that. You always try to soften stuff for him, so it doesn't seem as bad. I know when we were kids you were this parenting team, or whatever, but now we're all adults, you could just say if you disagree with him.'

Ruth pours the boiling water from the kettle into two mugs and thinks about what he's saying. If anyone else said something like that, she would be defensive. But this is Chris, and she knows he's probably right. 'Okay then, I disagree with him. I never wanted you and Max to move out, I want you here with me forever. I'd still be running your baths and reading you bedtime stories if it was up to me.'

Chris laughs, and the rush of relief that gushes through Ruth is so warm. 'I won't stay too much longer, I promise.'

'Remember that you can, though, if you want to.'

'Oh yeah? Is that what Dad would say?'

Ruth wants to say that she doesn't care. This is her nest, her family, and she won't let him push anyone out of it. But instead, she says nothing. She sits beside him, turns to face him, runs a hand along the length of his back. He used to like her rubbing his back to help him get to sleep, and some evenings she would be there for half an hour, her mind going over all the things she had to do downstairs, praying for the release that came with the deepening of his breath. And now, she would give anything for him to be six years old again, to need her like that. To believe that she was capable of fixing anything at all.

'What are you going to do?' she asks.

Chris shrugs. 'Start again. I've got a good CV, he'll give me a good reference. It will be okay.'

What she really means, but doesn't ask, is: what are you going to do about your heart? They sit there, side by side, dust dancing in the airy room, until he coughs and she stands and the spell is broken.

13

Debbie is woken by hammering on the door. It is Saturday, not yet eight. Who could it be? Postmen don't knock like that.

Jitu. She hasn't seen him for a few days. He's been calling in sick, messaging apologies. Debbie doesn't really mind. She and Matty have done longer days and she's earned some good commission, but she's been worried about him.

She waves him inside. It's pouring with rain and he's not dressed for it. Just jogging bottoms and a hoodie, and there are droplets of water in his hair and on his shoulders. He looks different, somehow diminished. Is it just the way he's standing, slightly hunched, when she's used to seeing him walk straight and tall? She leads him into the kitchen and puts the kettle on.

'What is it?' she asks, realising that she hasn't spoken since opening the door.

Jitu shrugs his hoodie off and then looks around for somewhere to put it. In his T-shirt, he looks more boy than man. 'It's all fucked,' he says.

Debbie waits, wonders. Could this be about a girl, or something to do with his family? They've spent many days together, walking up and down winding roads and chatting, but he hasn't really opened up to her about anything important. She doesn't really know him.

'It's uni. Look.' He pulls a crumpled piece of paper from his pocket and starts to unfold it. Debbie can see that it's been folded and unfolded a number of times, the creases worn. She has to go to the living room to get her reading glasses.

The letter is official-looking, on headed paper. From his personal tutor. It takes Debbie a while to wade through the stiff, formal language and understand what it's about. Plagiarism. Stealing, then. Jitu has been accused of using other people's words, passing them off as his own. They want him to come in for a meeting, in a couple of weeks.

Debbie takes a long, slow breath. She needs to ask him whether it is true, but she doesn't know how to phrase it. Surely they don't make these accusations lightly, though. Surely they must be pretty sure, for it to get to this stage. She makes tea, holds up the sugar, and he shakes his head. Nods for milk. The letter lies on the kitchen counter like a threat.

'What are you going to do?' she asks.

He shrugs, and when she pulls out a chair and sits at the small kitchen table, he follows suit and sits opposite her. Debbie knows nothing about university life. It's something that's always seemed like it's for other people. Richer people. More intelligent? But now, with this younger generation, it's for everyone. And perhaps Jitu's just not up to it, and he has too much pride to say so. This could be a cry for help, a shout out for someone to see that he's drowning. She thinks about the long hours he works with her, how she's often wondered whether he's missing lectures to fit it in. What a mess.

Debbie asks her question as gently as she can. 'Why did you come to me?'

Jitu looks at her then, and she sees that his eyes are red and hates to think of him crying alone. 'I don't know. I can't tell my family. They're so bloody proud of me. I'm the first to go to uni and my nani cried when I got my offer. And I wouldn't know what to say to any of my friends. And then I thought of you. I feel like you don't judge people.'

Is that an admission of guilt? Debbie takes it as one. 'What can I do to help?'

Jitu puts his head in his hands, his elbows on the table. When he speaks, she's lost in her thoughts and has to ask him to repeat what he said.

'Will you come with me, to the meeting? The letter says I can bring someone.'

Debbie feels a stabbing pain in her chest, just for a second, at the fact that he doesn't feel able to ask his mother. She checks the date and time on the letter, goes to the calendar that is hanging on the back of the door. With a biro, she writes 'Jitu meeting, university, 1 p.m.'

'Done,' she says. 'We'll have to think of something if we're due to be working.'

'Thank you,' Jitu says, looking at her, his eyes clear. 'Really, you don't know what this means.'

Debbie feels out of her depth, like she's swimming in the ocean and the seabed has fallen away beneath her feet. 'I don't know how much help I'll be. I don't know anything about academia. It will be my first time in a university building, unless those drinks at the Union count.'

He looks surprised, but doesn't say anything. And she realises that it's just about having someone there, about not being alone. She isn't expected to know how it all works. She is just a hand to hold. And that's fine. She can do that for this boy who's taught her so much about how young people think and speak. Sometimes, after a shift with Matty and Jitu, Debbie feels like she's shrugged off ten years. For a few minutes, they sit in silence with their tea. Debbie wishes she had biscuits to offer, or cake. Idly, she thinks about the possibility of ordering a cake from Ruth. Something elaborate and beautiful. It's not the kind of thing you do, when you live alone.

When Jitu gets up to leave, Debbie is relieved. There's a heaviness to the sadness he's carrying. It's spilled out into her kitchen and the air is thick with it.

'Are you coming back to work?' she asks.

'Yes. Sorry I've been off so much. But I need to get back to it. Money's tight.'

They are back in the hallway, in slightly too close proximity. Debbie feels panicked. Should she offer him money? A loan, or just a gift? She's not exactly well off herself but she's probably in a better position than him right now. She wouldn't mind giving Jitu money, but she doesn't want to tip the delicate balance of their relationship. It feels like they've moved from one thing to another, this morning, and she doesn't know exactly where the boundaries are. She is still feeling around. So in the end, she doesn't offer, though for the rest of the day, she wishes she had.

She spends a bit of time on her old laptop learning about plagiarism, about university policies, about what Jitu might face. It's guesswork, varying from one institution to another, and there are different levels of severity, too. Debbie wishes she knew someone who worked in that world, who she could ask, straight up, what might happen. But like she told Jitu, universities are an alien world for her. And then, when she's eating soup for lunch, her brain lands on Ruth, like a fly that's been buzzing and she only notices when it stops. Ruth has two sons, and Debbie thinks it's likely that they went to university. It isn't much, but it's more than Debbie has. She sends a text before she can have second thoughts.

> Ruth, could I ask your advice about something? Do you have time for another coffee?

While she's waiting for a response, she feels like she did when she was much younger, waiting for a boy to call. It feels like something in her stomach is expanding and contracting. It's not uncomfortable, it's more a fizzing feeling. But she doesn't have to wait long.

> I'm just in the middle of a wedding cake. Would four o'clock be any good?

Debbie hadn't expected Ruth to suggest today, but she's glad about it. Days she's not working, she finds it hard to give a shape to. She is grateful to have something to slot other things around. Outside, the rain has cleared. She decides, on a whim, to go for a walk. She sends a message to Pete, asking if he wants her to walk Bonnie, but doesn't wait for a reply. She'll go in that direction, just in case. After she's put her shoes on, Debbie remembers she hasn't replied to Ruth. She confirms that four is fine, invites Ruth to come to her house. Hopes that isn't crossing a line of some kind. But no, Ruth says she will see her then, and Debbie picks up her purse. She will buy biscuits while she's out.

* * *

'Plagiarism?' Ruth asks. 'How are you involved with this again?'

It is so strange, to just be finding your feet, working out what you are to each other, when it is clear that there is a strong genetic connection between you. She explains to Ruth about

Jitu, about working together, about the early morning visit and the letter. Ruth blows out a breath and Debbie recognises it as a mannerism she has, and there's a clutch of something in her stomach. Fear?

'Well, Max and Chris both went to university, but we never dealt with anything like that.'

Debbie wonders, for a moment, whether Ruth would say if they had. She doesn't know her well enough to judge, but she suspects Ruth cares what other people think of her and her family. That she would keep something like this under wraps.

'Where did they go?' she asks. Because as well as wanting Ruth's advice, she wants to get to know her better. And at the start of knowing someone, it's all about gathering facts, isn't it? Later, when you have the background and the context, you can chat freely, but before you get there, there's work to do.

'Manchester. Both of them. Nigel and I thought it would be better for them to go their separate ways at that point. They'd been together all through school, of course. At secondary, they weren't always in the same classes, but they sought each other out at break and lunch. We were worried that they were too dependent on one another. That they'd never find their own paths. Anyway, they both went to Manchester and we didn't think it was the right thing, but they were adults at that point.'

'Did they study the same subject?' Debbie asks.

Ruth nods. 'Business. It was like they decided by committee. Max is much more creative than Chris. I always thought he might go into something arty.'

'What do they do now?' As soon as she's asked it, Debbie can tell from the expression on Ruth's face that it's a difficult question, but she can't really take it back without drawing attention to it.

'Well, Max is an accountant. Self-employed, which is handy because he and his wife have got a baby. They live in Leicester. And Chris was working in finance in London. Quite the high-flyer. But he was made redundant recently, so he's moved back in with us for a while.'

It strikes Debbie that there's a chance she might meet him. This man, who may or may not be her blood relative. Who almost certainly is. 'So they struck out on their own in the end, then?'

'Yes, it was one of those things that I lost a lot of sleep over but that I needn't have worried about at all. There's a lot of that, in motherhood. After they graduated, Max went travelling for a bit, and Chris joined him for a month in Australia but then came back and started applying for jobs in London. And when Max came home, he lived with us for a couple of years and looked for jobs more locally.'

Debbie wonders what they look like. She is sure that Ruth will show her a photo if she asks. All her life, she's known mothers and they always have a photo of their children. Either on their phone or in their purse, and they're always ready to show them off. But something stops her from asking. It's a lot, all of this with Ruth, and she wants to keep it to the two of them for a bit longer. She isn't sure she's ready for wider family.

'You never had children,' Ruth says. It's half a question, the way she says it, but she isn't asking whether it's true. It came up the last time they met. She's asking why.

'No, no children.' Debbie thinks back to the years of waiting, hoping. The look on Richie's face that he tried so hard to hide when he looked at her, every time she got her period. She wouldn't mind telling Ruth, can imagine telling her. She thinks Ruth might be the type of person to cover Debbie's hand with her own to show she understands. But they are not there, yet.

'I'll ask the boys if they knew anyone who was accused of plagiarism,' Ruth says.

'Thank you.'

'Have you ever been married?'

Debbie is surprised. Has Richie really not come up? She has to remind herself that it's only been two meetings. It feels, somehow, like more. 'Yes, I was married for forty-one years. Richie. He died last year. Heart attack. It was sudden, unexpected.' Funny, how she can say his name and talk about what happened to him without getting choked up now. When did that happen?

'Oh, I'm sorry,' Ruth says, and she goes quiet.

Debbie imagines she's thinking about their lives, the differences between them. The emptiness of Debbie's. She feels she needs to explain, that it isn't all bad. 'I have a lot of people in my life, one way or another.'

Ruth nods. 'Who?'

'Friends. You don't know them.' Debbie is aware of how childish this sounds.

Ruth's expression changes, and Debbie can't read it. She wonders whether this is an expression she ever makes. Thinks hard about the way she would have to move her mouth and her eyebrows. Part of her wants to try it out, but she can't do it here, in front of Ruth. She will wait until she is alone. And then Ruth looks at her watch.

'I have to go, I'm sorry. My son, Max, he's coming for dinner.'

Debbie nods. She needs to go out in half an hour to walk Bonnie. Pete had replied earlier, to say that late afternoon would be best.

Debbie walks Ruth to her front door, and it's slightly stilted. She leans in for a hug, but it seems to take Ruth by surprise and she keeps her arms by her sides. And after Ruth's gone, Debbie thinks about how they may have once shared a womb, their limbs entwined. And now, all these decades later, they can't even manage a hug without awkwardness. But perhaps they will, in time.

14

Max must have arrived seconds before Ruth gets home, because when she lets herself in, her boys are standing in the hallway, their bodies pressed together in a hug. She stands there for a moment, unseen, and enjoys their closeness. When they were about seven, they used to sit in front of the TV with their feet in one another's laps. And so often, when she went to wake them in the mornings for school, she'd find that one had crawled into the other's bed at some point in the night. They would be lying there, fast asleep, their faces close, their feet touching, and when she woke them, neither of them would remember how they came to be sleeping in the same bed. There's a cry and the boys break apart. Max goes into the lounge, where the sound came from. Ruth follows him in, and Chris follows her. Layla's holding a distressed-looking Grace.

'She toppled over,' Layla says.

Grace can sit, now, and Ruth can see that Layla's pulled some cushions off the sofa to put around her. Ruth knows that when she falls, she cries out of frustration rather than because she's hurt. When Ruth is looking after her, she tends to use distraction in these cases, but Layla is rocking her. Max goes over and kisses his baby girl's head, and then Layla's, and it feels like such an intimate moment that Ruth is almost embarrassed to have witnessed it. She doesn't remember the last time Nigel touched her.

'Something smells great,' Layla says, and it spurs Ruth into action.

She's had a curry in the slow cooker for hours, and earlier she made naans and an apple tart for dessert. She just needs to get the rice on. So she goes to the kitchen, leaving the others to catch up with Chris. She's rinsing the rice when Nigel appears in the room.

'What was it she wanted?' he asks.

She'd told Nigel that she was meeting Debbie, because there was no reason not to, but now she wishes she hadn't. She doesn't feel like explaining. 'Oh, it was just a question about university stuff, for a student she knows.'

'What sort of university stuff?'

'Her friend's been accused of plagiarism and she's going to a meeting with him, at the university. But she doesn't know much about higher education, and she thought I might, with having the boys.'

Nigel looks puzzled, and Ruth has to concede that it's a bit strange.

'I think maybe she just wanted to get together again. I think we're going to be doing more of that. I'd like to ask her to come here sometime, to meet you and the boys.'

Nigel holds up his hands as if asking her to stop, or slow down. 'Don't you want to get to the bottom of what's going on first? To find out who she really is?'

Ruth thinks about the decision they made, her and Debbie, to leave all that for a while and just get to know one another. She is a bit surprised to learn that she feels strongly about it. It was Debbie's suggestion, but she is totally on board. She wants to know Debbie, and learning how they fit together could be painful, so why not put a pin in that, for a while at least? 'No. It's not important. I mean, it is, of course, but I just want to spend some time with her first.'

She knows that Nigel will shake his head at this, and he does. Ruth moves across the kitchen and picks up the kettle, pours water onto the rice she's washed, and Nigel says nothing, so the conversation is over. Except it isn't, because he brings it up again once they're sitting around the dining table.

'Has your mother told you about this business with her double?' He's looking at Max.

'What business?' Max looks from his dad to Ruth and back again, and Nigel gestures to Ruth to pick up the story.

Out of nowhere, Ruth feels that she hates him. Why bring this up, if he wasn't going to tell the story himself? Is he just stirring things up, making people uncomfortable?

'I met a woman who looks just like me,' she says, knowing even as the words leave her mouth that they don't quite capture it.

'Right...' Max says, and it's just like when she first told Nigel and Chris.

'She's her double,' Nigel says. 'They're as alike as the two of you.' He points with one finger to Max and then Chris.

For the first year or so of the twins' lives, Nigel found it hard to tell them apart. Ruth knew them, though. She always knew. Was that because of having grown them in her body? Did she have a deeper connection and a better understanding of these two little beings? It's strange, now that they are grown men, to see them together, to catalogue the similarities and differences. Sometimes, Max has a beard, but he doesn't at the moment.

Ruth wonders how it is for Layla, seeing Chris. Seeing a man who looks so like her husband, but isn't.

'How can that be?' Max asks.

Ruth gives Nigel a look that she hopes he can interpret. It says, simply, *Why? Why are you doing this?* Isn't it her story to tell?

'We don't know,' she says, tearing her naan and putting a small piece of it in her mouth. 'It's a mystery.'

It's Layla who speaks up next. 'That's wild. Have you got Kate looking into it?'

Ruth remembers what Kate said, about investigating. Reporting on the story. 'Not yet. We're just... taking it slowly. Getting to know each other.'

'Have you talked to Gran about it?' Chris asks.

Ruth shakes her head, feels close to tears. It's a slow loss, dementia. A series of losses. It's losing someone over and over. It's an ocean of grief. 'Can we talk about something else?' she asks.

Chris clears his throat and Layla gets up to check that Grace is asleep. They've put the travel cot up in Max's old bedroom, and when they're ready to go they'll prepare to transfer her to her car seat and Ruth will tell them to leave her sleeping, say that she'll drop her back in the morning. When Layla returns, nodding at Max to confirm that Grace is okay, Max starts a story about a new client he's working with, about the shoebox of receipts they provided and how Max is having to sift through them, emailing the client over and over to confirm that a holiday in Barbados can't be put through as a business expense for a plumber. Or a PlayStation. Or a conservatory.

'Good money in plumbing, clearly,' Nigel says.

After they've eaten dessert, Ruth offers to check on Grace. Layla is a nervous mother, and Ruth remembers feeling that way.

She wants to help. Layla is thin, always looks drawn. She smiles gratefully when Ruth says she'll go. Upstairs, she takes a deep breath, opens the door to the room that was Max's. Remembers the posters he used to have on the walls as a teenager. Bands and women. Cars. So aggressively straight. One of them has put up a temporary blackout blind and Ruth blinks to adjust to the dim light. Grace is curled on her side, her eyes shut, her body encased in one of those sleeping bags they have now. She looks so peaceful, and Ruth sits on the edge of the bed for a minute, just drinks her granddaughter in. She can see both Max and Layla in her face, even some of Nigel.

It's a powerful thing, genetics. She pictures Debbie, the expressions and mannerisms they share, as well as features, despite having lived their lives apart. She lands on what her mum said at the end of her last visit, about the twins belonging together. And that is it, she realises, that is what she feels when she's with this near stranger. Like they belong together.

The door clicks open and Max comes into the room. 'She okay?' he asks, nodding in the direction of the cot.

'Sleeping like a baby,' Ruth says.

Max sits next to her on the bed. 'Are you all right, Mum? You seem out of sorts, and all this stuff about this woman you've met. I'm a bit worried.'

'You don't need to worry,' Ruth says, putting a hand on his knee. It's what she's always said, a sort of mother's mantra. *Don't worry about me. Let me do all the worrying.* But it might be nice, she realises, for someone to worry on her behalf for once. 'Or maybe you do. I feel like things are shifting, and it's too fast. It's sort of scary.'

'Do you really think she's related to you?'

'She has to be, Max. It's like Dad said. She's my double.'

'So, a twin?'

Ruth nods, because it's the only explanation. 'But I don't know how.'

'Wow, that's massive. If you ever need to talk about any of it, I'm here for you.'

'You have your own life,' Ruth says, and they both look over at the cot, and Ruth sees how it makes Max smile, just seeing his baby. Max is a different type of father to Nigel, who rarely changed nappies or got up in the night when one of them was ill or had had a nightmare. Max is all in, hands on. Ruth wonders how much it's that times have changed, and how much it's just who Max is.

'That doesn't mean I can't listen,' Max says. 'Anytime. Okay?'

'Okay,' she says, and there's a wobble in her voice that she tries to disguise by clearing her throat. When she feels more steady, she speaks again. 'Do you want to leave her here tonight?'

Max raises his eyebrows. 'Are you sure you're up for that? You know she usually still wakes a couple of times in the night?'

'I know.'

'Thanks, Mum. An unbroken night's sleep will be incredible. Layla can pick her up in the morning.'

'I'll bring her back,' Ruth says.

'Okay, if you're sure. Thank you.' He gets up and heads for the stairs, presumably to tell Layla the good news.

Ruth remembers how it was, when she would have asked for sleep over anything else. With two babies, it felt like they tag teamed, one waking as soon as the other had settled into sleep. She remembers days when every minute felt like an hour, when she could barely keep her eyes open and her tears inside. These days, she sleeps badly despite having a silent house. It will be nice to have the company, she thinks, instead of lying there willing the time to pass. It will be nice to hold Grace in her arms, feel the warmth of her, breathe in the sweet smell of her body.

Debbie has never had this, never known this kind of love. The mothering, grandmothering kind. They are different. Both overwhelming. She can't imagine not having had it, having lived a life with just Nigel for company. What did Debbie say her husband was called? Rich, she thinks. No, Richie. She wonders what kind of a marriage they had, whether it was fuller and more loving than her own. Hopes so. Because if you only have one person for all those years, you'd want them to be more affectionate, more kind, than Nigel.

There's a shout from downstairs, Max calling that they're heading off. Making the most of their freedom. Ruth stands to go down and say her goodbyes, and it feels like a momentous effort. After they've gone, she will have a bath, ask Nigel or Chris to go to Grace if she wakes. Layla looks at her with enormous gratitude as soon as she appears in the hallway, and it feels too much. Ruth is embarrassed by it, can't meet her daughter-in-law's eye.

'Do you need her back at any particular time in the morning?' Ruth asks.

'No, whenever suits you. We have Baby Sensory in the afternoon but the morning is clear.'

Layla was an art teacher, before. Ruth wants to ask, suddenly, whether she's planning to go back, but it isn't the right time, here in the hallway, when she and Max are preparing to leave.

There's a moment between her sons that she just catches before Max opens the door. He puts a hand on his brother's arm and says, 'Call me, okay?'

Does Max know, about Chris's heartbreak, about his sexuality? Surely Chris hasn't kept it from his twin for all these years? Ruth knows that they know one another in a way she can never hope to come close to. That they have a secret language, almost. Is that something she might have had, with Debbie, if things had been different? Is it something they might have in the future, or is it too late, with so many years behind them?

'Mum?' It's clearly not the first time Max has said it.

'Sorry, love?'

'Thanks again, for having Grace.'

'Oh, it's nothing.'

'It's everything,' Layla says, and she leans in to kiss Ruth's cheek, and Ruth is oddly moved. They have a good relationship, she and Layla, but she doesn't consider them to be particularly close.

She stands at the door for a minute or so after they go, waiting for their car to reverse off the driveway. And then, when she closes it, Nigel rubs his hands together and says he really fancies a coffee. And somehow, Ruth doesn't end up having the bath she promised herself. She makes them all coffee (decaf for her and Nigel, who wouldn't dream of having a real coffee after about two in the afternoon these days), and then she loads the dishwasher, and then Grace wakes and no one else makes a move to go to her. It's ten o'clock before she knows it, and she goes to bed, leaving Nigel and Chris watching a panel show on TV. From upstairs, she hears them laughing and can't always make out which of them it is.

15

I knew the instant they were born. Ruth first, my body feeling like it was splitting in two. Then Debbie. The calm after the storm. The midwife handed them both to me and I didn't know how to hold them. I wanted to say, 'See? I can't do this.' Debbie had her eyes closed, but Ruth was looking at me. And even though she was a tiny baby, and she couldn't have understood, it felt like she was judging me for what I was going to do. And I knew she was the one who had to go.

Debbie was the easier baby, no question. Ruth screamed the house down if I fed Debbie first, but I wanted to. Debbie was my daughter, my baby. But she was so placid. Lay there on her back, gurgling. Curling a tiny fist around my finger. When you weren't there, I told the girls all about it. How Debbie was going to stay with me and Ruth was going to go away, and we'd never see her again. How it would be better for everyone that way. And I don't know whether they could hear me, whether language meant anything to them, but I felt better for being honest with them.

I waited a week, then two. I didn't want to. I wanted Ruth gone but I knew I needed to bide my time. I needed you to know this wasn't a post-birth idea, wasn't about me feeling overwhelmed and broken, though I did feel those things. And at the same time, I didn't want to give you too long to bond with her. Every time you picked her up, I felt cold.

And then, that time, you almost dropped her. You'd given her a bath and her skin was slippery. I don't know what happened, but all of a sudden she was squirming out of your hands and you were lurching forward to catch her. And I didn't feel the way I expected to feel. I felt scared. When you'd got her, and she was safe and wrapped in a towel, you passed her to me, and I really looked at her. Was I wrong? Could I do this?

16

At the end of their shift, Matty rushes off to see a friend but Debbie and Jitu pause for a few minutes, chatting. It's happening more and more, this, and it's funny because they spend hours together over the course of a week, but there always seems to be more to say.

'How's uni going?' she asks, making sure her voice is gentle.

Jitu shrugs. 'I sometimes feel like I might be okay if I was on a different course. Sometimes I'm in a lecture, and nothing that's being said means anything to me. I understand all the words, but I can't make them hang together with some meaning attached. And I look around and find that everyone else seems to be nodding along, scribbling down notes. It makes me feel like I'm a freak.'

'You're not a freak,' Debbie says. 'You're just maybe not cut out for this particular course at this particular time.'

'What are you doing for the rest of the day?' Jitu asks.

'I'm going to walk Bonnie now. In fact, I'd better get a move on. Want to walk her with me?'

'Nah, I'm heading home. I've got papers to not read properly.'

Debbie touches his arm and they move away from each other, and all the way to Pete's she marvels at this closeness they seem to have found, and how it makes her feel. Once she's picked up Bonnie and walked to the park, Debbie unclips the dog's lead and throws a ball, watches her tear after it. There is such joy in spending time with Bonnie. Sometimes, when she's at home after one of these walks, she lets herself get lost in a little fantasy in which Bonnie is hers. In which Bonnie is there to see her every day when she gets in from work. She's started walking Bonnie two or three times a week, and Pete insists on paying her, though she's told him there's no need. The first couple of times, he handed over cash and she felt awkward, like a teenage babysitter. It's better now he has her bank details and just transfers the money without a word. It's too much, though. Too generous. She keeps it in a separate account until she can decide what to do with it.

Debbie's going to let Pete know that she'd be happy to have Bonnie overnight, or even when he and Miles go on holiday. They seem like a couple who would go on a lot of holidays. Two big, busy jobs, no children. When Bonnie returns with the ball in her mouth, Debbie throws it again. Pete told her that Bonnie would literally do this all day and while Debbie hasn't tested the theory, she once did it for a full hour and Bonnie didn't tire of it. Today, though, she needs to get back. She's been invited to Ruth's, and Ruth's sister Kate is going to be there. The thought of it is enough to make her want to jump up and down with excitement. So next time Bonnie returns, Debbie clips her lead back on and the dog drags her feet to show she's disappointed, but they head for home.

'Debbie!' Pete has his headset on and Debbie never knows

whether he's on a call, so she just hands the lead over and smiles, all ready to turn and go. 'Time for a cuppa?'

She doesn't, but she wishes she did. She likes Pete. Likes his home, with its big, brightly coloured art and velvet sofas, colourful walls and neat, hidden storage. She's been in a couple of times, but she's never stayed for a drink. 'I can't today,' she says. 'Next time?'

Pete nods and smiles. It makes no difference to him, she thinks. He's just being polite. Still, she is thankful that they met that day in the park. Thankful that he's on the edge of her life. 'How are you fixed for tomorrow?' Pete asks.

Tomorrow she has a shift ending at two, so she says she could do three. Pete screws his face up. 'We'll both be in the office then. I tell you what, would you be happy to have a key?'

Debbie nods and he opens a drawer in the hallway unit, starts rooting around. 'Here.' He hands it over.

'Great,' Debbie says, and she leans down to give Bonnie a fuss and heads back down the path.

It's May, warm and bright but not hot, and Debbie is loving the long evenings, the almost-summer sky. She walks to Ruth's house, knocks on the door, and she's a bit taken aback when it isn't Ruth who answers, but another woman who looks a bit like both of them. Not the way they look like each other. Nothing like that. But still. She should have been prepared for this, but she wasn't, somehow. The woman – Kate, she must be – is staring at her and Debbie's staring back. And then Debbie clears her throat, and it's like it breaks a spell, and Kate steps back and ushers her inside.

'God, I'm sorry, you must think I'm so rude. Christ, Ruth told me but I didn't quite realise…'

'It's okay,' Debbie says, bending to take her shoes off. 'It's a lot.'

Ruth comes down the stairs then. 'Debbie, hi. I see you met my sister, Kate.'

There's an awkward moment when Debbie imagines they're all thinking about the fact that they are all sisters, but it passes quickly, and they are in the living room and Ruth's making coffee and bringing out a plate of brownies. 'I made too many,' she says.

Kate reaches for one and takes a bite. 'I love it when she makes too many,' she says.

Debbie takes one too, and it is heaven. Rich and squidgy. Richie used to love a brownie, and sometimes he had a go at making them but he always took them out of the oven too soon or left them too long. She wishes he was here, that he could try this one. She can imagine the blissful expression he would make. 'So good,' she says, and Ruth smiles. But she doesn't take one for herself.

'If I had a baking business, I'd be the size of a house,' Debbie says.

Kate laughs. 'Me too. But not Ruth. She never eats any of it.'

'I don't have much of a sweet tooth,' Ruth says.

'So...' Kate says, 'I don't know whether Ruth told you that I'm a freelance journalist?'

Debbie shakes her head.

'Well, I was thinking I could use my contacts to help you two work out your history. The women's magazines would love a story like this – all the news outlets would, in fact – so you'd be able to take your pick of who to speak to. And it would mean I could do the digging for you, try to work out how exactly all of this happened.'

Debbie isn't sure. She feels a bit blindsided. She thought she was just coming over for coffee, had had no idea that Kate had a professional interest in them. Plus, hadn't they decided to put all of that to one side and just get to know each other first? She is trying to formulate a response that covers all of this when Ruth speaks up.

'If you're unsure, you're not the only one,' she says. 'I'm quite a private person and the thought of there being photos of us in the papers is just...' She breaks off, shudders, and Debbie wonders whether her own mouth makes that shape when she is unhappy about something. 'Plus, my mother is still alive and I feel like I should talk to her about all this before we go looking for answers elsewhere.'

'Did you say she has dementia?' Debbie asks. She knows dementia, worked in a care home for a while, before she was at the Citizens Advice Bureau. She knows it is brutal, that it tears people apart. Where is Ruth's mother in that process?

'Yes,' Ruth says. 'It's quite advanced. Sometimes she remembers things and sometimes she doesn't. So it might take a while, but I feel like I owe it to her to try. If I don't, this whole media idea feels a bit like dragging her personal life into the spotlight, if you know what I mean.'

Debbie thinks of this woman, a stranger to her, deteriorating in a care home. She could be her mother. The woman who raised her, who she always knew as Mum, could have been nothing to do with her. But why?

'Could I meet her?' Debbie asks. She hadn't quite known she was going to.

Ruth looks a bit taken aback. 'Mum? I mean, I suppose so, although it might confuse her, seeing us together. What do you think, Kate?'

Kate sits back a bit. 'Do you realise that your accents are different, but your voices are the same? It's utterly bizarre. Anyway, sorry, about Mum. I'm not sure, to be honest. Maybe we could all go along one Sunday...' She turns to Debbie. 'We go every Sunday evening. And we could see how she is, bring you in if she's in good spirits.'

Debbie feels like she's asked something she shouldn't have and it's too late to take it back. She hadn't thought, about the way their confused mum might react to seeing her. She'd just wanted to nestle into this family, which she is starting to really like.

Kate looks at her watch and jumps up, says she has to leave. When she's in the hallway with her shoes on, she calls behind her. 'Think about what I said, okay?'

Debbie leaves Ruth to answer, and she does. 'We will. See you later, Kate.'

There is an ease between them that fascinates Debbie. Has she ever had that with anyone? With Richie, but that was different. He was her love, her husband. Friends? She's been close to people, over the years, but they've never had this sort of bond. This specific sort of friendly familiarity.

'She seems great,' Debbie says. 'How do you think she's taking all of this?'

Ruth tilts her head slightly to the left. 'I've been so focused on how I'm taking it that I probably haven't asked enough. I will, though. She's tough, Kate, but sometimes she hides her hurt. When we were kids she would only cry if she was in her bedroom with the door closed.'

Everything seems to lead back to their childhoods. Debbie feels like she's picking her way through landmines, trying to tread carefully but never knowing what is or isn't safe to say. 'I'm sorry about your mum. It must be hard.'

'It is,' Ruth says, and Debbie likes that she doesn't brush it off or underplay it. 'But it sounds like you had it tough with your mum too. For us, me and Kate, it's only been quite a recent thing.'

Debbie allows herself to go back there. The nights when

she'd wake to find her mum sitting on the edge of her bed, ranting, making no sense. When she'd have to call her grandmother and ask her for help. The days when she'd come home from school and her mum would be up and dressed, even making something for tea. Those were the worst days, in a way. Because Debbie allowed herself to believe in it every time. Wanted so much to believe that they'd turned a corner and were out of danger that the plummet the next time it all fell away was even worse. It isn't often that she does this. She's found, over time, that it's better for her own mental health if she doesn't. But meeting Ruth, it's made her question everything. An idea comes to her, starts to form.

'Would you like to go on a trip?' she asks.

'What kind of trip?' Ruth narrows her eyes.

'I don't know. Any kind. A weekend in Paris, a few nights in the Lake District, a week in Spain. I feel like it would be good for us, to spend some real time together with no distractions. Away from family and our work and all of that.' She's aware that this might be too much for Ruth, that she might have pushed too far, too soon. She's always been impulsive like this, and Richie was too, which is one of the reasons why their marriage worked so well. But she knows from experience that it's not a common trait. That most people like to mull things over, plan, prepare.

'Can I think about it?' Ruth asks.

And it's not a no, which Debbie is grateful for. She nods, tells Ruth to take all the time she needs. But she doesn't backtrack, doesn't say forget it, or it was a stupid idea, because she really wants it, and she doesn't know yet that Ruth will say no.

'I'm thinking about getting a cat,' Debbie says.

And Ruth laughs.

'What?'

'It's just, you can be so unexpected. I've never met anyone quite like you.'

Debbie leaves soon after that and she carries those words home with her, keeps them in her heart. She doesn't know whether Ruth thinks it's a good or a bad thing to be unlike anyone else, but Debbie thinks it's great. And how wonderful, for her and Ruth to be so alike physically, but worlds apart in other ways. There is so much to learn about each other. So much to discover.

17

'What are you thinking about?' Chris asks.

His voice startles Ruth, who is in the kitchen drinking a coffee and should be going over the plans for the day's baking but is actually thinking about Debbie, about the trip she suggested.

'You and Dad would be okay if I went away for a bit, wouldn't you?'

Chris frowns. 'Where are you going?'

'I'm not sure yet. I'm just thinking about going away. No more than a week.'

Chris slides onto the stool beside her. 'With Kate?'

'No.'

'So who with? I don't think I've ever known you to go away without either Dad or Kate.'

Ruth blows air out of her cheeks. 'It's not settled yet. I was just asking if you'd be okay.'

'Well, of course we'll be okay. You realise I managed to shop and cook and do washing and all of that for all those years I didn't live here.'

Does he live here now? Is this a permanent arrangement? Part of Ruth hopes that it is, for her sake, but for his, she hopes it's just a temporary blip. 'You know, you could do all those things while you're here. You don't have to regress to being your teenage self.'

He pretends to be hurt but can't maintain it, and soon they are laughing and the trip isn't mentioned again.

'What are you doing today?' Ruth asks. She is all for letting him wallow. She wants him to take the time he needs to fix his broken heart, but she's also worried about the long hours he's spending alone in his bedroom. The curtains closed, the bed unmade. Is this what depression looks like? And how do you know the difference between heartbreak and something that needs actual medical attention?

'I thought I'd call some headhunters,' he says. 'And then later I'm having dinner with Max.'

Ruth is at the sink, washing up the pan she made scrambled eggs in this morning, so he can't see her wide smile at these revelations. He must be starting to feel better, starting to feel that he can pull the strands of himself back together, if he's thinking about a new job. And she is always pleased when her boys make plans together, because there's a part of her that's always thought of them as a single entity, that feels on edge about them living their separate lives in separate places.

'Does Max know about all of it?' she ventures.

'About the affair? Or being gay?'

Ruth shrugs. 'Both, I suppose.'

'I told him I thought I was gay when we were sixteen. Even though I didn't *think* it. I'd known it for years at that point. He was cool about it, made some joke about it leaving more girls for him.'

Ruth imagines them having this conversation. They were

awkward at sixteen, not quite grown into their bodies, their limbs unwieldy. And they both had skin that broke out in spots regularly. Ruth remembers feeling that she wanted to keep them at home with her until their bodies had finished going through puberty. Wanted to protect them from school, and all the cruelty and pain that lurked there. 'And what about your... relationship?' She turns to look at Chris, her soapy hands dripping.

'He doesn't know about that. But I'll tell him. It's hard when you're mostly communicating by message. It's better to talk in person.' He reaches for an apple from the fruit bowl and bites into it.

Ruth starts to assemble the ingredients she needs for her first job of the day – a carrot cake and a Victoria sponge, both for a baby shower. She wants to keep Chris here, in the kitchen, but without asking him to stay. She's like a hunter, avoiding sudden movements that might scare him away. But when he looks like he's about to slide off his stool, she knows she's going to have to do something to hold him.

'It's Debbie,' she says.

'What's Debbie? Who's Debbie? Oh, your...'

There's no easy way to end that sentence. 'It's Debbie I'm going away with.'

Chris furrows his brow. 'Are you sure, Mum? You hardly know this woman. What if she's some kind of scammer?'

Ruth knows he is just concerned but she almost laughs. 'How would that scam work, exactly? She targets someone and then gets plastic surgery to look identical to them, before inviting them on a trip and somehow relieving them of their money?'

He holds his hands up. 'I get it. It's obvious that there's a connection. But that doesn't automatically make her a good person, does it?'

Ruth thinks about this, about what she knows of Debbie, the warmth she feels when she's with her. 'She's a good person.'

'See, this is what I mean! You're too trusting.'

Is she? Maybe she is. She'd prefer that to being overly wary, overly cynical. 'I know her,' she says. 'I don't know how to explain it, but I know her deep in my body. In my bones. The way you know Max.'

Chris shakes his head. 'It's not like me and Max at all, Mum. You know that. A childhood spent together counts for a lot.'

It does. She knows it does. But genes count for a lot too. That feeling of recognition, when you see a face so like your own. It's like coming home. And while she'll never know what it's like to grow up with a twin, Chris will never know what it's like to discover one later in life. She doesn't know what to say, so she says nothing, and Chris finishes his apple, throws it across to the bin where she's discarding eggshells, and leaves the room.

When the first cake is in the oven and she's washed her hands, she types a message to Debbie:

> I want to go on a trip, like you suggested. Let me know your budget and I'll find some options. And I was wondering, would it be okay to ask Kate if she wants to join us?

She sends it immediately, knowing that if she has a chance to overthink it, she will. But then she worries about the budget comment. It's the first acknowledgement between them that they live different types of lives. That Ruth lives in a comfortable, spacious home that she and Nigel own, while Debbie rents a terraced house on the less affluent side of town.

Ruth has always known that she's lucky, that she had a privileged upbringing and has led a charmed life in many ways. Why has it been different for Debbie, when they presumably started out in the same place, with the same opportunities? And when they were separated, however they were separated, could it have happened the other way? Could Ruth have been the one who ended up in Debbie's shoes – childless, widowed, without a home of her own – and could Debbie have ended up in hers?

And the part about Kate. Ruth has no idea how Debbie will take that, and there's a part of Ruth that hopes Kate turns them down even if they do invite her, but she feels quite strongly that she has to ask. It would be easy for the two of them to push Kate out, and she loves her sister too much to let that happen.

Her phone buzzes and it's Debbie messaging, with a budget and some ideas. She says it's fine to invite Kate. Ruth can tell that she's excited, that she isn't offended. She's an easy sort of person, happy-go-lucky. Ruth feels sure that whatever trip they decide on, they'll have a good time. Which hasn't always been the case with family holidays. Over the years, she's planned trips to Greek islands, American theme parks and Italian cities, and without fail, either Nigel, Chris or Max has found fault with them, and she's found herself unable to fully relax and enjoy the holiday she's spent so long planning. It comes to her, then, that perhaps her boys are spoiled, to a certain extent. Throughout their childhoods, she and Nigel always had enough money. Not a huge amount, but enough. So perhaps they indulged them too much, said yes too many times, and it's affected their expectations of life, their ability to enjoy things. Perhaps it's better, in a way, to be like Debbie. To take things as they come, to appreciate every little thing.

The oven timer goes off and shakes Ruth out of her wonderings. She reaches for the oven gloves. When she's made this next cake, she'll get her iPad out and do some research.

* * *

'I can't afford it,' Kate says over the phone.

Ruth debates offering to pay for her, bites her lip. 'I could—'

'No, Ruth. I hate owing people money, you know that. And besides, I feel like this is something the two of you should do on your own.' Ruth is pleased, and hates herself for it.

'How are you doing with all this?' she asks.

Kate breathes heavily. 'Thanks for asking. It's big, isn't it? Bigger for you, but still...'

'I really like her,' Ruth says.

'Yes, she seems very nice.'

Ruth hears Nigel's key turn in the lock and says her goodbyes. When she glances at the clock, she's shocked to see it's gone six. She hasn't done a thing about dinner. She and Debbie have been messaging back and forth all afternoon, sending links and TripAdvisor reviews and fixing dates. Nigel comes to stand in the living room doorway. 'How was your day?'

Ruth smiles at him. He doesn't always ask, and when he does, it means something. Such a small thing. Perhaps she should tell him. Perhaps, then, he'd do it more often. 'Really good, thanks. Yours?'

'Same old. What's for dinner?'

'I'm not sure. I've got a bit caught up in something. Chris is going out, so...' She breaks off, looks up at him. He's pissed off and not hiding it well. She was going to suggest they go out too, but she can see that wouldn't go down well. 'I could order us a Chinese?'

'Fine. I'm going up to get changed.'

When did her marriage turn into this? Brief exchanges of information, everything on the surface. Ruth cannot remember the last time they talked about a film, or even watched a film together, or shared their views on something in the news or in the paper. There was so much of that, in the early days of their relationship. Sometimes, they'd stayed up all night, just talking. Their pillows propped up against the headboard, their hands moving wildly as they emphasised their points. He used to read books she recommended to him. Used to pass her the morning paper, pointing to an article he'd just read. When did all of that die out? And how did she not notice?

Ruth orders a few Chinese dishes for them to share. Adds spring rolls at the last minute because they are Nigel's favourite. Perhaps they can sit at the table together and start to salvage something. She will tell him that she's missed talking to him, missed being close. But when the food arrives, Nigel says he's taking his down to the office pod in the garden because something's gone to shit and only he can sort it out. Chris comes down the stairs in clean jeans and a black T-shirt while Ruth is eating. He tells her he won't be late, grabs his keys. And when the door shuts behind him, Ruth feels more alone than she has ever felt. She reaches for a piece of sesame prawn toast, takes a bite. But it is tasteless. Her phone beeps, and she pulls it from her pocket. Debbie.

> I think Amsterdam. Three nights. Are you happy for me to go ahead and book it? Did you talk to Kate?

Ruth smiles. Amsterdam. She went once, when the boys were eight or so, and they complained about the walking she and Nigel made them do, and she didn't get to wander the streets, pretending she lived there, the way she wanted to. Yes, it was time to go back. She's checked the dates on the calendar but she hasn't yet mentioned anything about the trip to Nigel. She considers putting her shoes on and going to the bottom of the garden. Imagines how he will barely look up from his screen and will ask the same questions Chris did, about why she is doing this when she barely knows Debbie. No, she doesn't need his permission. She messages Debbie, tells her to go ahead, that Kate can't make it. She transfers the money. And she feels a fizz rising in her that is so alien she can't identify it at first. It isn't until she is loading her plate into the dishwasher that it comes to her. Excitement.

18

For Debbie, the journey is absolutely part of the holiday. Sometimes, it's one of the best bits. That's why her bag is bulging with snacks and magazines and puzzle books. Ruth is wheeling a neat, black suitcase and carrying a handbag that looks much more orderly. She puts a hand up when she sees Debbie, and they both smile, their faces mirror images. It's a bit breezy on the platform but in ten minutes' time they'll be on the train to London, which is the first leg of the journey, and it will all begin.

'Have you been before?' Ruth asks.

'No. I've always wanted to. Have you?'

'Yes. But it was a long time ago.'

Does Ruth mean when she was a child, as part of that family? Or with the family she's created since? Or maybe she doesn't mean either of those things. Maybe, for her, trips away with friends or her sister have been the norm.

'Richie and I used to love having adventures. We never had much money but we didn't really care where we went, so we'd buy those sale flights Ryanair do sometimes for a penny. The places we went! But I've always thought that any place has something to show you.'

Ruth is quiet, and then the train pulls in and they are finding their carriage, their reserved seats, lifting their cases into the luggage rack. Debbie opens her bag on her lap and starts pulling things out. A pack of cards, bars of chocolate, tins of gin and tonic. Ruth watches her unloading them, a smile on her face that gets wider and wider.

'You know how to travel in style, don't you?' she asks.

Debbie shrugs. Because why would you travel any differently to this? She offers things to Ruth, who takes the chocolate but refuses the gin, says she'll wait until a bit later in the day.

'Where did you land on getting a cat?' Ruth asks, biting a tiny corner off her bar of Galaxy.

Debbie has never seen anyone eating chocolate like that. Richie used to bite big chunks off, and she breaks the bar into sections, but this nibbling is totally new. It's almost as if she doesn't want to allow herself to have it. 'I'm still mulling it over. Are you a cat person?'

Ruth shakes her head. Then seems to reconsider. 'I was, as a child. When Kate and I were young, this tabby cat walked into our kitchen one summer day when we had the back door open and never left. We called him Jack. Kate used to carry him around like he was a baby and he just let her. Every night, he slept on the end of my bed.'

There's a faraway look in her eyes, Debbie notices.

'I'd forgotten about Jack. Nigel's allergic, so we can't have a cat now. What about you? Did you grow up with pets?'

Debbie shakes her head. 'We couldn't, really. Mum wasn't always there and I think she had enough trouble looking after me. It wouldn't have made any sense. But when I moved in with Richie, when I was twenty, we got a dog and a cat straightaway.'

'Did they get on okay together?'

Debbie thinks back, to the way they used to share a bed, the dog's legs flopping out onto the kitchen floor because there wasn't really space for them. 'The cat thought she was a dog, so that helped. We called them Bert and Ernie. Bert was the cat, a tortoiseshell, and Ernie was a springer spaniel. In the evenings, Richie and I would take Ernie for his walk and when we came back Bert would be sitting right by the front door, outraged about being left behind. And then we'd all pile in to the living room, all four of us on a two-seater sofa. It was chaos.'

Debbie wants to ask about Ruth's family life, but she doesn't know a way in. She hopes that if she keeps offering up bits of stories from her own life, Ruth will start to do the same.

'The boys had a rabbit, for a couple of years,' Ruth says, and Debbie smiles, encouraging her. 'It was a massive thing, great big feet. It escaped once and I had a call from a woman two streets away who'd found it in her garden. She had a girl in the same class as the boys and had known it was ours, somehow. I said we'd come to get it. Nigel was away with work, and it was pouring with rain, and I had to get the boys' shoes and coats on and drag them away from the TV. When we got there, cardboard box in hand, it was still hopping around the woman's garden, and we had a nightmare of a job trying to catch it. The boys were darting all over the place, and I was too, but it was just so fast. The woman and her daughter came out to help, in the end. It must have taken us about half an hour. And that was that. I decided then and there that this would be the last pet we had. When it died, about a year after that, I waited for the boys to ask if we could get another one, or something else, but they never did.'

Debbie chews over this story. She never said the rabbit's name, always referred to it as 'it'. Deciding never to have a pet again based on one bad day seems rash, to her, but what does she know? She has never had two children to worry about. Perhaps Ruth was just at capacity, and didn't need one more thing to look after. But what about now? Ruth works from home and wouldn't it be nice to have a dog around? Still, it isn't Debbie's business.

'Whose is the dog you walk?' Ruth asks.

'His name's Pete. The owner, not the dog. I met him in the park. The dog is Bonnie. She's a sweetheart.'

Debbie tilts her head, studies the way Ruth is looking at her. There's something in Ruth's eyes that she can't quite make out.

'I've never met anyone like you,' Ruth says.

Debbie wonders whether Ruth remembers that she's said this before. 'Oh. And is that a good thing? That I'm not like anyone else, I mean?'

Ruth bites on her bottom lip, and Debbie remembers doing that as a teenager. It's a habit she's managed to break. 'I think it's a really good thing. You're so much braver than I am. I feel like I'm learning from you.'

It's strange that she chose the word learning, because Debbie feels so stupid, sometimes, around Ruth. They haven't talked in detail about their education, but Debbie is sure that Ruth's was better than hers, that she stuck with it for longer. 'I think we all learn from everyone we meet.'

Ruth nods. 'I think you're probably right.'

There's a pause in conversation, and Debbie roots around in her handbag again, brings out her pocket-sized Amsterdam guidebook. She asks Ruth what's worth seeing, what she saw on her previous trip and whether there's anything she wants to return to. They make a loose plan. The Van Gogh museum and the Rijksmuseum. Anne Frank's house. Debbie wants to go to a coffee shop to try cannabis but she's not sure how to bring it up.

It doesn't seem like the kind of thing Ruth will be on board with. In the end, the decision's taken out of her hands because a voice over the tannoy announces that they will shortly arrive in London, and she starts to cram everything back into her bag and gather together the rubbish.

The train from London to Amsterdam is longer; a little over four hours. Debbie buys more snacks and they both choose a book at St Pancras, and they spend much of the journey reading companionably, pausing now and then to chat. Ruth has a nap and when she wakes, Debbie goes to the buffet car and gets them both a coffee. While she's queuing, her phone pings with a message and it's Jitu, saying he's missing her and he hopes she's misbehaving. She smiles, sends back a gif of an angel. Once she's bought the drinks, she makes her way back to Ruth and their seats, and it occurs to her that she feels totally comfortable with Ruth, as if she's known her and they've been travelling together like this for years. Is that something she should say? She knows she'd like to hear it.

'Here,' she says, passing Ruth the takeaway cup. 'It's a cappuccino. No lattes.'

Ruth shrugs, and it reminds Debbie of what she wanted to say.

'This feels good. Easy. Travelling with you,' she says, settling back in her seat.

Ruth doesn't respond at first, but Debbie can't help but notice the creep of a blush up her neck and into her cheeks. Is she embarrassed by what Debbie said? And why?

'I'm sorry, I didn't mean to embarrass you. I...' What? She what?

'Oh, it's all right. It's just, I'm not used to it. I'm used to arranging things for people and then getting moaned at for one reason or another. I usually feel like I'm getting everything wrong.'

This is a lot to take in. Debbie notices that the man sitting opposite them is listening in to their conversation. Has he spotted the likeness? He must have. What does he think of these women, these identical women, and the way they are interacting? 'What do you mean?' she asks.

'Well, I think it's just part and parcel of being a mum, really. You end up with a lot of admin to do and it's all pretty thankless. No one notices that their clothes are washed and ironed and back in their wardrobes when they need them. They only notice when they're not. When they've got a football match and their kit's still lingering in the washing basket. Or, more likely, on their bedroom floor.'

'But those years are long gone now, aren't they?'

Ruth rubs the back of her neck with her hand. 'They are and they aren't. Having Chris back home has brought it all back a bit, I think. They're always asking what's for dinner or where something is – him and Nigel, I mean. It makes me feel like I'm there to serve them. Anyway, it's just nice to be going away, to be leaving it all behind for a while.'

Debbie is quiet. When she pulled the front door of her house closed behind her this morning, she felt a strange melancholy that she didn't have anyone to call goodbye to, but then she remembered where she was going, and brightened. In her mind, Ruth has a busy, happy house, full of life and laughter. But perhaps that isn't the case. Debbie knows, from reading books and talking to friends and watching TV, that not all marriages are as happy as hers was. What is Ruth's marriage like? She hopes she'll find out more this weekend. For now, she reaches for her Americano and takes a sip, then scrabbles around for a packet of fruit pastilles and offers them to Ruth.

19

Ruth is shattered when they get to the hotel. They've been given a double room rather than a twin, and she isn't sure how she feels about it. She hasn't shared a bed with anyone other than Nigel for decades. Sometimes, Nigel tells her that she's been snoring. Wouldn't that be embarrassing, to snore in front of someone else? But Debbie doesn't seem to mind, so Ruth doesn't say what she was thinking of saying, which is that she could pay for a second room to avoid them having to share at all. They take it in turns to use the bathroom and Ruth finds herself turning on the TV to avoid the sound of Debbie urinating. She wishes she could watch an episode of *Finding Paradise*. But does she wish she was at home, curled up on her sofa? No, she finds that she doesn't. She recalls what Debbie said on the Eurostar, about her being easy to be with, and she resolves to soften. No one has ever said she's easy to be with before.

She reaches for her phone, calls Nigel. When she first told him about the trip, he didn't object to it (how could he?) but it was clear he wasn't happy. The thing was, he liked having her nearby to cook for him and do his washing, but he couldn't bring himself to admit that that was what he would miss, so he just stomped around for a couple of days like a sudden storm. Now, he answers after a few rings.

'Hello? Ruth?'

'Hi, Nigel, just letting you know we got here okay.'

'Great.'

There is a pause, and she leaves it for him to fill in. To ask how the journey was, or what their hotel is like, or how Debbie is. But it lengthens and yawns until she can't bear it any longer.

'How's your day going?'

'Ah, so-so.'

He's in the office, and she can picture him, his glasses in his hand, his forehead creased. She's struck by a yearning to go home to him, to really talk to him about what's going on in their marriage and their lives. But it is fleeting. 'Chris okay?'

'I've barely seen him.'

If she died, or never went back, would they just continue to coexist like that? Moving around each other, hardly speaking? No, Chris would move out. He wouldn't want to live that way. And then what would become of Nigel? He would get by on microwave meals and bowls of porridge, still going down the garden to his office pod despite the entire house being empty. As they've got older, she's thought a lot about what will happen when one of them goes. Look at Debbie. Her husband died suddenly, no warning. It could happen to anyone. Ruth's pretty sure that she'd cope all right, but Nigel would be a mess. She isn't sure he's ever used the washing machine.

'Well, I'd better go. Do some sightseeing.'

'Isn't it early evening?'

Ruth looks at her watch. It's half past six. 'Yes. Dinner, then. I'll see you on Tuesday.'

'See you then. Have a good time.'

These last words are grudging, and she knows he doesn't mean them. What does it say about him, about them, that he would rather she was there attending to his needs than away getting to know this new person in her life? She doesn't dwell on that too long.

'So.' Debbie claps her hands, lifts her suitcase onto the bed, and Ruth tries not to think about where the wheels have been. 'What's first? I want to go to one of the coffee shops.'

Ruth blinks. 'Where they sell cannabis, you mean?'

She has a sudden memory of Chris and Max talking about going to Amsterdam with university friends when they were about twenty. She knew she couldn't say no, knew that they were adults, but she hated the thought of them smoking weed and possibly even visiting prostitutes. In the end, the trip never materialised, and she was quietly relieved. If you'd told her then that she'd be here in Amsterdam, all these years later, talking about going to a coffee shop, she wouldn't have believed it.

'Yes. You don't have to smoke it, you know. They do cakes and everything. Have you ever tried it?'

'Cannabis?' Ruth knows her tone is judgemental. She tries to change it, finds she can't. 'No, I've never tried cannabis.'

'Me neither. But there's a first time for everything.' Debbie starts humming a tune as she takes her washbag and her pyjamas out of the case.

And Ruth is about to protest, about to say that she has no intention of trying drugs for the first time at the age of sixty-two, but something stops her. Because, actually, why not? Perhaps she could learn a few things from Debbie, who moves through the world in an entirely different way from her. Who is fearless where she is cautious, bold where she is hesitant. 'Okay,' she says. She wonders whether Debbie will look shocked, but she just carries on humming.

Out on the street, Debbie tells Ruth what she knows. They're looking for a coffee shop, not a café, and they're everywhere but Debbie's talked to Matty and Jitu and got the name of three that are particularly friendly for first timers. It doesn't take long for them to locate one of them. The scent of weed wafts out of the door and Ruth thinks of her boys, again, how they'd sometimes come home looking a bit guilty and smelling like this and she'd pretend not to notice. Her heart is hammering a bit, and she considers saying she has a headache, that she needs to go back to the hotel to lie down. But she doesn't. She follows Debbie inside and watches as she converses with the staff. No, they don't want to smoke. Yes, a brownie would be good. They'll share one, see how they go.

The coffee shop is full of sofas and when Ruth and Debbie sit down on one, they sink into the middle, towards one another. Debbie laughs. She seems so at ease.

'Did your friends say how it would make us feel?' Ruth asks.

'Just a bit spaced out and giggly, I think,' Debbie says. 'It can take a while to kick in. You're not supposed to have too much.'

Debbie has cut the brownie neatly into two and Ruth nibbles at the edge of her half. There's a slightly earthy taste to it, but otherwise you wouldn't know.

'Richie would have loved this,' Debbie says.

'Would he? I think Nigel would think I was losing it.'

Ruth considers taking a selfie with the brownie in shot and sending it to Kate. Kate would be surprised, Ruth thinks, but she wouldn't judge.

Debbie doesn't say anything, but there's a curious expression on her face, as if she's trying to work out how Ruth's marriage works. Ruth's finding herself trying to work that out too, more and more often. She won't tell Nigel or Chris about this, she knows. She'll tell them about the Van Gogh museum, and the canals. Anne Frank's house. That's if they ask at all.

'Chris is gay,' she says. It's the first time she's said it aloud, to anyone, and she is surprised that she chose Debbie.

'Your son Chris?'

'Yes. He just told me recently.'

'Good for him. Does he have someone?'

'No. He did, but it ended. That's part of the reason why he's come home.'

Debbie nods, takes her final bite of brownie. 'Home comforts.'

Ruth still has more than half of her piece of brownie to go, but she doesn't feel rushed. Debbie seems happy to relax on the collapsing sofa and drink her coffee.

'What do you think it says about us, that he kept it to himself for so long?' Ruth asks.

Debbie looks at her, her brow furrowed, and Ruth recognises the expression as one she makes when she's puzzling over a recipe. 'I don't think it says anything, necessarily. I suppose people are just ready at different times. I wouldn't worry about it. At least he told you eventually.'

'Not Nigel, though.'

'No?'

'No.'

They are quiet, and Ruth wants to say that she's pretty sure Nigel wouldn't take the news well, but she finds she can't. Because she can see that Debbie doesn't have a judgemental bone in her body, that she accepts people as she finds them, and she doesn't want Debbie to think badly of her husband. She goes back to her brownie.

'I don't know how it works, in a family, with secrets,' Debbie says. 'Richie and I, we were pretty open. But when there are more than two people in the dynamic and one tells another something, but doesn't want the third one to know... I guess that gets pretty complicated pretty quickly.'

Are they a family with a lot of secrets? Ruth's never thought of them that way. But now she thinks about Max and Chris sharing the secret of Chris's sexuality for all those years, and her, now, keeping it from Nigel. Perhaps you can never see your own family with complete clarity. Perhaps you always have a skewed sense of who your loved ones are, and who you are in relation to them. 'Let's talk about something else,' she says. 'How's Jitu? When's the plagiarism meeting?'

Debbie sighs. 'Ah, he's all right. The meeting's a week after we get back from here. He hasn't talked about it, really, since he asked me to go with him. He's a good kid. I think he's under a lot of pressure from his family, and maybe university – or just the course he's on – isn't right for him. We'll see.'

'I think it's great that you're supporting him,' Ruth says. She wonders whether Debbie will blush the way she always does at a compliment, but Debbie just smiles.

'Shall we go for a walk?'

Ruth has finished her brownie and their coffee cups are empty, so she stands up, half expecting to feel dizzy or sick, but she is fine. She follows Debbie back out onto the street, and the sun has set, the streetlights have come on, and everything looks beautiful.

They follow the path beside a canal and Ruth thinks about the map tucked away in her jacket pocket, but she doesn't get it out. It's nice, for once, to stop thinking. They'll find their way back to the hotel. And if they get lost, they get lost. Perhaps it will be an adventure. It's a little later that she starts to find everything she sees and everything Debbie says hilarious. Is she high? Is this how it feels to be high? She'd always imagined she would feel out of control, and scared, but this is joyous. Everything sounds clear and the smells of food from street vendors makes her salivate. And it is all *so* funny.

'Careful,' Debbie says, grabbing Ruth's hand and pulling her out of the path of a cyclist who's furiously ringing his bell. And the feeling of her hand in Debbie's is so comforting, Ruth doesn't let go. Not when the cyclist has passed, not when they've crossed the road, not until they get back to the shop near the hotel, where they load up on chocolate and crisps and fizzy drinks and take them up to their room, still giggling.

20

Debbie is awake, thinking, long after Ruth passes out. She feels like she's seen a different side of Ruth this evening, one who isn't concerned about rules and schedules. A looser, more fun version. She knows Ruth has it inside her to be more like that, but her family have worn her down. Debbie sees glimpses of that Ruth over the next couple of days. When she opens a can in the park and the drink fizzes out everywhere and she starts laughing and seems like she can't stop. When the man at the Rijksmuseum searches their bags and pulls out Ruth's travel hairbrush and looks at them like they might be terrorists and they collapse into giggles. It was a good idea, this trip. Debbie feels it's brought them closer, that she now knows Ruth in a way that might have taken months if they'd just met up now and again for coffee.

On their last evening, they eat mussels and fries and drink wine at a rickety outdoor table on a cobbled street. Ruth keeps folding up paper napkins to put under the table leg but never gets it quite right. They're finishing the wine off when Ruth suggests going back to the coffee shop. For Debbie, getting high on a brownie was fun, not dissimilar to getting a bit drunk, but she isn't too bothered about doing it again. She's surprised Ruth has suggested it, though. There's a look in Ruth's eyes that's close to pleading. 'Okay,' she finds herself saying, and when they've paid the bill and got up to leave, Ruth takes Debbie's arm and pulls her in close and it's so unexpected that Debbie feels close to tears.

The man behind the counter remembers them. 'The twins!'

Debbie is jolted by this. The truth is, the more she gets to know Ruth, the less she actually sees her. The less she is aware of their physical similarities. But of course it's obvious to anyone they see. And it's unusual, isn't it, to see twins together past childhood? Twins in their sixties. Twins who don't know how, or whether, they're twins. They brush it off and the man looks briefly troubled, as though he thinks he might have got something wrong. They order espressos, another brownie to share.

'What's been your favourite thing?' Debbie asks.

This is something she and Richie always did at the end of a holiday. It was a way of reliving it, but also seeing how it had been through someone else's eyes. Their answers were rarely the same.

'This,' Ruth says, taking a small, delicate bite of brownie.

'Getting high on cake?'

Ruth laughs, and Debbie thinks it isn't quite like her own laugh, though it's similar. Ruth's is somehow a bit deeper, a bit richer. 'Kind of. But I meant just being together, hanging out, as my boys would say. What about you?'

Debbie thinks. It's been a lot of fun. 'The mooching about,' she says. 'Just exploring the streets and finding things that weren't in the guidebook. That adorable chocolate shop and that tiny park where we saw kids playing in the sand.'

Richie always chose the big, concrete stuff. If he'd been on this trip with her, he would have said seeing the Van Gogh paintings up close. But for Debbie, it is all about the small moments, the things you stumble across on the way to something else. It sounds like Ruth is similar to her in that respect.

This time, they know nothing will happen until an hour or so after they finish eating the brownie. They order another coffee, stay put. When it comes, the high is like being wrapped in a soft blanket. Debbie feels it creeping over her, and she feels so content. Like her body is the exact right temperature, and nothing is hurting or aching, and her thoughts are still. She wants to tell Ruth how it feels for her, but she can't find the words. When the man from behind the counter comes over and asks if they want anything else, Debbie just shakes her head.

Ruth is talking about her granddaughter, about the pure joy of watching a baby grow and learn to do things when you don't have the everyday stress of looking after them, being responsible for them. She gets out photos, shows Debbie. The baby is called Grace, and she is chubby and dribbly and smiley, and Debbie thinks about the times when she's held a baby. They have been too few, but she can still remember the warmth and weight of a baby in her arms. The way it makes you feel scared, and awed. The way it makes things feel right.

'I wanted a child,' she says, feeling now is the right time to open up about this to Ruth.

Ruth turns to really look at her, and her eyes are glistening. 'You couldn't?'

'No. We tried for a long time.'

It's a six-word sentence that doesn't encompass the heartache and disappointment of those years. But it's the one she's settled on, the one she tends to use.

'I was lucky,' Ruth says. 'The boys came soon after we were

married and then we decided two was enough, so we didn't have to go through any of that agonising waiting and trying.'

Debbie nods. Imagines if it had gone like that for her. Richie would have been a good dad. The best. He was patient and kind, full of imagination. She's not so naïve she thinks they would have got it all right all the time. But she knows they would have done it with a huge amount of love and enthusiasm. It would have been more than she had, as a child.

'I'm sorry it didn't happen for you,' Ruth says.

Debbie has had a lifetime of people saying that things happen for a reason and at least she has all her time to herself, and this is the exact phrase she needed all along. She feels it nestle into her heart and fill a gap there. 'Thank you.'

They are quiet for a time. Last time, it was all giggling and joy. There's a more melancholy feel to it this time, but it's okay. Everything feels soft, like there are no sharp edges to catch yourself on. Debbie could stay like this for hours. She pleads silently for Ruth to know, for her to not break the spell. And she doesn't. It isn't until the high is starting to fade that they gather their things and go out into the street. It's started raining, and neither of them has brought an umbrella, so they walk quickly with their jackets pulled over their heads, back to the hotel for the final night. Debbie sees streetlights glinting in the puddles of rain that are forming on the street, and they look magical.

Back in their room, they take it in turns to use the weak hairdryer and make cups of tea. They've got into the habit of sitting propped up in bed with a cup of tea at the end of the day. It's funny how people fall into these rhythms, Debbie thinks. With her and Richie, it was a slice of toast at the kitchen table at nine in the evening. They would go over their days and make plans for tomorrow. They did it the night before Richie died, and when Debbie found him, she thought about the plans they'd made. Not falling down dead in the kitchen. Not that.

'Thank you for all this,' Ruth says, gesturing with her hands to take in the room and, beyond that, Debbie imagines, the whole city.

'I didn't do anything.'

'You suggested it. I wouldn't have done.'

'Why?' Debbie is curious.

'I think I find it hard to really think about what would make me happy. What I need, to recharge. I'm so used to thinking about everyone else. Plus we haven't known each other very long, and I don't think it would have occurred to me to suggest a trip so soon. But it's been just right. Perfect.'

Debbie thinks about the train journey home, about how they'll part at the end of it and she won't know when she'll see Ruth again. She wants to cling to her, to be a part of the family Ruth speaks of so often and so fondly. Every time Ruth mentions Kate, she feels a dark flash of envy, because she didn't have a sister and because, Debbie realises, she wants to inhabit the place Kate inhabits in Ruth's life. Not to push Kate out, but to sit alongside her in Ruth's affections. But she isn't sure it's possible; Ruth and Kate have had a lifetime together. She cannot say any of this, of course, because she's scared of frightening Ruth away completely. So instead she nods and says she has loved it, and she hopes they'll do it again.

That night, Debbie sleeps right through, which is unusual for her. She's often up going to the loo or drinking water or simply sleepless at three or four in the morning. Ruth wakes her with a gentle touch on the shoulder, and Debbie jolts, unused to being touched while she is sleeping.

'Time to go home,' Ruth says.

Ruth has already had a shower and Debbie can see that most

of her things are packed, while Debbie's possessions lie strewn around the room. Home. What is waiting for her there? Nothing and no one. Debbie isn't used to feeling like this, has always made the best of things and enjoyed her own company. But since meeting Ruth, it's like she's painfully aware of what's been missing for all these years. She doesn't say much while she gets up and ready, while they eat fruit and pastries in the hotel restaurant for the last time. And at the station, she doesn't really feel like stocking up on snacks for the journey. Ruth must sense this, because she takes on the role, gathering nice drinks and chocolate, making sure they have everything they need. Is this what sisters do? Fill in for each other, take on each other's roles when things are tough? Debbie doesn't know. She hasn't had a lifetime to find out, the way Ruth has.

'Are you all right?' Ruth asks.

They are half an hour into the long train journey and Debbie realises she needs to shake this sadness off to avoid putting a dampener on the whole trip. 'I think, spending this time with you, it's been wonderful, but it's made me realise what I've missed out on.' It feels easy to tell Ruth this truth. Easier than she'd imagined.

Ruth takes a deep breath, her skin reddening a little. She doesn't know what she's worth, Debbie thinks. She finds it hard to believe that her presence could make much of a difference to someone. 'Oh,' she says. 'Yes, we've both missed out, haven't we? But it's harder for you because you grew up with so little family.'

Debbie thinks back to her childhood, to nights on the sofa watching crime dramas that weren't really suitable, her mum's eyes never really focusing on the TV. To turning up at school without her PE kit, or her cooking ingredients, or her signed form, because her mum wasn't good at keeping up with those things. To looking around the hall whenever she was in any kind of production, hoping to see a familiar face. 'I don't think we were both adopted,' she says. 'I don't think that none of our parents were ours, biologically. I thought that was the most likely scenario at first, but not after I met Kate.'

Ruth doesn't seem surprised by the statement. 'I agree.'

'It's just, it would be a relief, in a way, finding out that my mum wasn't really my mum. That we weren't related. Because I've always been scared of becoming like her.'

Ruth covers Debbie's hand with hers and Debbie feels strangely moved by the touch.

'I'm sorry,' Debbie says. 'We've had such a nice time. I don't want to spoil it. It's just, I know we agreed to ignore it but it's hard, isn't it?'

'It is,' Ruth agrees. She is silent for a moment, and Debbie can tell she is thinking something through, deciding whether or not she wants to say it. 'Let's ask my mum. We'll do it soon. We'll go in to see her, together. See what she says.'

Debbie nods, and it's a tiny movement. She knows what Ruth is giving her. Because at least one of them is going to find out they've been lied to, that their entire life has been built on blocks that they're about to knock down.

21

Ruth glances at Debbie as they walk down the corridor towards her mother's room. Kate went in alone and Ruth and Debbie went to the café to wait. And after ten minutes or so, before Ruth had even started drinking her latte, Kate had sent a message.

Clear day.

So now they are doing it. Ruth feels like she is holding a bomb, about to drop it and blow up everything. But she can't not do it. Getting to know Debbie is great, but she has to know. Debbie's face is set in a sort of grimace, but Ruth is sure she's just anxious too. How quickly she feels able to decipher this woman's expressions, her tone. It is like they have always known one another. And perhaps they have, Ruth thinks. They've spent decades apart, but perhaps they knew one another in the months they spent becoming human, and perhaps a connection like that sticks.

When they reach the door, Ruth puts her hand out to open it, but Debbie says her name, stops her.

'I appreciate you doing this. You and Kate. And I want you to remember that this is your mum, no matter what we uncover.'

Ruth pictures her mum on the other side of the door. Sitting companionably with one of her daughters, no idea of what is about to happen. She nods, tries to convey to Debbie that she is grateful for her words. Hopes Debbie understands.

'Mum,' Ruth says, and there is a slight shake to her voice, and she knows that Kate will have picked up on it.

Joan turns her head and breaks into a wide smile. 'Ruth, I'm so glad you're here.'

'I've brought someone to meet you,' Ruth says. There is no going back now. She can only go on to whatever is next.

Debbie steps out from behind Ruth, into full view, and Joan looks from one woman to the other, her face unreadable. Time expands and contracts, loops like ribbon. The room is dead silent, everyone waiting for Joan's reaction. And when it comes, it's not what Ruth expected.

'I told him,' she says, a tear rolling down her lined face. 'I told him it wasn't the right thing to do.'

'What do you mean, Mum?' It's Kate, and Ruth is grateful to her for asking the question, because she isn't sure she could have done.

'I told Frank we shouldn't keep you apart, shouldn't keep you from one another.'

Joan's distress is clear on her face, and Ruth feels guilty for her part in causing it. She steps forward and takes hold of her mother's hand. She wants to convey that she forgives her, or that she will, in time.

Debbie clears her throat, then. 'I'm Debbie Jones. Ruth and I met a few weeks ago and it was quite a shock, as I'm sure you can imagine. Neither of us know what happened when we were born, why we weren't... raised together. We thought you might be able to help with that.'

'He said it was the only way,' Joan says, almost a whisper. All three of them lean in closer to hear her. And she is not speaking to them now, Ruth can see. She is lost in a memory. 'He just wanted both of you to be safe, to have the best possible chance of a happy upbringing.' She snaps back into focus, looks from Ruth to Debbie again. 'Did you have that?'

Ruth feels like there is something lodged in her throat, and no amount of swallowing will clear it. She nods.

But Debbie speaks. 'I don't want to be anything other than honest with you,' she says, her eyes fixed on Joan. 'I didn't have such a good childhood. My mother was unwell, on and off. She wasn't always able to look after me. And my dad was gone. It doesn't mean you did the wrong thing, all of you, but that's how it was.'

Would Ruth have said this, if Debbie's past was her own? She doesn't think so. Debbie is brave and honourable, won't just nod along to make things easier. Ruth feels like she's been nodding along her entire life.

'Mum,' Kate says, leaning forward in her chair and taking hold of one of Joan's hands. 'Are they both your babies? Did you have twins, and then have me? You don't have to tell us everything, but let's start with that. Is Debbie your daughter?'

Joan shakes her head, slow but firm. And Ruth feels like she's just been pushed out of a plane and she's freefalling, hoping against hope that her parachute will open. Because if Joan isn't Debbie's mother, then she isn't hers, either. And that's the truth of it.

'I'm sorry,' Joan says, looking at Debbie. Then she turns to Ruth. 'I'm so sorry.'

For a moment, no one says anything. The urge to say that it's okay is eating Ruth up, but she resists it. Because how can she say it's okay when she doesn't know what the story is? When her mother – this woman she's always believed is her mother – played some part in her being separated from Debbie for all this time? What would a childhood with her and Debbie and Kate have looked like? It's futile wondering, because she will never know.

Ruth sees the change come over Joan, as she has so many times before. Sees her face go from clear to confused. Knows what is coming. First, Joan drops Kate's hand.

'Don't touch me,' she says. 'Why are you here?'

No, Ruth thinks. No no no, not when we were so close. Just then, she feels a hand in hers, and it is Debbie's. It is exactly the reassurance she needs.

'It's Kate,' Kate says. 'I'm just visiting you, like every Sunday.'

'It isn't Sunday.'

Kate shrugs, stands. She and Ruth both know there is nothing to be done when Joan is like this. There's no talking her round, or making her see what is true and real.

'I'll go,' Debbie says quietly. 'I don't want to confuse her any more than she already is.'

'We'll see you outside in a minute,' Ruth says. Then she turns to Joan. 'Do you want anything, before we leave? Tea, or some biscuits?'

Joan sets her mouth in a firm line, says nothing.

'Mum,' Kate says. 'We're going to go now. We'll see you soon, okay?'

It is just as they're leaving, when Ruth has her hand on the doorknob, that Joan speaks again. 'I said it wasn't right, to split twins up like that. Twins belong together, don't they?'

Ruth turns back, but her mum isn't really looking at her.

Twins, she thinks. She knew it, of course she did, but this feels like confirmation. Is it a loss, or a gain? It's both, in a way. All her life, she's been missing Debbie without even knowing it.

* * *

They go to the pub where they always go after their Sunday evening visit, but everything feels a bit different to Ruth. It isn't the smell of the place, like meat grilling, or the sound, which is always a low buzz of chat. She can't put her finger on it, but it's like being somewhere she's never been before, rather than a pub where most of the bar staff know her name and her drink preferences. They order a bottle of red wine and take it into a quiet corner, and Ruth can feel people's eyes on them, the way she always can when she's with Debbie. Thank goodness for Kate. She looks around, defiant, as if daring anyone to come up and ask them.

'I don't know what to say.' Ruth twists the stem of her glass.

Debbie looks at her until Ruth meets her eyes. 'We can talk about something else, if you want.'

But Ruth knows they can't, not really. They have been pretending, up to now, that what is happening to them isn't really happening. And it's been easy to do it, in a way, because there's nothing solid, nothing to grip on to. But they've done it now. In bringing Debbie and Joan together, they've set something in motion and it can't be stopped.

Kate pours them all a glass, a small one for herself, because she's the designated driver, and Ruth finds the glugging noise reassuring. When did she last get really drunk? Years ago, decades, even, she and Nigel used to drink wine and talk about politics and music and books and films, their mouths becoming more and more stained as the bottles emptied. Sometimes two, sometimes three. The morning after, she always felt like death, but she never regretted those nights. They held the two of them together. Now, she can't remember the last time they shared a bottle or had a proper conversation.

'Let's think about what we know,' Kate says. It's the journalist in her. She even roots around in her bag and pulls out a small spiral notebook and a biro. 'You two are twins, yes. We all think that's a definite?'

Ruth and Debbie nod and Kate writes it down. *Ruth and Debbie = twins.*

'What else?'

'Well,' Debbie says. 'If you think we can put faith in what your mum said, then she isn't my biological mother. Which means...'

'She isn't mine either,' Ruth finishes. Perhaps if she says it enough, both in her mind and out loud, it will start to feel true.

Kate writes *Joan – not Ruth and Debbie's mother*. She taps her pen against the paper, and Ruth knows she's working up to something. 'Do you think she's mine?'

Ruth hadn't even considered that Kate would be questioning her own lineage. But of course she would. She's thorough. She leaves nothing unchecked. Ruth is about to say that she remembers Joan being pregnant with Kate, remembers Kate being born, but it isn't really true. There are family stories she's heard so many times they feel like memories, photographs she's pored over. How can she know what is memory and what has been planted? Still, she feels as sure as she can that Kate's parents are who they've always thought they were.

'I think so,' she says.

'You have her eyes,' Debbie says, and Ruth and Kate both turn to her. 'The first time I met you, I noticed that you had different eyes to Ruth, and when I saw Joan tonight, it clicked.'

'But we all have blue eyes,' Ruth says.

'It's more the shape than the colour,' Debbie says. 'Maybe you two are too close to see it. That happens, with people you love, doesn't it? You don't really see them clearly.'

Ruth looks hard at Kate, then pictures their mum. But it's no good. Everything is confused in her mind. 'So maybe we're not sisters?' The words are out almost as soon as she's thought them.

'We're sisters,' Kate says, covering Ruth's hand with hers. 'Just like Mum's your mum. It's not all about biology, is it?'

They drink in silence for a few moments, and Ruth wishes she knew what they were thinking.

'If your mum isn't our mum,' Debbie says, 'perhaps my mum is.'

Ruth has considered this, nights she hasn't been able to sleep, and also this evening. Debbie's mum is the next likely candidate, isn't she? Ruth thinks about what she knows of this woman, who brought up Debbie alone but struggled with her mental health. She can't make it fit. She has lived too long with the lie.

'Is she still alive?' Kate asks.

'No.' Ruth and Debbie say it at the same time.

'I'm sorry,' Kate says.

Ruth is sorry, too. Because what is the value in finding out you have a different mother to the one who's raised you if she's already dead when you discover her? How can it be that she might have missed her own mother's funeral?

'Do you have any photos of her?' Kate asks.

Debbie nods. 'Not with me, but at home. I'll get them out. We can look through them.'

'That sounds like the next step, then.' Kate writes in her notebook. *Debbie's mother = Debbie and Ruth's mother?*

It's the question mark that does it. Ruth is a mess of feelings.

Her sister, beside her, trying to tread so carefully. Trying not to upset anyone. And her twin, on her other side, still so unknown to her. She picks up her glass and drains it, pours herself another.

'Will you tell us about her?' she asks Debbie.

22

Debbie is glad of Ruth's question. Because although her mother wasn't the best mother she could have had, she was hers, and Debbie loved her, and now she's gone and there is no one to ask for stories about her. Hasn't been, until now. She takes her time, thinks back.

'When she was well, she had this great sense of humour. Really sharp. We'd play tricks on each other, have sarcasm competitions. Her imagination was incredible. She could make up a story on the spot, and it always had something woven in. A lesson or a moral or something that had come up in our lives. I felt like she could have been a wonderful teacher.'

Ruth must have told Kate about Debbie's mum's mental health, because they both nod like they understand. It's so easy to focus on someone's illness, so hard to pull out the things they were great at when they were well. Debbie is just getting started.

'She planned this trip for us, the summer before I went to secondary school. We both liked reading, so she made a list of places in some of our favourite books, and plotted this route between them. Dorset for the Famous Five, the village in the

Pennines where the Bronte sisters grew up, Roald Dahl's home, where she was hoping we might get to spot him if we hung around long enough. This was before the internet, so it took hours of research and phone calls.'

'Did you? Spot Roald Dahl?' Ruth asks.

Debbie pulls her cardigan around her, remembering. 'No, we couldn't go in the end. But I never forgot that she did it.'

'What did she like to do, other than reading?' Ruth is hungry for these details, and Debbie is happy to provide them. She doesn't mind doing some sugar-coating, either.

'She was great in the kitchen. We didn't have a lot of money and she could make a meal out of anything. And there was almost always a cake in the tin – fruit or plain sponge or sometimes chocolate.'

Something flashes up in Ruth's eyes and Debbie knows what she's thinking. That perhaps she got her own love of baking from the mother she never knew. It's one of the many things they'll likely never know.

'Each time she was well for a period, I'd think maybe this time it would last. Maybe the clouds wouldn't come again. But they always did. One day, she wouldn't get me out of bed for school, and that would be the start of it. Granny would start coming over, and I'd know it was only a matter of time before I was packing up and moving back in with her for a while.'

Debbie remembers the fear she had, each time, that she wouldn't see her mother again. She used to cry herself to sleep. It didn't matter how much reassurance her granny gave her, how much she promised that her mum just needed some time to get better.

'People didn't talk about mental illness then, you remember. That's part of the reason I'm so proud to do what I do now, for Hopeful Horizons. Back then, mental illness was a shameful secret. If anyone at school found out I was living with my granny, I'd say that Mum had broken her leg. I must have said that three or four times. Nobody questioned it. And I just felt so alone with the secrecy of it all.'

Debbie looks at Ruth and Kate, sees the bond that exists between them. As she's spoken, they've moved slightly closer together. She doesn't think they're aware of it. But how different might things have been for her, if she'd had a sibling to share all of this with? She corrects herself. If she'd known she had a sibling. Maybe two.

'When did she die?' Kate asks. 'How old were you?'

Debbie has been waiting for this to come up. She's told Ruth that her mother passed away, but not when. Ruth probably assumes it happened in the last decade or so. 'I was fifteen,' she says.

Ruth and Kate both put a hand to their mouths in a gesture that is so similar it would be funny if the circumstances were different.

'Fifteen! I had no idea.' Ruth's face is a picture of concern.

When it happened, everyone looked at her like that. Her friends' mums, teachers. The trouble was, none of them actually wanted to do something about it. Debbie wasn't bitter about it; she knew how it was. Everyone had their own family, their own life. No one was looking to take in a fifteen-year-old orphan. She'd gone to her granny's, pretended not to notice that she wasn't really wanted there either. 'Well,' she says, and then stops, because what is there to say?

'Your grandmother took you in?' Ruth asks.

'Yes.' There is no point in elaborating, in mentioning that Granny herself died three years later. That Debbie was fully alone in the world from the age of eighteen. Legally an adult but still so young. She thinks of the girl she was then, lost and scared. There's no telling what might have become of her if she hadn't met Richie. If he hadn't taken her under his wing, taught her how to be loved properly. She doesn't know she is crying until Ruth comes and sits close beside her on the sofa, puts an arm around her body.

Kate slips away, comes back with another bottle and some crisps. And Debbie realises how hungry she is, that she didn't eat dinner before they went to the home. She does this, sometimes. When it was her and Richie, she always thought about the meals they'd have, but now it's just her, she often ends up having toast or a boiled egg. Filling up on chocolate and cake. She wonders whether it's like that for these two women. They've looked after other people for years and years, but have they looked after themselves? When Kate pours her another glass of wine, Debbie drinks it quickly and then realises she's feeling a bit drunk. Fuzzy and relaxed. 'What about your mother?' she asks them. 'Before the dementia, I mean. What kind of a mother was she?'

Kate and Ruth exchange a glance and somehow, between them, it's decided that Ruth will do the talking. Is it because she's the older one? Because she's better at this sort of thing? Debbie doesn't know, but she hopes that, in time, she will.

'She was very good at the little things,' Ruth said. 'Remembering people's birthdays and finding them a really thoughtful gift. Making costumes for school plays. Reading with us every night. I didn't value all of that fully until I had my own children, I think. She made it all look so easy, but I know it isn't.'

Debbie tries to imagine that sort of childhood. Always having the money and the signed form for the school trip, being in the right clothes, in the right place, at the right time. There is so much to mothering, she thinks. Her mum did what she could. She did her best. There's a ringing sound and it takes Debbie a minute to realise it's her phone, inside her bag. She's used to messages but she rarely gets calls. 'Hello?' In her attempt to catch whoever it is, she didn't check on the screen for their name.

'Debbie? It's Pete. With Bonnie?'

Debbie hasn't walked Bonnie for a week or so, what with the Amsterdam trip and work. She's surprised to hear Pete's voice. He usually messages her. And he sounds a bit frantic. 'Hi, Pete, everything okay?'

'Not really. I have to take Miles to the hospital – suspected appendicitis. Is there any chance you could look after Bonnie for us? It might be overnight. I'll pay you, of course.'

'No need for that. It's fine. Do you need me to come to yours? I've had a drink though, so I'll have to walk over.'

Kate taps Debbie on the knee, mimes driving.

'Oh, scratch that, I've got a lift. I can be there in ten minutes.'

Pete sighs, and Debbie can hear the relief in his voice. 'Thank you so much, Debbie. You're a lifesaver.'

After she's ended the call, Debbie explains the situation to Ruth and Kate, who are already gathering their things together. There's wine left in the bottle, but nobody seems to mind.

'So where does Pete live?' Kate asks, her car keys in her hand.

'On that new estate over near the football club.'

Kate whistles. 'Very nice.'

Pete's on the doorstep when they get there, Bonnie at his feet. 'Debbie, thank you! I'll just get Miles.'

'Do you need a hand?' Debbie asks. 'There are three of us.'

Pete smiles gratefully and Debbie gestures for Ruth and Kate to get out of the car. They all traipse inside, where Miles is lying on the living room sofa, his hand clutched to his side and agony written all over his face. Between them, they get him up and out of the house. He leans on Pete and Debbie, while Kate and Ruth open doors and keep hold of the dog. It isn't until they're in the car and ready to go that Pete properly looks at the women Debbie is with. He does a comedy double take.

'This is my sister,' Debbie says. She stops, seeing Kate. 'And her sister. It's complicated. I'll explain another time. Good luck. Hope you feel better soon, Miles.'

Miles lets out a strangled thank you and the car starts moving, leaving the three women and Bonnie on the street. Debbie crouches down so she's at Bonnie's eye level. 'Want to come home with me, Bonnie? Let's get your things.'

They go back inside, and Ruth and Kate help Debbie locate Bonnie's lead, her bed, her food.

'I can walk her from here,' Debbie says. 'I don't want to make your car smell of dog. But would you mind driving this stuff round? I live on Manor Road.'

'Come in the car,' Kate says. 'Really, it's no problem.'

When they pull up outside her house, Debbie expects Ruth and Kate to stay in the car, but they get out and help her with Bonnie's things. Debbie puts some food down for Bonnie in a cereal bowl and rubs her head. She knows that dogs are sensitive, that they pick up on things. She'll have to spoil her tonight. She'll let her sleep on her bed, if she wants.

'Well,' Ruth says. 'I suppose we should get going. It's been an eventful evening.'

Debbie thinks back to the visit to their mum, which feels like it happened days ago. 'Thanks,' she says. 'For the lift and helping with Bonnie and, just, all of it. Letting me into your lives. Taking me to meet your mum. You could have just shut the door on all of this, never called.'

Ruth is standing in the hallway, perfectly still. She has good posture, doesn't slump or slouch. 'I don't think there's any going back now.'

Debbie isn't sure what she means. Does Ruth regret getting involved with her? It's something she worries over all evening, while she watches old sitcoms on TV with Bonnie on her lap. At midnight, she gets a message from Pete to say Miles is having emergency surgery and to check Bonnie is okay. Debbie replies with a photo of the two of them snuggled up together. She goes to bed shortly after that, and as she'd expected, Bonnie trudges up the stairs after her, but she doesn't get up on the bed. Perhaps she's not allowed to at home. She settles down by the side of the bed and Debbie manages to wrestle a blanket under her. In the early hours, she wakes up to the sound of snoring and thinks, for a second, that Richie is next to her. And in the morning there's another message from Pete to say it's gone well and he'll be round to collect Bonnie as soon as he can. He says he'll transfer some money and Debbie tells him not to be silly. She tells him, too, that there's no rush to pick Bonnie up, that they are perfectly happy.

And it's true. It's the happiest Debbie's felt for a while. It's the company, she decides. It's having someone to talk to, even if they don't talk back. After breakfast, they go for a long walk, out across the fields towards the villages that lie next to the town. Bonnie finds a stream to paddle in and a stick to carry, and she is content. It's catching, her contentment, Debbie thinks. It's something she brings you.

23

I really tried. Tried to love her, to love both of them. It wasn't in me. So I told you what I thought, that we should give Ruth up, give her away. You didn't say anything at first. Your mouth dropped open. You said that Ruth was our daughter, that you loved her just as much as Debbie. That they were equal to you. And I just shook my head. You were gentle, didn't shout and scream. You asked if I'd been having intrusive thoughts again. And it was that one word, again, that undid me.

You knew about my past. You'd always known. The way the walls started closing in sometimes when I was growing up. The hospitals I stayed in, if you could call them that. The one I was taken to against my will when I was seventeen. You'd listened to all of it and promised me you wouldn't let it happen ever again. You'd sworn on it.

So when you said you thought we should talk to a doctor, you knew how I'd react, didn't you? I was terrified and furious and I felt like the only person I really trusted had let me down. That's when you came up with the plan. You would take Ruth; I would keep Debbie. It was crazy, but it was a solution. We talked about it like it was hypothetical, until we talked about it like it was real.

I remember the morning you took her. The way you held on to Debbie, tears streaming. I didn't look at Ruth. Couldn't. I told you to just take her. And sometimes I regret that. Sometimes she comes to me in dreams and she can't forgive us for what we did. She looks like Debbie, but with a harder edge. And I want to push her, to escape from her. Because we thought we were ending things that day. But it was really just the beginning.

24

Ruth's body is in her son Max's kitchen, but her mind is everywhere.

'I think everything you need is in the changing bag,' Layla says.

'Great.' It's Ruth's cue to make a move, but she doesn't get up from the kitchen chair she's sitting on.

Grace is asleep in her car seat, a blanket covering her little body.

'I should get to work,' Layla says. 'Unless...'

'Unless?'

'Unless you'd like a cup of tea, while she's napping?'

'That would be lovely,' Ruth says. She is grateful for a chance to pause, to stop rushing around.

While Layla makes the drinks, Ruth imagines opening up to her daughter-in-law about what's been happening in her life. About Debbie, and her mum. People often ask whether she and Layla are close, and she's not sure how to answer. They like and respect each other, she's sure of that. But she's never confided in Layla about anything important. Perhaps today is the day.

But when Layla puts the cups on the table and takes a seat, she starts talking almost immediately and Ruth sees that it is her who has something to get off her chest.

'I'm pregnant again.'

Ruth is surprised but tries not to show it. She scans Layla's face for a clue about how she feels, but there's nothing there. She does the maths. Grace is nine months old now, so she'll be about eighteen months when the new baby comes, if Layla is very early on in the pregnancy. Two under two. People used to talk about that, when she was in the thick of it, about how hard it was. And there she was, with twins. As if she can sense Ruth's thoughts, Layla speaks again.

'I know you had two together, but I just don't know whether I can cope with two babies. I feel like Grace sucks me dry as it is. I feel like a husk of a person.' There is a subtle note of panic in her voice, and Ruth catches it.

Something about Layla's words takes Ruth back into it, the intensity and bone-deep tiredness of those early days.

'What does Max think?' she asks. And then she's cross with herself, for bringing it back to her son, who won't be the one most affected. It is Layla's body that will go through this. 'Actually, ignore me. I'm more interested in what *you* think.'

Layla smiles, looks grateful. 'He's blindsided, too. We had it all planned out. We were going to try again when Grace was three, and in the meantime we were going to save like mad and try to get a bigger place.'

Ruth remembers that saying about making God laugh by telling him your plans, knows better than to say it aloud. 'If it isn't the right time, you don't have to have this baby.'

Layla tilts her head to one side, looks surprised. 'I didn't expect you to say that.'

Should she tell her? It's something she hasn't spoken of, even with Nigel, for decades. But she isn't ashamed of it. 'I had an abortion, when the boys were about eight. Max doesn't know, but I can tell him, if you think it might help. We'd decided two was enough and were using contraception and... it failed us. I thought it was just one of those things. That we'd have the baby and it would be fine. But I didn't want to do it all again, truth be told. I knew so many women who'd had a second or third or fourth that way, by accident. Sometimes it worked out well and sometimes it didn't. And then I realised that women do have a choice, that it's a choice I believe in, and I took it. I've never regretted it.'

There are tears in Layla's eyes. 'Thank you for telling me that.'

The silence of the room is disturbed by a cry, and both women look down at Grace, who has woken and is red in the face. Angry. Hungry.

'I love her so much,' Layla says, and it's almost defensive. As if Ruth has suggested she might not.

Ruth stands, goes to pick Grace up. Holds her against her shoulder and rubs small circles on her back. 'I know you do.'

Neither of them has drunk their tea.

'I suppose I might as well feed her, now she's awake,' Layla says, and Ruth nods.

In the early days, when she was getting used to breastfeeding, Layla used to go to her bedroom to feed Grace. Now she does it anywhere, pulling her clothes out of the way, revealing discreet layers. How tired she must be, Ruth thinks, remembering the sluggishness of those early months of pregnancy. She will do more, have Grace more. Whatever Layla and Max decide.

When Grace is fed and back in her car seat and Ruth is ready to go, she puts a hand on Layla's arm and is surprised when Layla pulls her in for a hug.

'I'll let you know what we decide. But for now, could you keep it to yourself?' she asks.

Ruth looks her dead in the eye. 'You don't have to tell me anything. If you and Max come over with news in a few weeks' time, so be it. If you don't, you don't.'

Layla nods, her eyes grateful. Something has shifted between them. They are closer, now, and Ruth is glad of it.

She gets in her car and starts to drive home, but when she gets close, she turns off in the wrong direction. She is going to see her mother, she realises. She needs to ask her about what she said when she visited with Debbie and Kate. She needs to know for sure, one way or the other, about where she comes from. As she lifts Grace out of the car seat, she thinks about the fact that she's never brought Grace here, to see her great-grandmother. She knows Max and Layla have, now and again. She hopes it won't confuse her mum to see her with a baby.

Joan's in the lounge, playing Scrabble with one of the other residents. She looks up and beams when she sees Ruth and Grace, reaches out a hand for Grace to grab on to.

'Do you mind if we finish this later on, dear?' she asks her companion, who shakes her head and turns to face the TV. 'Let's go back to my room,' she says to Ruth.

In her mum's room, Ruth pulls out the foldaway changing mat and sits Grace down on it, pulls the cushions from the armchair to place around her. She rarely tumbles over now, but the floor in here is hard. Joan settles in the armchair and Ruth perches on the edge of the bed, ready to go to Grace if she is needed. She roots around in the changing bag again, finds a squeaky giraffe toy and gives it to Grace to hold.

'Which of my grandsons are you?' Joan asks.

Oh. Ruth was hoping for another clear day but it seems her mum's trapped in the past, mistaking Grace for one of her boys.

'This is Grace, Mum,' she says. 'Max and Layla's little girl. Your great-granddaughter.'

Joan frowns but doesn't challenge it. How terrifying must it be, to live like this? Ruth takes a deep breath. If she's going to do it, she needs to do it now.

'Do you remember when I came in with Kate and Debbie?' she asks.

Joan's frown deepens. 'Debbie?'

'My twin.' It's the first time she's said it aloud, and it feels nonsensical, because the word is so connected in her mind to the boys.

'How did you find her?'

Ruth's mouth feels dry. The question suggests that Debbie was hidden from her deliberately, doesn't it? 'She found me. It doesn't matter. I just need to ask you something.'

They look at each other, the only sound in the room Grace's sucking noises as she mouths the giraffe toy.

'Are you my mum?'

It's a monster of a question, one Ruth never expected to be asking. But if Joan is fazed by it, it doesn't show on her face.

'No.'

It's what Ruth was expecting to hear, and she's also told herself that she can't fully trust what her mum says one way or the other, but she still feels like all the air's been knocked out of her. Winded.

'Was Dad my dad?' She has to keep going now, one shock after the other.

'Yes,' Joan says. 'I met him when you were a little baby, not much older than this one.' She gestures to Grace, who breaks into a big smile.

Ruth gets down on the floor and pulls Grace into her arms. It's just something to do. She doesn't know what to say, or do.

She holds Grace tight, feels her granddaughter's warm body against her own. It anchors her. When she looks at her mother again, her eyes are drooping. There's a slant of sunlight hitting her chair, and she is basking in it, like a cat. Ruth knows that what she's said is true. So her dad, then, and Debbie's mum? That must be it. She can't for the life of her think why they would have separated them, severed all ties. But it's the only thing that makes sense. For ten minutes, Ruth sits with Grace on her lap, playing clapping games and whispering nursery rhymes. And then, when she is sure her mum is properly asleep, she gets up to go.

Back at home, she busies herself with taking care of Grace. She gets out the playmat and all the toys, helps her stack bricks and put together two-piece wooden jigsaws. She reads to her, one bright picture book after another. And at lunchtime, she gives Grace a thin strip of toast, a sliver of cucumber, a stick of cheese. Baby-led weaning. She wishes it had been around in her day, so she wouldn't have had to do all that boiling and pureeing. When Nigel comes in for his sandwich, he sits opposite the highchair and makes funny faces until Grace throws her head back and laughs, and it makes them laugh, too.

'I thought I might take her to the park this afternoon,' Ruth says.

'Sounds good.'

She's aware of the secrets between them. Chris's sexuality, and now Layla's pregnancy. What her mother just told her. She feels as though they're getting further apart, and that is less scary than it used to be. Grace has a long nap after her lunch and Ruth bakes cookies, and then they go to the park and Ruth pushes her on the swing. How is it that so much time has passed since she was pushing her boys, one hand on each swing? But here is Grace, proof that the years are speeding by.

It isn't until she's dropped Grace home and got back in the car that she breaks down. She cries all the way home, aware she should pull over and get herself together, but somehow unable to. Her mother is not her mother. Debbie's mother, who she'll never know, is really hers. She knows that Joan has been her mother in all the ways that really count, but it is still a deep shock. Still painful. She hadn't expected anything to derail her like this, so late in her life.

Ruth calls Debbie that evening, tells her about the visit. Debbie is quiet, and Ruth knows she is formulating her response, picking her words.

'She said your dad was your biological dad?' she asks.

'Yes. And you've seen her, she gets confused, but I'm pretty sure it's the truth.'

'So they each took one of us,' Debbie says. 'What a strange arrangement. It's like *The Parent Trap*!'

Ruth remembers the film, about teen girl twins who find one another. Wishes Debbie had turned up on her doorstep many years ago.

'So now we know,' she says.

'Now we know.'

'But we don't know why.' Ruth wonders whether they ever will, or whether it will be something to pick at and worry about for the rest of their lives.

They arrange to meet at Mildred's again in a couple of days and both promise to bring photos of the parent they each knew. Ruth busies herself after the call, wiping the tops in the kitchen and doing a load of washing. Nigel and Chris are watching a quiz show on TV, the sound turned up loud. She is going to tell them. She isn't keeping it from them. It's just that they haven't asked, and she doesn't quite have the words. That night, lying in bed while Nigel snores beside her, a thought comes to Ruth, clear as crystal. She might leave her marriage.

Has she known it, deep down, for a long time? She has definitely known it recently, but hasn't faced up to it, hasn't let the words form into a sentence. She turns her head to look at Nigel and her heart squeezes. She has given him most of her life, and he has given her most of his, and it isn't enough. It was, once, but it isn't now.

25

Debbie opens the door and the Jitu on the doorstep both is and isn't the young man she knows. His dark hair, often wild and unkempt, is neatly brushed, and his usual joggers and hoodie have been replaced by navy chinos and a white polo shirt. She suspects there's even been an iron involved.

'Ready?' he asks.

'Ready.' Debbie picks up her bag from the hall table and joins him on the other side of the door.

Though this meeting has been hanging over Jitu for a while, they haven't discussed it at work because Matty doesn't know. Is Jitu ashamed? Debbie suspects so. Matty is one of those students who can go out five nights a week and still ace all his assignments. Work hard, play hard. That sort of mentality. Not everyone's cut out for that.

They are quiet on the walk to the university campus, passing streets they've trawled up and down, asking for money. For help. Not on their behalf, but for other people. Debbie thinks about how that kind of help is so much easier to ask for.

'Just here,' Jitu says, and they turn onto a footpath that leads them from a main road and into a quiet campus, with students riding bikes and gathered in groups, laughing. The Students Union bar where Debbie went with them a few weeks ago is in a different part of the university, on the other side of the main road. Debbie likes this part more. Tries to envisage her younger self here, casually chatting to friends, taking three years from her life to make something of herself, to explore ideas. It never felt like an option for her, and that's okay. But she can't help wondering what her life might have been like if it had been.

When they reach a stark, five-storey building, Jitu juts his head in the direction of the door.

They are about to enter when she asks him to stop. They stand to one side so they're not in anyone's way, and Debbie puts her hands on Jitu's shoulders. 'I need to know where we stand, what you want to come out of this,' she says. 'I can't help if I don't know. And I need to know... if what they're accusing you of is true.'

It's ludicrous that she hasn't brought this up before now, but there it is.

Jitu can't meet her eye. 'It's true. It was so stupid, but I was struggling, had two assignments due the same day and I'd been working most days, and I found these passages online that just fit the brief I'd been given exactly. I told myself it wasn't cheating if I attributed them properly, but by the time the assignment was done, I'd used so much of it that that would have been mad. I was running out of time. I just handed it in, pretended to myself that no one would know.'

Debbie nods. She isn't shocked. It's just as she suspected. He'd taken on too much and something had to give. 'And what do you think they'll do? Do they throw people out for this? Make them repeat the module? Or the year? Do you know?'

Jitu makes a face, his nose scrunched, and for a second

Debbie can see how he would have looked as a little boy. A little boy who'd been asked to do something he didn't want to do. 'I don't think they'll kick me out. But I sort of wish they would.'

They're out of time. If they don't go inside now, they'll be late, and Debbie doesn't want them to get off on the wrong foot any more than they are already. She puts a hand on Jitu's shoulder and guides him towards the door, and then they are in the lift with a handful of students who are laughing about something that happened in a bar last night. She wishes she'd said it would be okay, or something reassuring like that. Debbie follows Jitu out of the lift on the fourth floor, along a dimly lit corridor to his tutor's office. Debbie knocks on the door and a voice calls for them to come in. She's not sure what she was expecting but it isn't this. One man and one woman sitting in easy chairs at one side of a coffee table. Books everywhere. On bookshelves but also in stacks on the desk and on the floor. Two plastic chairs set out for them.

The man stands. 'Thanks for coming in, Jitu.' He turns to Debbie, tries to hide his confusion about who she might be. She is clearly not this boy's mother. 'Nice to meet you. I'm Professor White.'

Debbie clears her throat. 'Debbie Jones,' she says. 'I'm a friend and colleague of Jitu's.'

The woman stands, then. She is another academic, who introduces herself as Tamsin Peak. There is a lot of handshaking, and finally everyone sits down. If she didn't know better, Debbie would think they were here for a positive reason. Everyone is so polite and charming. Is this just how people are, in this kind of institution? She has nothing to compare it to other than school, which was nothing like this. University, she supposes, is all adults who've chosen to further their education. It stands to reason that there'd be a lot of mutual respect.

Professor White does the talking. He has pages from Jitu's assignment on the table in front of him, marked up with red pen. He has printouts from the internet, also marked up. He is showing them how one has been copied from the other. And there's no denying it. It's clear as day.

'Do you have anything to say?' he asks Jitu.

Debbie looks at Jitu beside her and thinks, for one awful moment, that he's going to cry. She doesn't mind how much he cries afterwards, in her kitchen or outside on the street, but she wills him to hold it together now.

'I panicked,' Jitu says. 'I was underprepared and I was running out of time and I made a stupid decision. I should have just not handed it in, asked for an extension or something.' He is muttering, talking to his shoes.

'We have to take this seriously,' Professor White says. 'You understand that?'

Jitu nods.

'Let me ask you this, Jitu. Is this the first time you've plagiarised?'

Debbie didn't think to ask that, just assumed it was. But one glance at Jitu's face tells her she was wrong. His skin is pale and she wants nothing more than to take hold of his hand, which she suspects would be clammy, but it doesn't feel appropriate.

'No,' Jitu says. It's so soft you could almost miss it, but the room is quiet.

Professor White shuffles his papers, and Debbie wonders whether he already knew the answer before he asked the question.

'Could I say something?' she asks.

Everyone's eyes turn to her and she feel momentarily intimidated. Professor White nods for her to speak.

'I work with Jitu,' she says. 'We go door to door asking people to sign up for charity donations. He's been working a lot. I'm sure you know it's hard for some of your students, financially. I suspect Jitu took on too much, out of necessity, and made some poor decisions to get himself out of a tight spot. That's understandable, surely? Could he redo the relevant assignments over the summer?'

Professor White puts the papers down, steeples his fingers. 'I'm afraid we can't be too lenient with this sort of thing. We run all submitted work through a checker but it doesn't pick up everything.' He turns to Jitu. 'Jitu, tell me, what do you think would be an appropriate response?'

Jitu looks like he's been cornered, which Debbie supposes he has. His eyes flit from her to the two academics, and every second of silence feels loaded. Debbie feels awkward and uncomfortable, as if she's the one being taken to task.

When it becomes clear that he isn't going to speak, Tamsin steps in. 'Sometimes students repeat the year, when there have been multiple incidents of plagiarism.'

'I can't afford to do that,' Jitu says.

'Well, there is financial help available, and we can talk about—'

'No,' Jitu says. It's the first time he's sounded sure. 'I'm in enough debt as it is.'

There is silence, and it stretches out into the corners of the stuffy room.

Ten minutes later, Debbie and Jitu leave. They are quiet in the escalator. Jitu is no longer a student at the university, but Debbie is pretty sure he's pleased about that.

'Do you want to get a drink?' she asks. 'It's on me.'

He nods, looks grateful, and they head to a pub he knows that he says will be quiet in the daytime. Inside, Debbie orders two pints of lager and they take them into the garden.

'How do you feel?' she asks.

'Just, sort of, lighter,' he says. 'But also anxious, because I can't tell my family.'

'Surely they'd understand that higher education isn't for everyone? You said you were the first in your family to go, so it's not as if they've done it.'

'That's just it,' Jitu says. 'All their hope and pride is resting on me. They think it's a ticket out, to a better life. And I just need to work something else out before I tell them. So it isn't all bad news.'

Debbie takes a sip of her lager, says nothing.

'Listen,' he says. 'Thanks for coming with me. It meant a lot, not to have to turn up alone. You're a good person, Debbie.'

She feels tears prick her eyes. She knows this. She is a good person. She's always prided herself on it. But this boy, this almost man, has come to mean something to her in such a short space of time. It's crept up on her. And she's so grateful to have been able to do something to help him.

'What now?' she asks.

Jitu looks at his glass, swills the liquid and takes a big drink. 'I think I'll have a few more of these, and try not to think about what's next.'

'Will you have to move out of your flat?'

'It depends what comes up. I'm paid up for another month. It's a private rental so it doesn't matter that I'm not a student. But the charity work isn't enough to pay the rent. I'll need a second job.' He nods at her empty glass. 'Another?'

Debbie nods. 'Go on, then. One for the road. I'll get them.'

'No,' he shakes his head. 'Let me. Please.'

So she does. While he is at the bar, she tips her head back, lets the early summer sun warm her. She has an hour before she's due to meet Ruth. The photos she promised to bring are in her bag. She didn't know how long the meeting would be, so she brought them in case she had to go straight from there to Mildred's. She didn't envisage she would be in a beer garden with Jitu, toasting his new-found freedom.

'Excuse me,' a voice says.

Debbie turns, sees a dapper-looking man of around her age who looks familiar.

'Do I know you?' he asks.

Is it a line? Debbie thought she was past the days of being flirted with in pubs. But she assesses his face. She's sure she's seen it before. Perhaps someone whose doorstep she's stood on. And then it comes to her. The man who'd lost his wife. The thousand lottery tickets.

'Hopeful Horizons,' she says. 'You were so generous.'

She sees it dawn on him, notices how expressive his eyes are as she spots the exact moment he moves from confusion to recognition. He holds out a hand. 'Russell.'

'Debbie.' It feels so formal, shaking hands.

Jitu's back with the drinks and he looks at Russell and then at Debbie, and Debbie thinks he's asking if he should make himself scarce. She shakes her head. 'Russell, this is my colleague and friend, Jitu. Jitu, Russell.' She isn't sure how to introduce him, because surely it's not her place to say that he made such a generous donation. They shake hands, and it feels a bit like they're all in a business meeting.

'Well,' Russell says, 'I'll leave you both to it.'

Jitu waits until Russell's out of earshot before he grins and says, 'He's into you.'

Debbie feels the colour creeping up her neck. She isn't one for getting embarrassed, which leads her to conclude that there is something there for her, too. They're just finishing their drinks and preparing to leave when Russell approaches their table again. Jitu's in the middle of a story about his uncle getting drunk at a wedding and crashing into the table with all the food, but he dries up as Russell stands there, waiting.

'I don't want to interrupt,' Russell says, 'and I can see you're about to leave. I wanted to give you this. Have a lovely day.'

Debbie tries not to look at Jitu, whose eyebrows are lost beneath his hair. She thanks Russell and waits until she's out on the street to open the neatly folded piece of paper. On one side, in neat handwriting, he's written:

I'd love to take you for dinner sometime.

And then his phone number, his name. She hugs Jitu goodbye, bats away his teasing, and heads to Mildred's to meet Ruth.

26

Ruth is looking at a photo of Debbie's mother – *her* mother – trying to see a resemblance. Maybe there's something about the nose. But it certainly isn't startling. It isn't obvious. Opposite her, Debbie is leafing through the photograph album Ruth brought, and Ruth notices Debbie stop dead when she first spots him. Their father. Ruth's looking at it upside-down but she knows the photo well. It's grainy, black and white, taken by Joan, she presumes. She's standing beside her father and Kate's sitting on his knee. They all have the same eyes, she sees now. The same face shape.

'I know him,' Debbie says. 'I... knew him.'

It's so unexpected that Ruth has a sensation of falling and actually grips the chair she's sitting on to make sure she's steady. 'How?' she asks.

There are tears in Debbie's eyes and she is pressing down on the photograph album as if she's scared the picture might disappear. 'He called himself Thomas.'

'His middle name,' Ruth says. 'His first name was Frank.'

And then she wishes she hadn't interrupted, because what if Debbie clams up?

'I only met him a handful of times. He'd come to visit, have some lunch with us, maybe go to the park. Mum said he was an old friend. I never even thought...'

Ruth feels cheated, knowing that Debbie had some level of access to both of their parents, when she did not. She knows it's selfish. Childish, too. But there it is. She feels it and there's nothing she can do about it.

'I wonder why he didn't use his real name,' Debbie says.

'I suppose it was to do with stopping you from piecing it together, in some way.'

There is a moment of stillness, and Ruth turns her head away, unwilling to let Debbie see how hurt she is. 'What were they like together?'

Debbie seems to consider this. 'Like friends, I suppose. Not close ones. I would never have guessed that they'd once been a couple.'

'But didn't you think it was odd, this man on his own, no family, just turning up like that?' Ruth is frustrated, and she knows that Debbie is not the person to take it out on, but she can't seem to help it. It's like Debbie has always had the key to all of this, and she just hasn't bothered to ask any questions.

'I was a child,' Debbie says. 'And it was only every few years. I didn't give it much thought. And then it stopped. I must have been thirteen the last time. I didn't think much about it, and then Mum died, so...'

There is a pause, and they both reach for their cups.

'We look like him,' Debbie says. 'I can't believe I never noticed that.'

Ruth conjures up a mental image of her father, compares it to the woman sitting opposite her. Which is essentially comparing it to herself. She remembers people saying, 'Don't you look like your dad?' She never paid much attention to that kind of thing, secure as she felt in her place in the world, in her family. She spins the album round, flicks through and finds one of the four of them. Joan has her hand on Kate's shoulder; Ruth stands in front of their dad. She combs back through memories. Were there any clues, that Kate was fully theirs and she was not? In the way they behaved, the way they treated them? She doesn't think so. That feels like something to be grateful for.

'He was a good man,' Ruth says. 'A bit distant, but I think a lot of men were like that then. It's different now, isn't it? But he was kind and he worked hard, and he always listened if you went to him with something. Always had time.'

'How long has he been gone?' Debbie asks.

'Coming up for six years. He was a few weeks away from turning eighty. Lung cancer.'

She is back there, in the stuffy room which had a hospital bed where the dining table once was. He'd been adamant that he wanted to die at home, and it had made things more difficult for all of them, but they'd wanted to go along with his wishes. It had only been a matter of weeks from his diagnosis. They hadn't had time to get used to life without him. She was used to it now, though. Had done her grieving. Every so often, something would catch her unawares. One of those big band songs or spring flowers or something silly like malt loaf. But most of the time, she was all right. How was it for Debbie, who'd found and lost him all at once?

'2018?' Debbie asks.

Ruth looks across at her, wondering why it matters. 'Yes. February. He said he wanted to see the snowdrops come up, and he did.'

'He had forty years more than Mum. It doesn't seem fair, somehow.'

'Was it sudden, with your mum?'

'Yes. Stroke.'

Is it better, to have time to say goodbye? To get a chance to say the things you've held back, or assumed were taken for granted? Ruth remembers that Debbie's husband died suddenly too, and she wishes she could offer her something, or someone, to fill the gaps in her life. But Joan is nothing to Debbie, and Joan is the only one left.

'Have you thought any more about what Kate said?' Ruth asks. 'About going to the media with the story?'

Debbie meets Ruth's eyes and Ruth cannot read them. But it doesn't matter, because a moment later she speaks. 'I think we should do it. We might find some things out. And what have we got to lose?'

Our anonymity, Ruth thinks. *Our privacy*. Right now, the story is theirs and theirs alone. They can choose who knows what, can ignore the way people look at them when they're together and leave them to wonder. But if they open the door to media scrutiny, they'll give all of that away. Still, Ruth is in favour of doing it, too, because they know the facts but they don't know the why of it all. She lay awake last night, trying to think of all the ways the papers could hurt them. She can weather it. They can, together. 'I'll call her,' she says. 'When I get home.'

They part soon after, and Ruth senses they're both keen to move this thing along, now they've decided. Kate doesn't pick up Ruth's call, so she leaves her a voicemail, and Kate calls back less than ten minutes later.

'You're both sure?' Kate asks. 'Because I think this could be big. It's the kind of good news story the papers and chat shows love.'

'Chat shows?' Ruth feels her mouth go dry.

'I don't know for sure, but I wouldn't be surprised. You know, breakfast TV, that sort of thing.'

'And you'll try to find out why it happened? Why they separated us?'

'Of course.'

Ruth wonders whether she should ask Kate to wait while she checks with Debbie about the possibility of going on TV. But then she reasons that no one can make them do anything, and she tells her sister to set things in motion. After the call, Ruth sits with a cup of tea beside her, lets it go cold.

When Chris comes down the stairs, it's a welcome relief from the thoughts that are spinning in her head. Ever since he came home, he's mostly worn jogging bottoms and T-shirts that have seen better days, but now he has jeans on and a black T-shirt and he looks like he's done something with his hair.

'I've got a date,' he says.

'Wow. Who and where?'

'Guy called Alex. We're meeting at the Stag in town.' He looks at his watch. 'In twenty minutes. I need to go.'

Ruth has got used to having him as a buffer at the dinner table. When he's there, it's not so noticeable that she and Nigel have little to say to one another. But she can't stop him going out, and she knows he'll be gone again before long. He just needed some time to lick his wounds.

When Nigel comes in the back door, she's putting the dinner out. Pie and mash and peas.

'I was just about to come down and let you know it's ready,' she says.

'Where's Chris?'

'Oh, he's gone on a date.'

'Really? Who's the lucky girl?'

Now is the time to tell him, she thinks. Up until now, she just hasn't brought it up. But if she doesn't say it now, she will be wilfully misleading him. She hands Nigel his plate to take through to the dining room, says one word that she knows will change things forever. 'Boy.'

Nigel doesn't say anything as they sit down, but Ruth can see he's heard. He doesn't like it. He's doing that thing he does with his teeth. Not quite grinding. 'He said that, did he?'

'Yes.' He doesn't say anything, and Ruth busies herself cutting into her pie, watching the steam curl in the air above it. But it's like a scab she can't help but pick. 'What do you think about that? About him being gay?'

Nigel seems to flinch slightly at the word 'gay'. And then he shrugs. 'Up to him, isn't it? Wouldn't have been my choice for him, though, I have to say.'

There's a lot to unpack in that. 'Don't you just want him to find someone and be happy?'

Nigel picks the salt shaker up and puts it down again. He's been told his blood pressure is high, that he needs to be careful. 'It's not as simple as that, is it?'

To Ruth, it is. 'Why not?'

'Because everything's going to be harder for him. Having a family, all of that.'

'Maybe he doesn't want a family.'

'Has he told you that too?'

Ruth shakes her head. She can't help but notice it's the most they've had to say to each other for a long time. 'I just don't think we should assume anything. There are different ways to live a life, to be happy. We need to let him find his.'

Nigel makes a sound that isn't a word. More like a grunt. And then his head is down and he's eating fast, the way she's always hated, as if he thinks someone will take his food away from him if he doesn't finish it in five minutes. She thinks of how long the pies took to make, the rolling out of the pastry, and how quickly they're consumed.

'He was having an affair with his boss, back in London,' she says. Is she deliberately taunting him, trying to provoke the reaction that she's pretty sure is in there?

Nigel looks up, his face screwed up. 'It's a bit sordid, isn't it?'

'What is?'

'Affairs and all that.'

Ruth laughs. 'Affairs are nothing to do with being gay.' She pierces him with a look, daring him to contradict her. It was years ago, all of that. Him coming home late or not at all, her trying to keep things normal for the boys.

Nigel puts his cutlery down with a clatter. 'I feel like I can't say anything, in my own home. You've got a comeback for everything.'

Ruth almost feels sorry for him, but her mind snags on the 'in my own home'. He's always thought of it as his, paid for with his salary. The boys were her domain, her baking business bringing in pin money for bits and pieces. She feels sick, suddenly. Because she knows her marriage is over. That she can't stay with him even another week. She thinks for a moment about breaking the news to Max and Chris, about how it will make them feel, but no. They are adults and they have their own lives now. She has stayed in this unhappy home for long enough.

'Nigel,' she says.

There must be something in the way she says it, something soft that reminds him of the way they used to be with each other, because he looks up with a hopeful expression. 'Yes?'

'I can't bear this.'

'What?'

'This.' She gestures around them. 'Us. I'm not happy. I don't remember when I was last happy.' That's not quite true. She was happy in Amsterdam with Debbie. But she wouldn't tell him that. She isn't cruel.

Nigel splutters a bit, puts his knife and fork down. 'What are you saying? I thought we were talking about Chris.'

'We were. And it just shows the huge gap between us.' She stands up. 'I'm going to sleep in the spare room tonight, and then starting tomorrow I'll look for somewhere else.'

Nigel's eyes widen as he sees she is serious. 'Somewhere else? Just because I'd rather our son wasn't gay?'

'Not just,' Ruth says. 'But partly that. I love those boys in a way you never could. Unconditionally. You need them to fit in little boxes that you've devised. And it's not right.'

If he is going to say anything else, she doesn't hear it, because she walks away from the table, out of the room. And he doesn't follow her. Thank God, at least, for that. Ruth gathers her toothbrush and nightdress, her phone charger, her book, and takes them into the spare room. Sits down on the bed, feeling like all the air has been sucked out of her. Has it always been leading here, this relationship? Would it have ended up like this no matter what she did or didn't do? She isn't sure, but she is sure that she's doing the right thing. She feels affection for the man downstairs, the man she's shared her life with. But not love.

Without thinking too much, she picks up her phone and types out a message:

> I'm leaving Nigel.

And she thinks she will send it to Kate, but she doesn't. She sends it to Debbie.

27

Debbie's walking Bonnie in the park when Ruth calls. She has to juggle the lead and the poo bags around a bit before she can answer.

'Can we meet?' No hello, nothing.

Debbie's thrown, but not so much that she has to hesitate before giving her answer. She tells Ruth where she is and Ruth says she'll come to meet her straightaway, so Debbie spends the next twenty minutes walking Bonnie around in circles so they're still in sight of the bandstand, where she told Ruth to come. The previous night, after Ruth's text, they had a bit of back and forth, but Debbie doesn't feel she understands what's going on, or what's led to this huge decision. When Ruth does appear, she looks her usual self. Debbie isn't sure what she was expecting. Red eyes, sunken shoulders? Before she can second-guess it, Debbie pulls Ruth in for a hug, and she feels her sister's body relaxing against her own. These two bodies, which existed side by side as they developed, lay side by side as newborn babies.

'What's happened?' Debbie asks. She releases Ruth from the hug, holds her at arm's length.

'There was no big row,' Ruth says. 'It's more of a slow decay. I think I've known for years, deep down.'

Debbie swallows, nods. Not once in her life with Richie did she consider leaving him. Not once did she worry that he would leave her. She was lucky, until she wasn't.

'Where will you go?'

Ruth gestures towards a bench and they sit down, Bonnie pulling at the lead to stray further than the small circle she has access to. 'I'll call Kate. She'll put me up.'

Debbie turns that over and over. The future tense. Does that mean Ruth hasn't broken this news to Kate yet? Does this mean that Debbie was the first person Ruth told? It feels childish, in a way, to wish for that. But at the same time, it would mean a lot. Debbie isn't sure how to ask, so she doesn't, but she tucks it away. The hope of it.

And then Debbie's brain moves on to the practicalities. She remembers Ruth saying that Kate's son still lives with her and her daughter is back and forth from her house like a boomerang, that it isn't a spacious house. Where will Ruth sleep? Debbie could offer up her spare room. What would that be like? Waking up and knowing there was someone else in the house, having to close the door when she was dressing. Having someone to go over the day with, to make a cup of tea for. She thinks she would like it, but there's something stopping her from saying the words. Does Ruth want her to say them? Or would she think it was forward, too soon? There's no way to test it, other than just saying it. So she doesn't. Perhaps she will, another time.

Ruth reaches down and gives Bonnie a scratch behind her ears, and Bonnie tips her head back in delight. Debbie's about to ask if Ruth fancies a bit of a walk when Ruth's phone rings.

'Oh, this is Kate now. She must have sensed I needed her.

Kate, hi, I was going to call you...' She goes quiet and Debbie can't help trying to imagine what's being said on the other end of the line. 'Tomorrow? I mean, I'd have to talk to Debbie.' Debbie's head swivels round at this. 'No, I'm with her right now, actually. I'll call you back.'

Debbie waits for Ruth to speak, knowing this must be about them and not about Ruth's marriage.

'We've been invited to go on *Breakfast Time* tomorrow morning.'

Debbie can't tell from Ruth's tone whether or not she's in favour. 'And? What do you think?'

'I'm not sure, really. My head's a mess, Debbie. I've just walked away from my marriage and it's not long since I found out my mum's not my mum.'

Debbie nods. 'It's a lot. You didn't tell Kate about Nigel.'

'No, she didn't give me a chance. She said she's on a tight deadline for something else but she needs to know about this asap. Tell me what you think.'

What does Debbie think? She tries to picture it, being in a TV studio with all those lights and people rushing around out of shot. Everyone wearing a lot of makeup, their hair styled and sprayed in place. It's the scrutiny she's unsure about. People looking closely at her and Ruth, trying to decide what they think about these women who look so alike but have only recently met. But there's excitement too. And she decided to sign up for this, so she might as well keep going.

'I think we should do it,' she says.

'Then we will,' Ruth says.

'It's not only my decision...'

'I know, but I think I just need someone to tell me what to do at the moment. "Come on, Ruth, one foot in front of the other," that sort of thing.'

Debbie looks across at Ruth's hand, which is resting on the bench between them. She's still wearing her wedding ring. Hasn't thought to take it off, probably. Debbie still wears hers. She puts her hand on top of Ruth's, just lightly, just trying to show her that she will be here, that she will do all she can. And Ruth must understand the gesture, because she gives Debbie a shaky smile.

'Do you know,' Ruth says, after a few moments of silence, 'when we were going out, me and Nigel, I was desperate for him to propose. Marriage felt like this goal we were all aiming for, almost like it didn't matter who, as long as you made it down the aisle. How silly we all were.'

'Has it been a bad marriage, on the whole?' Debbie asks. 'Have you been unhappy?'

Ruth looks a bit wild-eyed, as if it's the last question she was expecting, and she takes a while to formulate her answer. 'No, not unhappy. Just, not happy either, you know? No excitement or passion or tenderness. Just coexistence. I didn't notice really, for the years the boys were at home, because there was so much going on. Always someone's football kit to wash or someone's presents to be wrapped. I let those boys fill my life completely, and didn't notice until they'd gone that there wasn't much else.'

Debbie nods, though she doesn't know how this is. She can imagine, but only so far. A friend had once told her that when she first sniffed her baby's head, she felt like she'd unlocked the secrets of the universe, that she understood in that moment why she was here on this earth. And that's always stayed with Debbie.

Bonnie is getting really fed up, so Debbie stands. 'I need to get her back. Do you want to walk with me?'

Ruth shrugs her shoulders. 'Sure.'

There's a bit of a breeze and Debbie notices the way the blossom's fallen from a particular tree. It looks like a pink bed of feathers underneath, and she imagines laying Ruth down there, telling her to take her time in coming back to herself. To rest, to recuperate. There's no rush.

'What do you think they'll ask us?' Ruth asks.

And Debbie is thrown for a moment, has forgotten entirely about Kate's call and the breakfast show. 'I don't know,' she says.

'I suppose it's more that people will want to look at us like we're in a zoo. They'll compare us, you know, even though we look almost exactly the same.'

Debbie thinks about that. About what people might say. She knows that Ruth has aged better than her, keeping her figure slimmer and taking better care with her skin. She doesn't mind, much, about that sort of thing. But it might hurt, mightn't it, to hear it spoken? 'If it's awful, we just won't do it again,' she says, as if it's simple.

Ruth taps at her phone screen as they walk. 'I'll let her know we're in.'

'When will you tell her, about Nigel? About wanting to stay with her?'

'Oh, she said she'll call me when she's finished this interview she's writing. Her deadline is midday, so there's plenty of time.'

When they reach Pete and Miles's house, it's Pete who answers the door. It usually is.

'Thanks, Debbie,' he says, reaching to take the lead and the poo bags.

'How's Miles now?'

'Oh, almost fully recovered. It's going to be a battle to keep him from going to the gym for the next few weeks. But, you know, doctor's orders. And this is your sister, I think you said that night?' He looks at Ruth, then back to Debbie, confirming his own suspicions.

'We're twins, but we only just found each other,' Debbie says.

'Wow, that's like a film!'

He doesn't follow it up with any questions, and Debbie's pleased. 'I need your bank details. You transferred way too much.'

Pete bats her words away. Debbie wonders what it must be like, to be so free and easy about money like that. She doesn't push it, doesn't really know how.

'Same time on Friday?' she asks.

'If you could. You're a star.' Somewhere behind him, a phone rings. 'I'd better get that, see you both!'

On the pavement outside, Debbie isn't sure whether Ruth's coming with her or not. 'I'm going home now,' she says, 'but I don't have work for another couple of hours, if you want company.'

Ruth looks like she's about to say yes, then doesn't. She nudges a cigarette butt along the pavement a bit with the toe of her trainer. 'I think I'll go home. I can't stay away forever.'

Debbie nods. 'Have you told Max and Chris yet?'

'No. It's silly, really, but I'm worried about hurting them. I know they're not children, but I remember reading years ago that kids tend to blame themselves when their parents split up. I'd just hate for either of them to think it was anything to do with them.'

Debbie pulls her cardigan around her a bit tighter as the wind picks up. 'I think they'll want to support you,' she says.

'I'd better face the music. Thanks for listening, this morning. I picked up the phone and called you without even thinking. Do you think there's something in all that stuff about twins feeling each other's pain and just understanding each other completely?'

Debbie wasn't expecting the swift topic change, or for Ruth

to be suddenly more sentimental than Debbie's ever seen her. She thinks about what Ruth said. It isn't something she's given much thought to in the past. Because why would she? Twins have been a focus of Ruth's life, but for her, until all this, twins were something she never really considered or discussed. 'I don't know. I guess we'll find out, won't we?'

They hug, and it feels slightly awkward, but Debbie knows they'll get there. That they'll find the way their bodies fit together. Before she walks away, Debbie speaks again. 'You know you can call me, anytime.' She means it, too. She doesn't mind late-night or early-morning calls, doesn't mind being woken from sleep if she is needed. Because everyone wants to feel needed, don't they? And Debbie has thought she isn't, since Richie's death. But now, here's Ruth, a twin sister with a broken marriage, suddenly all over Debbie's life like spilled milk, dripping.

28

Nigel is in his office pod when Ruth gets home, and she starts gathering some of her things together, hoping he won't suddenly appear. She's folding pyjamas and T-shirts when she becomes aware of someone standing in the door, and jumps as if in fright. But it isn't Nigel; it's Chris.

'Going away again?' he asks. He sounds a bit affronted, as if he's still a child, or even still lives here permanently.

'Chris,' Ruth says, one hand on her chest to show he's made her jump. 'I didn't see you there.'

He's leaning against the doorframe, his arms folded across his chest.

'How was your date?' she asks.

'Not too bad. Did you tell Dad that I'm gay?'

'Yes,' she says, looking him in the eye. 'Was I not supposed to?'

'No, it's fine, it's just... he's behaving a bit weirdly with me, so I wondered.'

Ruth sighs, then rushes to speak so Chris will know she's not sighing at him. 'He's finding it difficult.' She's about to say

'Which is why...' and tell him about leaving, but she stops herself, because then he really would have reason to think the split is his fault. 'Listen,' she says instead, 'things haven't been right here for a while. Strangely, you coming home has highlighted that. When you're not here, we just coexist in this house, coming together for meals but barely speaking.'

'What are you saying?' Chris asks.

Isn't it obvious? Ruth wants to ask. 'It's over, our marriage. I'm leaving, for a while at least.'

'God, Mum. Why? At this stage of your life?'

What does he mean by that? If you've managed to get to this point, you might as well just stick it out until the end, like a fairground ride you're not enjoying but which can't be stopped partway through? Does he think of them as so old that there's no point making positive changes to their lives? She suspects he does.

'Chris, I'm just not happy. This, being here with your dad, isn't making me happy any more.'

Ruth sits down on the bed beside her folded clothes, suddenly overwhelmed by it all. She's only been pulling together enough to last her a week or so. She can come back for more. But when she thinks about all of it, the furniture and the books and the gardening tools and the kitchen equipment, it feels insurmountable. When two lives have been merged for decades, it is never going to be easy to pull them apart. She and Nigel have grown around each other, the way plants do, and now they'll have to find their own roots.

'Where will you go? To Aunt Kate's?'

Ruth nods. When she saw Debbie earlier, part of her thought that she might offer for Ruth to stay with her. Her house isn't large, but it's big enough for the two of them. But Debbie didn't offer, and she's not going to ask. She looks at her watch. It's almost two and she hasn't even thought about lunch. But Kate's piece should be done by now. She will call her, when this exhausting conversation with Chris is over.

'Does Max know?'

'No,' she says. 'Let me tell him, will you? I don't want him to think that he's the last to know.'

Chris doesn't verbally agree but Ruth knows he won't go against what she's asked.

'Are you sure about this, Mum? It feels like you've met this long-lost twin sister and gone a bit mad. Going to Amsterdam, now this...'

Ruth presses her lips together hard. What can she say to this accusation? That she hasn't gone mad at all. More that she's come to life, looked around her and realised that she's not satisfied, not happy. 'It's nothing to do with that, love. I'm sorry you had to find out like this, coming in and seeing me packing my things, but I don't think there's ever an easy way, is there? You've just got to trust me. This is the right thing for all of us.'

'Not for Dad,' Chris says, and then he disappears back to his room, leaving Ruth to think about what he means by that.

Is this the right thing for Nigel? Ruth thinks it will be, in time. They're not giving each other anything, haven't for years. It's not only about affection, and attention, and sex – all of which have been absent for a long time. They don't support one another, share ideas. None of it.

After she's packed her clothes and toiletries, thrown in a couple of books, Ruth goes downstairs and pages through her baking diary. She has a few jobs coming up in the next week, so she starts putting baking trays and ingredients into a plastic bag. This is what she's doing when Nigel comes in.

'Is this strictly necessary?' he asks.

His voice is flat, his words have an unkind edge, and Ruth

thinks about their wedding day, about promising to love and cherish one another, and wonders whether anyone can ever believe they've gone from there to here.

'Don't make it harder,' she says. 'I know you feel like it's come out of nowhere. I'm happy to talk it all through. But not right now.'

Nigel says nothing, and when she looks at him, he looks like a lost boy. She wants to give him a crash course on the things she does for him. On how to use the washing machine and the dishwasher and the hoover. But he'll work it out, won't he? He's run a business for thirty years. He isn't stupid. Ruth knows that he will miss her, but thinks it might only be in a practical sense. He'll miss her when he spills something on the carpet and doesn't know what she uses for stains, or when he fancies a lasagne and doesn't have the first idea about how to make one or how inferior shop-bought ones are. He won't miss her when he's lying in bed. Won't miss the warmth of her skin, or the way she laughs. And that feels a bit like a tragedy, somehow.

In all the hurry to get out of there, Ruth forgets until she's standing on Kate's doorstep that she hasn't actually told her sister what's going on. Hasn't asked, even, if it's okay to stay here. When Kate opens the door, she looks from Ruth's face to her bags and back again, taking her time.

'Can I stay?' Ruth asks. 'Just until I sort myself out. I've left Nigel.'

Every time she's said it, it has felt like such an obvious thing, so clearly right, so she isn't quite prepared for Kate's hand to fly up to her mouth, for her mouth to be hanging open when she removes the hand. She looks like a cartoon character, Ruth thinks.

'Left him? For good?'

'Yes,' Ruth says. 'Now, any chance we could do this inside rather than on the doorstep?'

Over coffee, Ruth fills Kate in, and Kate does a lot of nodding and agreeing and then hugs her. All the things she expected. But then she tells Ruth that they'll have to share a room, if that's all right, because the other two bedrooms are currently being occupied by James and, at weekends, his daughters. She doesn't say that she's expecting a call from Connie anytime, expecting her and her daughters to turn up again, but Ruth knows it's true. It's such an intimate thing, lying beside someone while unconscious, when your body could do just about anything to betray you. But she and Debbie got on okay in Amsterdam, and she and Kate will manage just fine. She thinks of sharing with Kate when they were kids, how they used to beg to have sleepovers in each other's rooms, and wonders when she changed.

Once she's got herself a bit settled in, Ruth takes over the kitchen to make the Bluey cake she needs to have ready for the following day, and soon there is flour and blue food colouring everywhere. When Kate enters the room, she looks a bit taken aback.

'I'll sort it all out, and I'll make dinner, don't worry,' Ruth says.

'I wasn't worried,' Kate says. 'It's just, I was thinking. Are you sure you want to do this TV interview tomorrow, with all this going on? I mean, they'll crucify me if we cancel this late in the day but...'

'It's fine. I'll do it.'

'And do you need to let Debbie know, you know, about you and Nigel? It's bound to come up in conversation.'

Ruth looks at her sister, says nothing. And she sees the exact moment it dawns on Kate's face, that Debbie already knows. That Ruth went to Debbie first. She sees the hurt that realisation leaves, and she wants to take an eraser and rub it out. But it's done, and there's no taking it back.

'Is this how it's going to be, now?' Kate asks. 'You and her telling each other everything and me on the outside? Why was it my doorstep you turned up on, and not hers?'

She didn't offer, Ruth thinks, but she knows it will make everything worse if she says that. She tries to think about how this must all feel to Kate, but her head is too full with how it feels for her.

'I'm feeling my way, with all of this,' she says.

Kate's expression softens a bit, but she doesn't come over to Ruth, doesn't close the gap between them. Doesn't open her arms to offer a hug.

That night, they lie side by side, their backs to one another, and Ruth knows it will take a long time for sleep to come. At home, she would get up, take her book and read it in another room, but she thinks Kate might be asleep already and she doesn't want to disturb her. The more she thinks about the five o'clock alarm, the further she feels from sleep.

When Kate speaks into the darkness, Ruth isn't expecting it. 'Did you ever love him?'

Ruth doesn't answer immediately. She combs back through memories, gets to the early ones. Sees them laughing together, their hands always touching each other's bodies. 'Yes,' she answers, knowing it is the truth. What she doesn't know is when that changed. Was it when the boys came along, with their needs so gaping and endless? There was a holiday in Crete, when the boys were around ten. She remembers it because it was the first holiday that felt like a break. The boys were good swimmers and sensible enough to be left to their own devices a bit, and Ruth read one paperback after another on a sun lounger, in the shade of a plastic umbrella. She can picture the boys, Max's sunburned nose and the goggle marks around Chris's eyes. She can see them with water dripping from their bodies, freckles spreading across their noses. But when she tries to picture Nigel, there's simply nothing there.

'I'm sorry for being a bitch,' Kate says into the darkness. 'I just felt like I should have known, if you weren't happy.'

'I think I was doing a really good job of pretending,' Ruth says.

And then there is silence again, and Ruth finds herself drifting off to sleep much more quickly than she'd expected. When the alarm goes, at five, she feels almost rested.

29

Debbie feels a fizz of excitement every time she reminds herself that she's actually going to be on television. It feels childish, and she doesn't share it with Ruth, but she wishes she could tell Richie. It's the kind of thing he would really have got a kick out of. Right now, she's having her makeup done, and each time she sneaks a look in the mirror, she sees a woman who looks like her, but better. Ruth is in the chair next to her, with the hair person. When they've both finished, they'll swap. And Kate is rushing around somewhere, bringing them coffees and offering pastries and telling producers what Ruth and Debbie will and won't talk about.

'Are you nervous?' Ruth asks.

The truth is, Debbie isn't. But she suspects Ruth is, so she says she is a little, because it feels like the kind thing to say. There's a message on Debbie's phone that her brain keeps going back to, since she received it on the drive down to London. The television company sent a car, and Ruth was quieter than usual, so she had plenty of time to mull it over. The message is from Russell, the widower who she met on his doorstep and then in the pub when she was with Jitu. They've been messaging back and forth a bit and now he's asked for the second time if he can take her out for dinner, and without letting herself pause to overthink, she said yes. So tomorrow, once this is out of the way, she will get to meet him properly, and there's a fizz of excitement about that, too. Who would have thought, a few months ago, that there would be multiple things in her life that she was fizzing about?

The makeup artist and hairdresser swap over and Debbie can't help but smile at her own reflection.

'Ten minutes,' Kate says, coming into the room. 'Do either of you need anything?'

They say there's nothing. And then time seems to compress and the hair and makeup people have finished and Debbie notices that they've made their hair look as similar as possible, which she hadn't expected but perhaps should have done, and they're being ushered out to the set and the lights are hot and intense. The presenter is called Tom Oakham and Debbie cannot quite compute that she is in the same room as him, this man who is so often talking to her out of her TV. He used to present a show about cars that Richie loved. He shakes their hands and smiles and Debbie can see that he's wearing a thick layer of makeup, and for a second she thinks about telling Richie afterwards, before remembering that of course she won't. Can't. Someone does a countdown from five and then Tom is speaking and they're live and Debbie suddenly feels like she'll burst out laughing or swear or do something else that's inappropriate.

'Have I got a story for you today,' Tom says. 'Imagine you were just going about your ordinary life and there was a knock at your front door and when you opened it you were faced with your mirror image. That's what happened to Ruth Waverley and

Debbie Jones a couple of months ago. They found out at the age of sixty-two that they are identical twins, having previously known nothing about one another's existence. Welcome, Ruth, welcome, Debbie. Tell our viewers, how on earth did this come to be?'

Ruth looks at Debbie, gives a small nod to indicate that she should tackle this question.

'Well,' Debbie says, and then she clears her throat and starts again. 'Well, it's taken us a while to work things out, and we still don't have all the answers, but we think our biological parents split up when we were very young and our dad took Ruth and our mum kept me and we lived hundreds of miles away from each other.'

'So you both grew up with one parent?' Tom asks.

'One biological parent, yes,' Ruth says. 'I had a stepmum, too. Who I thought was my mum.'

'I have to say, you both seem very calm about this. If this was me, I'd be furious. How dare they make those sorts of decisions for you and keep you apart for all those years?'

Debbie feels a kernel of anger in her gut. But it isn't directed towards her mother, or the father she never knew and never will. It's directed towards him. Tom. What does he know about any of it? He's just looking for something sensational, something people will talk about. Of course he is. 'I think everyone probably did what they thought was the best thing at the time...' she starts.

'But how can it be the right thing – the best thing – for twins to be kept apart like that? Don't you feel sad about all the years you missed?'

Does she feel sad? Debbie isn't sure about that. Yes, she would have loved to know Ruth all her life, but she didn't, and that's that. It's only when Ruth speaks that she realises she hasn't, and they're on live TV, and Tom Oakham is waiting for an answer.

'Our mum had mental health problems,' Ruth says. 'We don't know our dad's reasons for taking me, but I think we both want to believe that he had them.'

'If that's the case, if she couldn't cope, why would he leave Debbie there?' Tom is sitting opposite them, using his hands to make big gestures. Seemingly irate on their behalf.

'We don't know,' Ruth says. 'But they were our parents, so we'll give them the benefit of the doubt, if we can.'

'Am I right in thinking that both of these parents are no longer with us?'

'That's right,' Debbie says. She has a flash of an image, then, of her mother. The way she was when Debbie was a child and she was well. Pink cheeks and fun.

'But this stepmother of yours' – he tilts his head towards Ruth – 'she is still alive, is she not?'

It sounds like an accusation.

'She is,' Ruth says. 'Yes.'

'And what does she have to say about it all?'

'Well, she has dementia, so it's not straightforward to get any answers out of her. But she's confirmed that I'm not her biological child.'

'Ah,' Tom says. 'Dementia.'

He says it like it isn't true, like it's an excuse she's making, and Debbie feels hot and uncomfortable and wants this to be over. And it almost is. Tom Oakham turns to look directly into one of the cameras.

'Do you know anything about this strange and puzzling story? Did you know either of Ruth and Debbie's parents, Frank Simpson and Lizzie Cooper? If you can shed any light on this delicate matter, we'd love for you to get in touch by phone, email, or via our social media on the usual accounts – check the bottom of the screen now for details. Ruth and Debbie will be with us all morning and we'll keep you all updated if there's any news. Now, if you're a fan of the soaps, you'll no doubt be aware of the ongoing serial killer storyline in *Coronation Street*, and we've got the man himself here on the sofa after the break.'

They go back to the green room, where the *Coronation Street* actor is eating a muffin. Debbie feels shell shocked. But Kate bustles in and says she thinks it's gone well and would they be interested in featuring in *Good Housekeeping* magazine? Debbie glances at Ruth, tries to read her. For her, it all feels a bit like a runaway train. It's not that she wishes they hadn't done it, not yet, but she'd expected it all to happen more slowly. Just shows what she knows about the media. Absolutely nothing.

'I'm in if you are,' Ruth says.

And Debbie nods, thinking that if Ruth can handle this alongside the ending of her marriage, she can too. 'When?' she asks.

Kate frowns at her phone. 'Early next week, I think. I'll check. Also, I'm expecting the tabloids to get in touch any time now. They often pick up stories that have been on the breakfast shows and vice versa.'

Debbie goes to the toilet just so she can lock herself in a cubicle and be on her own for a moment. She takes some deep breaths. Says, in her head, to Richie: 'Look at me now, love.' Realises that she hasn't talked to him for a long time.

When she feels calmer, Debbie goes back to the green room and helps herself to a coffee. She tries to focus on the dinner she's going to have with Russell. It's her first date since Richie's death, her first date since she was a teenager, and she hasn't told a soul. But Ruth told her about her marriage breakdown, didn't she? So doesn't she owe it to her sister to be open?

'I've got a date,' she says, and the words feel strange and foreign in her mouth.

Ruth turns her head to look at her. 'Who with?'

'His name is Russell. I met him through work. The fundraising.'

'Wow, I wouldn't have expected that to be a good way to meet people.'

Debbie considers this. 'Most of the time, it isn't. People are mostly trying to get rid of us. But on this occasion...' She trails off, unsure how to finish the sentence.

'On this occasion it's worked beautifully,' Ruth offers.

'Well, we'll see. I haven't been out with anyone since Richie. And sometimes you have to rip the plaster off, don't you?'

Ruth doesn't get to answer, because a runner puts his head around the door of the green room and says they've had a call and they want Ruth and Debbie back on the sofa in three minutes.

'What did the caller say?' Kate asks, but he's already gone. She turns to Ruth and Debbie. 'Fuckers. They want to get your reaction live on TV. I can refuse, if you want.'

Debbie looks at Ruth and they both shake their heads in unison. They need to know, even if the circumstances aren't ideal. Debbie feels a bit sick, but she stands still while the makeup artist touches up her face and then Ruth's, and she goes back out.

'Now,' Tom Oakham says to the camera, 'our first story this morning was about Ruth Waverley and Debbie Jones, identical twins who've only recently found out about each other. We asked you to get in touch if you had any information, and you didn't let us down. We've got Pamela Whitmore on the phone. Let's see what she's got to tell us.'

Ruth widens her eyes at Debbie and Debbie gives her the

smallest of nods. Yes, she knows who Pamela Whitmore is. She lived next door when Debbie was a child. She was a teenager, then. Must be an old lady now.

'Hi, Pamela, this is Tom Oakham.'

'Hello, Tom.'

Debbie wouldn't have recognised her by her voice, but there is something familiar about it. She remembers playing out in the street, Pamela the eldest, bossing all the others around. She remembers going home in tears once, because Pamela said she was cheating at a game of tag. How would you even cheat at tag?

'I believe you saw our segment about Ruth and Debbie and have some information to share. Is that right?'

'That's right, Tom. I lived next door to Debbie and her mother in my teenage years. With my family, I mean. I'm a bit older than Debbie. Ten years or so.'

Tom turns to look at Debbie. 'Do you remember Pamela?'

'Yes,' Debbie says. Her mouth feels dry, and she thinks about the fridge full of drinks in the green room. The jugs of water, the tea urn.

'And do you remember Debbie's father being on the scene? Or there being a twin sister?'

'I do,' Pamela says.

Debbie feels like the sofa she's sitting on is slipping away from her. She and Pamela were never friends, but how could she keep something like that a secret? She almost misses the next thing Pamela says.

'There were lots of rows, lots of screaming. Debbie's mother, she wasn't quite right, as I know Debbie and Ruth have mentioned. Frank did his best, but he was working all the hours and those two babies were always crying, and it was just too much, I think. One day, it really came to a head. You could hear them out on the street, never mind through the wall. I distinctly remember him saying that there was nothing wrong with Ruth and he was going to take her away with him and she'd never see either of them again. And the next day, they were gone. None of us ever saw him again.'

Debbie wants to get up and run off set. She shouldn't be hearing this kind of thing, about her own life, in this way. And what could possibly have been wrong with Ruth? She feels like she's being abused, set up. And then Ruth's hand sneaks into hers and she is instantly calmed. She can do this. It isn't what she would have chosen, but she can do it.

'Extraordinary,' Tom says. 'Well' – he turns to Ruth and Debbie – 'does that fill in some of the blanks for you at all?'

Debbie looks at Ruth, and her face is pure humiliation. 'Yes, thank you,' Ruth says, using a tone that leaves no one in doubt about how she really feels.

Tom wraps things up and when there's another advert break, he beams at them. 'So that was useful, wasn't it? It will be a ratings winner, too! If we get anything else that we think will be of interest, we'll pass it on via your—'

'How dare you?' Ruth asks.

Debbie isn't expecting the venom, and she jumps a little.

'These are our lives, not some juicy bit of gossip.'

Tom Oakham holds up both hands in front of him. The universal sign for 'now hang on a minute'. He brushes at his hair, which has fallen a little into his face. 'I can assure you, we take this kind of thing very seriously...'

But Ruth has heard enough, and Debbie is glad when she stands and pulls Debbie up with her, marches them off the set and into the green room, where Kate is waiting for them, her head tilted to one side.

'I'm sorry,' Kate says. 'He's a dick. Let's go.'

Out in the street, Debbie takes full breaths of clear air and feels a little better. But the whole drive back to Loughborough, she keeps replaying Pamela's words. *Nothing wrong with Ruth.* Since they've worked out what happened, she's felt like she was the one who was left behind, because she wasn't deemed good enough. But it sounds, now, like their dad took Ruth to protect her. But from what? From whom? Their mother?

30

It might sound strange, but it was only after you'd gone that I thought about the fact that I'd never see you again. It had all been about the girls, up to then. I think you believed I didn't love you, that I couldn't, that that was part of how I was broken inside, but it isn't true. I cried myself to sleep for months after you left.

I got on with things. There was no other choice. My mum helped out; I think you'd known she would. She'd moved to be closer to us during the pregnancy, after all. I believed, with Ruth gone, that things would start to look brighter, so it took me by surprise when it all got worse a few months later. I couldn't get out of bed. My mum found me there, Debbie screaming in her cot. Asked me how long the baby had been crying, and I had no idea.

I begged her not to call the doctor, but she said it was a matter of safety. That she couldn't leave me alone with Debbie, knowing that I might not be up to looking after her. That's when I missed you the most, I think. Because you'd promised you wouldn't let it happen again. And you'd done the hardest thing in trying to keep that promise.

I don't know how long that first hospital stay was. Mum brought

Debbie in and it was a comfort of sorts. I missed her starting to crawl. Mum reminded me that I was missing all that with Ruth, too. I told her to get out. I still remember the look on her face when she snatched up my remaining daughter and left.

31

Ruth feels like she's still processing it all when she and Kate are dropped off at Kate's house. Layla's on the doorstep, Grace in her arms, and it's so unexpected that Ruth doesn't know what to say at first.

'I know you're going through a lot of stuff,' Layla says, and Ruth waves her hand through the air as if to say she isn't. 'But do you have time for a coffee?'

They all go inside, and Kate offers to take Grace while they talk. So Ruth and Layla go to the kitchen and Ruth makes the drinks, and it feels strange, to be serving someone coffee in a house that isn't hers. She wants to ask Layla whether she's made up her mind, because surely that's what this visit is about, but she promised she would never bring it up again, and she is a woman of her word.

'I lost it,' Layla says.

Ruth nods. 'The baby?'

'Yes. I was still trying to decide. *We* were. Although I think Max was in favour of going ahead with it. I think he'd decided we'd make it work. And then I started bleeding and it was all over. And there's a part of me that doesn't feel like I can grieve, because I might have chosen this path.'

'Oh, love,' Ruth says.

'And I hate to bring this to you, with what's happening with you and Nigel, and with you and Debbie, but I don't know who else to talk to. I hadn't told my mum. I don't think she would have been so understanding. And I feel like Max is cross with me, like I somehow caused this to happen.'

Ruth makes a mental note to have a word with Max. To plead with him to go easy on her. It is hard, for women, the whole procreation business. They're damned if they do and damned if they don't and mostly damned no matter what the hell they do.

'It's helpful to think about something else for a bit,' she says. 'Have you been to hospital?'

'Yes,' Layla nods. 'I'm fine, they don't need to...'

Ruth doesn't need her to finish the sentence. She knows what can sometimes happen, what has to be done if the foetus doesn't completely come away of its own accord. She thinks of Debbie, all those years spent trying to get pregnant, how unfair it all is.

'I'll talk to Max,' Ruth says. 'The last thing you need is for him to be acting like it's only him that's going through something. He should be looking after you.'

Layla looks tired and sad, and if she didn't know she was in her early thirties, Ruth would have guessed she was anything up to a decade younger.

'Thank you,' she says. 'It's hard, with Grace, because you can't just take a day off and let yourself wallow.'

Ruth remembers how that was. Never having a day off. Illness, sadness, tiredness. Just having to plough on, regardless. 'Why don't you leave Grace here with me for the day?' she asks.

'Go home and relax, or take yourself out for lunch or something.'

Layla brightens a little. 'Really?'

'Really. I'm here to help.' Ruth thinks about the cakes she needs to make, then pushes the thought to one side. Layla's need is greater.

'I suppose everything she needs is in her changing bag.'

Kate comes into the kitchen, then, with a red-faced Grace. 'She needs a change,' she says. 'Want me to do it?'

Layla looks like she might cry.

'Changing bag's in the hall,' Ruth says. And when Kate has gone, she turns to her daughter-in-law. 'You don't have to do any of this on your own. Remember that.'

When Layla's on the doorstep, almost ready to go, Ruth asks her a question. 'How's Max taking the news about Nigel and me?' She feels almost selfish asking, when they're going through this loss of their own, but she has to know. When she spoke to Max about it on the phone, he didn't say much at all.

Layla looks down at her feet. 'He's okay, Ruth. He said it probably should have happened years ago.'

* * *

Ruth can't quite let go of that thought. Not while she's singing nursery rhymes to Grace, or taking her for a walk to see the ducks on the pond. Not while she's baking during Grace's nap. Why did Max know, when she didn't? And how would things be now if it had happened years ago? Would she be in a new relationship, living in a different house? Would she never have met Debbie? She feels like she's holding a knitted scarf and there's a loose thread and she knows she could pull the whole thing apart if she's not careful.

It's Max who comes to collect Grace, straight from work. Ruth notices how his face changes when he sees his daughter.

'Is Layla okay?' he asks. 'She just sent me a message asking me to pick Grace up from here.'

Ruth feels like she needs to be careful. Does Max know that she knows, about the pregnancy, the miscarriage? Layla didn't say. 'She just looked like she could do with a break, so I took Grace for her.'

'Thank you,' Max says.

Ruth offers coffee, knowing Max will decline. He is always in a rush to be home after work, and Ruth has thought, often, that perhaps that's what it's like in a happier marriage. Feeling that pull to be together, wanting to share the highs and lows of your day. Were she and Nigel like that, in the early days? It's too far back to remember. Maybe they were.

When Max and Grace have gone, Ruth leans back against the front door and takes some deep breaths. Kate is out at a yoga class and James is still at work. It's the first time Ruth's been truly alone for days. And that's when it comes crowding in, what was revealed this morning. Her dad taking her out of necessity. Insisting there was nothing wrong with her. She calls Debbie.

'Why did she think there was something wrong with me, do you think?' She can't quite say 'Mum' yet, and she doesn't need to, because Debbie will know who she means.

'I don't know,' Debbie says. 'It doesn't make any sense. Were you ill as a child?'

Ruth thinks back to stories her parents told her about chicken pox and ear infections. 'Nothing out of the ordinary, as far as I know.' She hasn't been ill as an adult, either. Nothing more serious than colds and tummy bugs. The only times she's stayed in hospital were for the births of her sons. She has been so lucky. She could have been like their mother, in and out of mental institutions. Either one of them could have inherited that kind of life. Ruth realises they've never really talked about it. Not about how it relates to them. 'Debbie, have you ever had mental health problems, like she did?'

She doesn't regret asking it but she does hope she hasn't crossed a line. It's a balancing act, this relationship they're building. Ruth feels as though they are close, because of the circumstances, but it hasn't been all that long. She has to keep reminding herself of that.

When Debbie speaks, her voice is a little hushed. 'Depression,' she says. 'Not all the time. Bouts of it. I'm on medication. But I've always been terrified of it morphing into something bigger.'

Ruth understands, then, the true impact on Debbie of the way she was raised, the demons her mother – *their* mother – faced.

'What about you?' Debbie asks.

'No, nothing like that.' Something flits across her mind. A decade or so ago, she'd felt herself slipping away. Menopause. And when she'd gone to the doctor to ask for HRT, a surly cover GP had tried to give her anti-depressants. But she'd gone back, when her usual female GP was available, and been given the HRT, and things had felt almost immediately brighter.

There is a brief silence, and Ruth imagines they are both thinking that they got off lightly. Debbie breaks it with a change of subject.

'I have that date tonight. I'm in my room, trying to decide what to wear like a teenager.'

'I'm sure he won't care what you're wearing,' Ruth says.

'No, you're probably right. But focusing on the outfit stops me from focusing on the fact that I haven't been on a date for decades and I don't really remember how to do it.'

'I bet it's like riding a bike,' Ruth says. She doesn't know either, of course. Will there be dates in her future? Nerves, and choosing outfits, and all of that? She hasn't considered it until now, in all honesty. There's a big part of her that is sure it's all behind her. Romance, and sex. Intimacy. Where do you even start with all that, after a long marriage? But here is Debbie, being brave after losing the man she loved. Perhaps Ruth should follow her example. Not now, but in the future.

Ruth's just put the phone down when she hears voices in the hallway. Kate's and, she's pretty sure, Nigel's. She opens the kitchen door and Kate gives her an apologetic look and a shrug, and Ruth is furious that Nigel has barged his way into her sister's house without permission from either of them.

'Ruth,' he says, his voice all bluster, 'isn't it about time you came home and we talked about this?'

Ruth puts one hand on her hip and really takes Nigel in. She knows you don't see a person when you're with them every day, but she's been away from Nigel for a week and he is so far from the man she pictures when she thinks of him. Older, more red in the face. She remembers showing Kate a photo of him, when they were first going out, and Kate's eyes widening in envy. It is laughable now. It isn't that she wouldn't have loved him, wouldn't have stayed with him, because he's got older. That's happened to both of them, of course it has. But she feels as if they both got in separate cars on their wedding day and they've been driving in different directions for years. They are so far apart now that she's sure there's no way back to one another.

'I'm not coming home,' she says. 'But we can talk.' She gestures to Kate's kitchen table and Nigel pulls out a chair and Kate disappears into a different room. Ruth makes a mental note to apologise, later, for taking over Kate's house like this, for making her feel she has to keep out of certain rooms while Ruth talks to various members of her family.

'You don't just throw away thirty-seven years of marriage,' Nigel says.

And he's right. You don't. Unless you realise that you've effectively thrown away those years by staying. 'Nigel, I'm not throwing it away. It wasn't right, between us. It hadn't been for a long time. And I think when you get over the shock of it, you'll see that.'

He shakes his head, and when he looks up at her, Ruth is astonished to see that there are tears in his eyes. He's not a crier, Nigel. She could probably count on the fingers of one hand the times he's cried during their marriage. 'I don't know who I am without you,' he says.

Does Ruth? Does she know who she is without Nigel, after being part of Ruth and Nigel for so long, after writing out birthday and Christmas cards from the two of them for what feels like an eternity? Maybe she doesn't, but she's prepared to find out. She's aching to find out.

32

'I can't believe you were on TV and you didn't tell me,' Pete says.

He's at the counter, making coffees, and Debbie's sitting at the huge table. Bonnie is in her bed in the corner of the room, snoring quietly.

'I didn't tell anyone.'

'Well, next time, please do. I don't watch much daytime TV but I'd make an exception for you.' He crosses the room and puts a mug down in front of her. It says LGBTea on it, and she laughs.

'Do you have time for this?'

Pete glances at his watch. 'Barely.'

'Do you like it, working so hard?'

He looks unsure, like it's something he's never been asked. 'I love my job. I suppose it gives me a purpose. We don't have kids, don't plan to, and when I was out of work for a while a few years back I felt wretched. Like I didn't know what the point of me was.'

Debbie has never felt this way about a job but she does understand it. Everyone needs to feel useful. 'What about Miles?'

'He's much more work-to-live than live-to-work. He doesn't hate his job, but he loves it when Friday comes around. Likes gardening, and cooking. Obsessed with films. What about you, Debbie? What's at the centre of everything for you?'

Debbie thinks. Richie's face comes into her mind, and then Ruth's. 'People,' she says. 'I just can't get enough of people.'

* * *

Later, Debbie decides on wide-legged jeans and a white top with a floral print that the woman in the shop had said was 'very boho' but which Debbie had just liked the look of. When she gets to the restaurant, Russell is already there, which throws her a bit, because she's dead on time. He stands as she approaches the table, and she questions what she's doing for a moment. How can she sit opposite this man who is not Richie and share food and conversation? If he hadn't already seen her, she might have changed her mind. But he has, and she isn't cruel, so she accepts his kiss on the cheek, sits down opposite him.

'You look lovely,' he says.

He looks neat and well-put-together, like always. 'You too,' she says, and he laughs, as if this is unexpected.

After they've ordered a bottle of wine, Russell leans in, motions for Debbie to do the same. 'This is the first date I've been on since I lost my wife,' he says. 'And we were together since we were twenty. I don't know how things work any more.'

Debbie laughs, grateful for his honesty. 'I'm the same. Lost my Richie last year after forty-three years together. I suppose we just... give it a try and see what we think?'

Russell pours them both water from a carafe, takes a sip. 'To Richie,' he says. 'And to Gail.'

It's enough to make Debbie's eyes prick with tears, but she brushes them away. 'What was she like, Gail?'

Russell shakes his head. 'I mean, I'm pretty sure this isn't how it's supposed to go. Talking about our past loves.'

Debbie takes a moment to consider this. She pretends to look at the menu, though she's already decided she's having the Thai green curry. 'So much of who I am is bound up in who Richie was, in who we were together. I don't think I could get to know someone very well if I left him out of it.'

'You're right,' he says, almost immediately. 'I haven't thought about it like that, but Gail is everywhere in my home. I say phrases I picked up from her nearly every time I open my mouth. I have books she thought I'd like on my bedside table.'

'We don't need to pretend they didn't exist,' Debbie says. 'It's fine to acknowledge that we loved them, and we probably always will, and to make a bit of space for a new person at the same time.'

The waitress comes to take their order, and they choose the same meal, and share a brief smile about it. When she's gone, Russell goes back to the conversation they were having before. 'I feel like you've got it all worked out, how to start again without dishonouring your husband in any way. I'm still working on that.'

Has she got it all worked out? She wouldn't have said so, but perhaps she should just take the compliment and smile. They muddle through their main course and dessert, finding things in common and bringing up their old loves when it feels right, and Debbie feels like she's had a pretty good time, so she's a bit crestfallen when Russell says he thinks it's been a bit of a disaster.

'What do you mean?' she asks.

'Well, it's all just a bit clichéd and boring for a first date, isn't it? Dinner at a middling Thai restaurant. What sort of nights out did you and Richie like?'

Debbie thinks back to dates they went on. Sometimes dinner, of course, sometimes drinks, but he was always taking her to unexpected places, too. Greyhound racing, bowling, a rock concert. Once, memorably, Seattle, after she fell in love with it through watching *Frasier*. A memory flashes up, and she knows what her answer will be.

'Karaoke,' she says.

Russell raises an eyebrow. 'Karaoke. Watching or performing?'

'Both,' she says, shrugging. 'I don't mind if it's not your thing. We didn't do it all the time, but whenever we did, I had a brilliant time.'

Russell already has his phone out, his reading glasses on, and Debbie knows he's trying to find a place. After a bit of scrolling and tapping, he smiles. 'Aha! Karaoke at nine tonight at the King's Head on Rose Street. Fancy it?'

Debbie does. She hasn't been to karaoke since Richie died. It's not the kind of thing she'd do on her own. They pay the bill, Debbie insisting on splitting it fifty-fifty despite Russell wanting to cover it himself, and spill out onto the street. Russell links her arm as they walk and it feels okay. It's half nine so when they get to the pub the karaoke is in full swing. There are two women in their forties belting out 'I Know Him So Well' and most of the tables are occupied. At the bar, Russell orders them mojitos and Debbie finds they're surprisingly good for a pub that's a bit rough and ready. She spots a table in the corner and points, and they head over there.

'So,' she says, 'is this your first time?'

Russell nods. 'Gail was quite shy. I'm not, really, but she

wouldn't have dreamed of coming somewhere like this.' After a pause, he smiles at her. 'Are you going to sing?'

Debbie has been thinking about what she'll sing. Whether she'll sing has never been up for debate. 'Of course! I'm going to put my name down now. Do you want me to put yours down too?'

Russell holds up one hand. 'Give me a bit of time. I might need a couple more of these.' He raises his glass, and she clinks it with hers, and then she goes over to the man running the karaoke and flicks through his book, checking he's got the song she wants.

When her name is called, Debbie goes up to the front and she can feel Russell's eyes on her even when she's not looking in his direction. It's nice, she thinks, knowing that someone is watching. That someone cares. She's chosen 'Jolene', a song she's always loved, and she stumbles a little on the first line but recovers it, and from then on her voice is in good shape. There's a burst of applause when she finishes and she feels her skin reddening a little, and when she goes back to the table, Russell has this incredulous look on his face.

'That was amazing! Wow. I was sort of expecting a few bum notes or wrong lyrics, but you completely nailed it.'

Debbie takes a sip of her drink, mimes taking a bow. 'There's nothing like singing for giving you an adrenaline rush. For me, anyway. It beats driving on a racetrack or white-water rafting, all of that. What is it for you?'

Russell is gazing at her with a look she can't quite place. 'I'm not sure I know,' he says.

And Debbie almost says that they'd better start finding out, but it's too soon, isn't it, to make such an assumption? To allude to her being a part of his life, for longer than this evening. She stops herself, goes to the bar for another round. And when she gets back, Russell tells her that he's made a decision, that he's put his name down. He won't tell her what he's going to sing, but he does warn her that his voice isn't a patch on hers.

Debbie feels a fizzing of excitement. She needs someone who will match her in this way. Who'll take risks and chances, and have fun doing it. They sit through an awful performance of 'Purple Rain' and a half-decent one of a song Debbie doesn't recognise, and then it's Russell's turn, and he flashes her a 'What the hell am I doing?' look, but he goes up there, takes hold of the mic and gives the audience an almost smile. Debbie doesn't recognise the song at first but then the lyrics come up and she smiles. It's 'I Walk the Line' by Johnny Cash. She finds she's glad he's picked something that Richie never would have done, and he makes a decent stab at it, given it's his first time. When he finishes, Debbie stands and cheers, and he's grinning when he gets back to her.

'You did it,' she says, and before she knows what she's doing, she's pulling him into a hug, and the warmth of his body against hers feels so nice.

'I did it,' he says with a little shrug.

'And you were good! Honestly, you had me thinking we'd have to leave straight after, out of embarrassment.'

'And you don't want to leave?' he asks. 'You want to stay for another drink, and maybe another song?'

Debbie checks in with herself. It's something she tries to do a lot, rather than just answering with the first thing that comes into her head. 'I do,' she says. 'Yes. I do.'

Much later in the evening, they sing 'Islands in the Stream' together, and by the time they leave the pub, Debbie's face hurts from smiling. Russell walks her home, and she thinks about inviting him in for coffee, but the truth is, she isn't ready for that.

'I'm not going to try to kiss you,' Russell says, standing

outside her front door. 'I just... wanted to tell you that, so there's no confusion.'

'Thank you,' she says.

'But don't think it's because I don't want to kiss you, because that's absolutely not the case. I'd just like to take this a bit slowly, if that's okay with you?'

'That's fine with me. That's perfect, in fact.'

'I've had a really fun night. Thank you.'

Debbie's had a really fun night, too. The best for a long time. 'Can we do it again?'

'I really hope so,' he says, and then he starts to walk away, turning back once to hold up a hand in a wave. 'Goodnight, Debbie.'

'Goodnight, Russell.'

Inside, Debbie feels a bit dizzy. She's drunk more than she usually would. So she gets a big glass and fills it with water and sits on the sofa to drink it before going to bed. Knowing she'll have to get up several times in the night to go to the loo, but hoping that it will at least temper the hangover. She's a little restless, a little wired. She finds herself turning on the TV for a bit to wind down, because she knows she won't sleep if she goes to bed feeling like this. A couple of times, she reaches for her phone, but it's too late to call anyone.

And then it hits her. Something good has happened, and she wants to tell Ruth. She lets a smile creep across her face, closes her eyes. In the morning, she will send her sister a message, telling her she's met a man she likes. It feels so teenage, so silly. So good.

33

Ruth takes a deep breath and goes into her mum's room. Joan is sitting in the armchair, and she looks up and smiles.

'Ruth! It's so good to see you.'

A clear day. Ruth is relieved. There hasn't been one since Joan told Ruth she wasn't her biological mother. 'It's good to see you too, Mum.'

She has come armed with questions but it's a sunny day and the window is open, the warm air blowing in, and suddenly they don't seem so important.

'Shall we go for a walk? Maybe have a coffee?' Ruth asks.

'I'd like that.'

They link arms on the walk, and Ruth can't help but notice how brittle her mother feels, how small. She remembers a summer day when Chris called her out to the garden. He was four or five, crouched over on the grass. There was a bird, injured, and Ruth had shuddered at the thought of touching it but Chris was so upset. He'd insisted they try to save it. So Ruth had found a shoebox and put a tiny dish of water in it and she'd picked up the bird, feeling its heart hammering, its legs like sticks. That is what touching her mother feels like, now.

Ruth finds them a table and settles her mother before going up to order. She gets them coffee and a salted caramel brownie each. It feels extravagant, but don't they deserve this? A small treat in what must feel, to Joan at least, like the relentless march of days.

'I'll get them next time,' Joan says, and Ruth just nods, like she always does.

'I've been spending time with Debbie,' Ruth says.

Joan furrows her brow. 'Debbie?'

'My sister. My... twin.'

She sees the recollection dawn on Joan, knows she remembers. She'll have to dive in, won't she, while she has the opportunity? Because they don't know how long it will be until her mother doesn't know her at all. Doesn't remember anything from her life, let alone a decades-old secret. She thinks about the questions she wants to ask, how she can get to them without going into detail about the TV show and the woman who called in.

'Mum, was Dad married to Debbie's mum before you? Lizzie?'

Joan nods.

'So that's why my birth certificate says Elizabeth Simpson.'

Joan winces slightly, and Ruth wonders whether it's because she feels guilty about the lie. But she has to go on, now she's come this far.

'Mum, I heard somewhere that Dad had to take me because there was something wrong with me. Is that right?'

Her mum tuts. 'You were perfect. That woman wasn't in her right mind. How she could think that Debbie was all right and you were – how did she put it? – possessed. I'll never understand it.'

'Possessed?' Ruth's mouth is dry and it's hard to get this single word out.

'She'd been in a mental hospital before, of course.' Joan sips at her coffee and smiles, as if this is a perfectly normal conversation that they're having.

'She had?'

'Yes, when she was sixteen or so. And Frank had promised her he'd never let it happen again. So when she started saying those things about you, it's no wonder he was worried.'

There's a pause but Ruth decides not to fill it. Perhaps her mother will just go on, if she leaves the space for her to do so. And she does.

'He told her he thought they needed to get some help, for her sake and the babies', but she wouldn't hear of it. Got very agitated. Said it was you, Ruth, that there was something wrong with you and you needed to be sent away. Locked up. That she was fine. Of course, Frank knew it wasn't true but what could he do? And then he came up with a plan. To take you both away from her, raise you himself. But when he told her about it, she was outraged. Begged him to take Ruth and leave Debbie. She threatened to kill herself if he took them both. And in the end, he agreed. Oh, but it broke his heart, leaving one of his daughters behind like that. Never seeing her again. It would, wouldn't it? When I met him, you'd just turned one and he was like a shell, empty inside. But we made it work, in the end. You, me and him. And then Kate, of course. A perfect little family. But he never stopped thinking about Debbie.'

'He used to visit her,' Ruth says.

Her mum's face darkens a little. 'I told him it wasn't a good idea, but he couldn't stay away.'

She stops speaking, her eyes focused on something Ruth can't see. The past, she supposes. So that's the truth of it. Her dad gave up Debbie to keep her safe. And her mum? Well, she didn't want her, did she? Ruth knows that it must have been a symptom of her mental ill-health, but it still stings to know that she was unwanted by the person who should have loved and protected her. And why her? If she and Debbie were two identical babies, why was it Ruth who was demonised? She knows that she'll never know the answer. Ruth looks at Joan, feels a rush of gratitude for her. She didn't have to treat Ruth like a daughter, but she did. Just the same as she treated her actual daughter. Not everyone would do that, she knows.

'This brownie is good,' Joan says, as if it's a perfectly ordinary day.

Ruth brushes away tears, takes a bite of her own. It is good, but not as good as the ones she makes, which took her a good few months to perfect. People always say they're the best they've ever had, and yet Ruth very rarely has one. Why is that? Why has she always felt she has to deny herself pleasure? 'I'll bring you one of mine, next time,' she says.

Joan smiles. 'I'll look forward to that.'

When they get back to the home, it's almost lunchtime, so Ruth says goodbye and leaves her mum in the dining room. Back at home, she sets up a WhatsApp group for her, Debbie and Kate, because she's sick of messaging one and then the other with the exact same information. She sends a message:

> Thought this group might be handy. Are either of you free this afternoon? I just got some more info out of Mum.

They're together within the hour, Kate abandoning an interview transcript that she says she needs to get back to later,

Debbie rushing the end of her walk with Bonnie. Ruth tells them in as much detail as she can remember, and Kate's eyes get wider and wider as she goes on.

'I wondered whether it might be something like that,' Debbie says.

Ruth and Kate snap their heads round to look at her, and Debbie laughs.

'You look so similar when you do that. Sorry, I mean, I didn't know anything, obviously. Just that Mum had problems with her mental health, so it sort of stood to reason that that might have been a factor in the breaking apart of the family.'

Ruth had assumed the same, but she hadn't quite realised how serious their mother's mental health issues were. It's hard, she reflects, to imagine your biological mother thinking you were evil, dangerous. Possessed. As a newborn baby. She thinks of her boys, the way they gazed at her, the way they needed her for everything. The way she needed them right back. But no, she can't go too far down this road. She isn't sure she'll find the way back, if she does.

'Have you unearthed anything, Kate?' she asks instead.

She shakes her head. 'I've been digging, in between other jobs. Lots of interview requests. You can pretty much take your pick of the papers and the women's magazines, so we could go one of two ways. Say yes to everyone or offer someone an exclusive.'

Ruth feels tired, unsure why it is they're doing this. Hasn't she got her answers now? She isn't sure she can face being paraded around from one photoshoot to another, especially not now she has this information about the way it all happened.

'Exclusive?' Debbie suggests, and Ruth is glad.

'I agree. I'm ready to put it all to bed, I think.'

Debbie looks at her and Ruth can't quite make out her

expression, but it looks like hurt. She doesn't have space in her brain to untangle it. 'I need to get changed,' she says. 'I'm having dinner with Max. Help yourself to more tea, if you want it?'

Debbie starts getting ready to leave. After she's gone, Kate looks at Ruth. 'Dinner with Max? Just you and him?'

'Yes.'

'Sounds nice. Enjoy.'

Just you and him? Ruth hears the words over and over as she slips into a floral print dress and applies mascara and lipstick. She knows why Kate asked it. Usually, she'd see Max with Layla and Grace or with Chris. Rarely alone. But she has engineered it this way, because she wants to talk to her son about Layla and the baby they're not going to have.

Ruth drives to Leicester and parks in a multi-storey car park that she knows she'll hate going back to later, in the dark. She uses her phone to navigate to the Indian restaurant Max suggested, and as she approaches from one direction, she sees him coming from the other. From a distance, he looks like any other young-ish man at the end of a day at work. His shirt open at the collar and his hair swept to one side by the wind. It's only when they get close to each other that he becomes her boy. The one who couldn't tie his shoelaces for years, who used to pick daisies and dandelions for her and put them in a glass. Who would never hear a negative word said about his brother, would fly into a rage at the smallest slight.

She holds out her arms and he walks into them, and they go inside.

'This is nice, Mum,' he says when they've been seated. 'How are you doing? Chris says Dad's a mess.'

Chris hasn't said this to her. But then, she supposes he wouldn't. Is Nigel really a mess? And if he is, then why? He can pay someone to clean his house and cook his meals, if he wants to, and that was really all she was doing for him, these past few years.

'I didn't come to talk about that,' she says.

Max looks surprised. It's more like her, she thinks, to go along with things. To let the conversation go where others steer it. But not tonight. This is too important.

'Layla told me, about the pregnancy. And then about the miscarriage.'

'Oh.'

'Please don't say that I told you. She came to me in confidence, but I want to say that I'm sorry you're dealing with that and also that I hope you're taking care of her.'

Max juts his chin very slightly and Ruth recognises it as a gesture he makes, unconsciously, when he feels attacked. 'We're taking care of each other,' he says. 'And of Grace. It's full on, you know?'

'I do. And I know how much you do, how hard you work, but losing a child can be so hard on a woman, and I just want to be sure you're seeing her.'

The waiter comes to take their order and Ruth wonders whether he can feel the tension between them. It's pulsing. They both order biryanis and sparkling water, and when the waiter nods and leaves the table, Max looks at her hard.

'You don't know everything about how to keep a marriage going,' he says. 'Clearly.'

'Max.' Ruth touches his hand, which rests on the table. He was always like this, fiery and quick to anger. Full of love and cuddles five minutes later. How does Layla cope with that? 'I'm not preaching to you, I promise. And I know you're going through this too. I just thought Layla seemed sad and a bit defeated when she told me. That's all. I don't want her to feel like it's her fault or—'

'You know she wasn't sure she wanted to have it?' Max asks.

Ruth can tell he's trying to shock her. She keeps her gaze level. 'I do, yes. And I encouraged her to do whatever was best for her.'

He is deflated, wrong-footed.

'Look, Max, I haven't told you this before because it never seemed relevant. But I had an abortion when you were eight. I hadn't got pregnant intentionally and you and Chris were a handful and I just didn't want to do it all again.'

Max opens his mouth to speak but no words come out.

'Max,' she says, her voice soft. 'I don't think men know what it takes out of a woman. Being a mother, choosing whether or not to be one, trying to be the best one they can. It's the hardest work I ever did, the hardest thing. One of the reasons your dad and I are no longer together is that he didn't appreciate all I did for the two of you, didn't see how it overwhelmed me and offer his support. I don't want you to make the same mistakes. That's all. I love you, Max, and I would never do anything to hurt you. And I love Layla, and I want you to be the best partner to her you can be.'

When she's finished speaking, she feels exhausted. Max doesn't say anything for a moment. He crosses his arms, and doesn't uncross them to eat when their food arrives. Ruth pours them both a glass of water, begins to eat. At the end of dinner, they would usually argue about who's going to pay the bill. But she's not sure that's going to happen this time. She wishes she could fast-forward to that part, to going home, and it feels like a shame.

'Chris said you've changed, and it's true,' Max says.

'What do you mean?'

'Since you discovered this Debbie.'

The use of 'this Debbie' makes Ruth want to throw something. Debbie is her sister, her twin. An extension of her that she's only just found, more than halfway through her life. How dare he?

'How about I worry about Layla, and my family, and you worry about yours?'

It stings. Ruth half expects him to get up and walk out, but he loves food too much. Once, as a teenager, he told her he hated her and then inhaled a huge portion of lasagne before storming off to his room. The thought makes Ruth smile, and he catches it.

'What? What's funny?'

'I was just remembering something. Max, sometimes it feels a bit like you and Chris want to keep me in a little box, so you know where I am and what I'm doing. You don't like it when I break out and do what I want to do.'

'That's nonsense,' Max says.

Ruth reminds herself that he's hurting. There's little point to carrying on with this. She'd thought he might be prepared to listen, but his ideas are fixed and he's not moving. All she can do is offer Layla support if she needs it. So she stands, her food barely started, rifles in her purse for some money to leave.

'I'm going to go,' she says.

Max doesn't say anything, because this is unprecedented. Always, she's been the one talking him down, being patient. Well, she's had enough.

34

On their second date, Debbie tells Russell the whole saga about her and Ruth. He listens attentively and asks questions that make her look at things from a different angle. And then, when she says she's ready to change the subject, he tells her about his work as a property developer. He buys flats and houses at auction, renovates them, then sells some and keeps others to rent out. He tells her that he often rents to people he knows other landlords would turn down. People who've been in prison, or had addiction problems, or who don't have references.

'Why?' she asks.

'Just because those people need somewhere to live too. If you've got sober and you can't get a place to live, I'm guessing your chances of relapse increase quite significantly. Whereas if you give people a chance, they often surprise you.'

Debbie admires him for this. She likes the fact that he keeps surprising her. 'Have you ever regretted it?'

Russell shrugs. 'Once or twice. Let's just say, there's a reason why getting references is a good idea. But I can afford to make the odd mistake, so I just keep going.'

'You're like a modern-day Robin Hood,' Debbie says.

Russell shakes his head, lifts his glass to drink. 'No, that isn't right. I do pretty well from it all myself. I just try to help people a bit, too. Another drink?'

They are at a place that sells cocktails and desserts. Debbie's working early in the morning, so she chooses from the mocktail menu. Later, they've promised themselves an ice cream sundae.

Debbie is having fun. Russell is so different from Richie in some ways, so similar in others. She's enjoying the challenge of getting to know a whole new person from scratch. It feels different to what she's doing with Ruth, too. With Ruth, she feels like she has the rest of her life to learn about her and simultaneously like she knows her already. With Russell, it's all excitement and butterflies. It's like her heart is in a hurry.

They're just starting on their second drinks when there's a commotion near the door and Debbie looks over to see a man being marched out. And when she glances across for a second time, she sees that it's Jitu. She's on her feet, heading over there. On the street outside, a doorman gives Jitu a push, and he ends up sitting down in the road. He's more drunk than Debbie's ever seen him. More drunk than she's ever seen anyone, possibly. He puts one hand down to try to push himself back onto his feet, and a car comes around the corner and blasts its horn while swerving to avoid hitting him.

'Jitu!' Debbie calls out. She reaches out a hand and pulls him up.

He doesn't look surprised to see her, or pleased. Just defeated. Debbie keeps hold of his hand, feeling like he'll fall again if she lets go. She saw him a couple of days ago, at work, and he seemed fine, if a little quieter than usual.

'What can I do?' she asks him. That's when he starts crying.

There is nothing contained about it. He sobs, falling into her arms.

Debbie hears a voice behind her. 'Shall we get him home?' She hadn't realised Russell had followed her out here.

'Will you help me?' she asks.

Russell shrugs. 'Of course.'

They take an arm each and start walking him in the direction of his flat, but Jitu is resistant.

'Not to Warren Street,' he slurs.

'Why not, Jitu?'

'Because I don't live there any more.'

They come to a stop in the street, the three of them.

'Where do you live now?' Debbie asks.

Jitu shrugs one shoulder and Debbie feels her heart breaking for him. She knows, in that instant, how it must feel to be a parent. How you must live their best and worst moments with them, feeling what they are feeling.

'Jitu,' she says, making her voice as soft as possible. 'Do you have anywhere to go?'

He slumps, shakes his head. Debbie looks up at Russell. 'We'll take him to mine, then.'

Russell doesn't question it. It takes them half an hour to make the five-minute walk, Jitu stopping to be sick more than once. At Debbie's front door, he swipes away tears, as if there's someone inside that he wants to keep all this a secret from. Debbie makes them all a coffee, and when she brings them into the living room, Russell is on his knees, taking Jitu's shoes off. Jitu looks barely conscious.

'He can just sleep here, if he passes out. I don't like our chances of getting him upstairs,' she says.

Russell looks at her, narrows his eyes a fraction. She waits for him to tell her that Jitu is not her responsibility, but he doesn't.

'Nice place,' he says instead, and she realises this is the first time he's seeing where she lives.

'It'll do.'

They sip their coffee in the quiet room. Debbie thinks about saying sorry for the way their date has deteriorated, but she doesn't need to. She can see that Russell doesn't mind. That he understands.

'Listen,' he says after a long pause. 'Do you want me to stay? Just so there's someone else here to help with Jitu, if he needs it? You have a spare room, don't you?'

Debbie is so grateful to him that she doesn't immediately know what to say. So she just nods, and then she leans back and rests her head on his shoulder, and it feels strange, because she knew all the ways her body fitted with Richie's, but she doesn't know Russell's body yet. Still, she doesn't move, and he puts a hand on the top of her head, and it feels comforting. Safe.

* * *

In the morning, Debbie wakes to find Jitu gone and Russell making coffee. She looks at him, eyebrows raised. He's wearing the clothes he was wearing the night before, because she didn't have anything to offer him, and he looks sleep crumpled.

'I came down about ten minutes ago, and he was already gone,' Russell says.

Debbie looks at the oven clock. She's due at work in just over an hour, and Jitu is on the same shift. She can't imagine that he'll turn up, but then, he has up to now.

'Have you got time for a coffee?' Russell asks.

She makes toast, and they sit at the kitchen table, and it feels strangely intimate, like they've skipped forward a few steps.

Debbie has to keep reminding herself that they haven't spent the night together. Not really.

Russell flashes her a smile, and then she says she needs to get in the shower, and he says he'll get out of her way. For a second, Debbie wants to say she doesn't want him to. That it's been nice having him here, having another person in the house. But it's too soon for an admission like that, so she just thanks him again, tells him to let himself out, and when she comes downstairs again after showering and getting dressed, the place feels oddly empty.

On the walk to their meeting point, Debbie thinks about what she'll say to Jitu if he's there, whether she'll make an excuse for him, to Matty, if he's not. And when he is, she's so relieved that he's safe and she wants to take him in her arms, but he's looking shifty and unsure, so she just says hello and looks down the street to see if she can see Matty coming.

'Thank you,' Jitu says. 'For last night. I don't really remember. I hope I wasn't an arsehole.'

Debbie feels like she might cry, suddenly. 'No,' she says. 'You were just...'

'Hammered?'

'Lost,' she says.

Matty arrives and they make a start, heading into a warren of council housing. And after that there's only chit chat, bits of small talk, and no way or time to ask someone if they're all right. If their life is intact.

At one point, Debbie mentions Russell and Matty teases her gently, and she hopes for Jitu to join in, for it to feel like a normal day for the three of them, but he doesn't. There's something off in the dynamic and Debbie knows they all feel it. Eventually, Matty says he'll take a couple of the side streets and meet them back on the main road further down, and Debbie wonders whether he just wants a bit of time to himself or whether he senses that she and Jitu need to talk. Still, they don't. They trudge up and down paths and ring doorbells and have one-sided conversations, until Debbie can't bear it any more. She puts a hand on Jitu's arm, and he pulls it away but doesn't move.

'I've got this money put away—' she says.

Jitu shakes his head. 'Debbie, I'm not about to take money from you.'

'It's not really like that, though. It hardly feels like mine. Pete gives it to me for walking Bonnie, and I've told him not to, but he always does. And I love walking her, I don't need to be paid for it. So I just put it in a different account and it's been building up. I want you to have it.'

Jitu rubs his hand along his jawline, thinking. 'It doesn't feel right.'

'Well, it's what I want. Think about it.'

He reaches for her then, gives her a tight hug. Debbie doesn't want to pull away from him, but they need to keep moving. They've been a bit slower than usual, and Matty will be waiting. And then her phone rings, and she realises she forgot to put it on silent this morning. She takes it from her pocket, prepared to decline the call. But when she sees Ruth's name, she knows, somehow. Not what has happened, but that Ruth needs her to answer.

'Hello?'

'Debbie.' Ruth's voice sounds strangled, thin. Debbie knows this kind of phone call. She thinks about Ruth's sons, about her granddaughter. Prays it isn't them.

'I'm here, Ruth. What's happened?'

'It's Mum. I just had a call from the home. She's gone. Heart attack, in her armchair. I don't know what to do, Debbie.'

'I'll come,' Debbie says, and even as she says it, Jitu is nodding at her, silently agreeing to cover. 'I'll come right now.'

35

'It's stupid, but because of the dementia, I didn't even consider anything else happening to her,' Ruth says.

They are in Kate's kitchen, stalling for time. Debbie is going to take the three of them to the home, and none of them want to go.

'No, it's not stupid. I'm the same,' Kate says.

Ruth looks at Debbie, and Debbie reaches for her hand and gives it a squeeze. She hopes Kate doesn't mind that she asked Debbie to come. She needs her. 'Shall we go?' she asks, and they trudge out into the hallway to put their shoes on.

At the home, a woman Ruth doesn't recognise shows them in. 'I'm so sorry for your loss,' she says. 'Would you like to see her?'

Ruth silently catalogues the dead bodies she has seen. Her father's, her aunt Edith's, and once, a motorcyclist at the side of the road. She saw the sheet being pulled over his face.

'I would,' she says, and Kate nods. 'We'll go in together.'

'I'll wait out here,' Debbie says.

The woman points Debbie in the direction of the lounge and

then takes Ruth and Kate to their mother's room, though they know the way. Joan is in the bed, looking small and like her body is empty, which it is, Ruth supposes. The woman leaves, closes the door behind herself. Just before it shuts, she tells them to come and find her before they leave, and Kate says they will. Then, silence. Ruth can tell without looking at Kate that she is crying. She goes into big sister mode. Pulls a plastic chair to the side of the bed and tells Kate to sit. She stands on the other side. Ruth feels she should take hold of her mother's hand, but she still remembers the shock of her father's, how cold and stiff it felt, and she doesn't.

Across the bed, Kate does. Ruth watches the tears roll down her sister's cheeks and feels them on her own, as if they are contagious. Which they are, in a way.

'I love you, Mum,' Kate says. 'I'm sorry it wasn't always easy these past few years. I hope you're at peace, now.'

Ruth feels Kate's eyes on her and knows she should say something too. But what? It's so complicated, the way she's feeling. This woman was a mother to her in all the ways that matter, but it hurts to have found out she wasn't in that one crucial way so close to the end of her life. But then the words come, and she lets them.

'Kate and I used to talk about clear days. The days when you knew who we were and where you were and you seemed like the old you. But those other days, when you were confused and lost, those were precious too, in their own way. I hope we offered some comfort. A bit of light in the dark. And I'm glad it's over for you, now. Rest easy, Mum.'

Something in those words must tip something in Kate, and her tears turn to full-on sobs that Ruth worries she'll choke on. She walks around the bed and leans over the chair to take her sister in her arms. 'It's okay,' she says into Kate's hair. 'It's okay, it's okay.' Repetitive, rhythmic, the way she did when they were children and Kate had come to her with a physical or emotional wound.

Ruth doesn't know how much time has passed when they leave the room, but she knows Debbie won't mind. They find her in the lounge, half watching a lunchtime chat show, and the three of them go to the office together to fill in some forms and make decisions about funeral directors. Ruth takes charge, as she always has with Kate, and it makes her wonder, idly, which one of her and Debbie would have been the leader, if they'd grown up together. It was Max, with her boys. Born a few minutes after Chris but slightly bigger and always the one to come to her when they had something to ask. But she and Debbie don't know that about themselves, do they? And they probably never will.

Once they've done all the admin they need to do that day, they drive away from the home and Ruth thinks about how many times she's made this journey, and how she'll probably only make it a couple more. There'll be the room to clear, and then all ties to this building, which has been a part of her life for several years, will be severed. Will she end up somewhere like this at the end of her life? It's too much to think about.

'Do you want to go home?' Kate asks over her shoulder on the way back. She's in the passenger seat, Ruth in the back.

'Home?' Ruth asks. 'My house?'

'Yes. You don't have to, of course, I just wondered. Bad news always makes me want to hunker down.'

'No. I'll stay with you if that's okay.'

Kate tries to smile, and it fails but Ruth is grateful for the effort. 'That's fine. Take as long as you need.'

It's these words that make Ruth realise Kate thinks she will go home eventually. She doesn't see this as a permanent break, as the new normal. It reminds her that she should start looking into where she is going to go. She can't share her sister's bed forever. As soon as the funeral is done, she'll make arrangements. But, oh, the funeral. The thought of it, of sitting in a draughty church or a clinical room at the crematorium. Ruth has never felt close to any of the people she's loved in those types of places.

Debbie swings her car onto Kate's driveway. 'I can come in, make the tea, help out with anything you need?'

Ruth suspects that Kate would prefer it was just the two of them, but she still feels this tug at the thought of Debbie leaving, so she says yes without looking at Kate, and the three of them troop inside.

They're halfway through a pot of tea when Kate stands up. 'I'm going to go to Mum's house.'

'Now?'

'Yes. I can't just sit here. You don't have to come.'

This is Kate all over, and Ruth tells Debbie that once the door is closed and they can hear Kate starting up her car. Even when they were children, Kate couldn't sit still for long. Ruth would lie on her bed with a book on rainy days, but Kate would move all the furniture around in her bedroom or bake cookies or design an obstacle course in the living room. For the second time that day, Ruth wonders what Debbie was like as a child. How she would have fitted in to the dynamic Ruth and Kate have.

'We'd talked about selling the house,' Ruth says.

'To pay for her care?' Debbie asks.

'Yes. I think we would have done it in another year or so. It's been sitting empty since she went in there, and we knew she wasn't going back.'

'Hard, though.'

Debbie's look isn't easily readable, and Ruth suspects she's thinking about clearing out and selling her own mother's house.

'All those things you keep, just in case,' Ruth says. 'And then your children end up having to decide whether to give them to a charity shop or chuck them away.'

'What's Kate looking for, do you think?'

Ruth doesn't know. 'Photos, maybe. Letters. Something to give her some kind of connection.' Then, out of nowhere, Ruth remembers they have the magazine interview and photoshoot tomorrow. 'Tomorrow. I'd forgotten...'

Debbie furrows her brow, then Ruth sees it dawn on her. 'The interview. We can postpone, surely?'

Ruth doesn't know. There will be people lined up. Hair and makeup. Clothes. Plus the person who will interview them. She thinks that perhaps it will be good for her, to take her mind off things. 'I'd like to go ahead, if Kate would. I'll ask her.'

It's like a wave of exhaustion hits her then, and she tells Debbie she thinks she needs to lie down. She goes to the living room, lies on the sofa and pulls a blanket over the lower half of her body, rests her head on the arm. She doesn't ask Debbie to stay but she hopes she will. And she does. The next thing Ruth knows, the light in the room has changed and her arms are cold. There's a slightly bitter taste in her mouth. She takes a moment to orient herself. She is on Kate's sofa. Her mother is dead. Both her mothers are dead. She calls Debbie's name, but her voice is a croak. She clears her throat, calls it again.

Debbie comes into the room and Ruth feels a sense of calm wash over her.

'How long have I been asleep?'

Debbie tips her head from side to side, as if to say she isn't sure. 'An hour, maybe?'

'Is Kate back?'

'Yes. She's in the kitchen.'

Ruth feels a stab of jealousy at the thought of the two of them talking without her being there. And then she dismisses it as stupid. They are grown women, not little girls fighting over whose best friend is whose.

'You should come in, when you've woken up properly,' Debbie says. 'She brought something back from your mum's house.'

Ruth knows, then. She isn't sure how. Could Debbie have silently passed a message on to her, underpinning those everyday words with a more urgent missive? She knows that Kate has come back with the key to it all. That the remaining secrets are about to be unlocked.

'Hey,' Kate says when Ruth enters the kitchen. 'How are you feeling?'

Ruth ignores the question. 'What did you find?'

Kate looks startled by Ruth's abruptness, but she shakes it off. 'Letters. To Dad, from' – she looks at Debbie, then at Ruth – 'your mum.'

Ruth feels like she hasn't quite shaken off the sleep she just had. 'Wouldn't we have found those with Dad's things?'

Kate holds her hands up in a shrug. 'Either it was Mum who kept them or she hid them away when he died. It doesn't matter, really.'

'Where are they?' Debbie asks.

It's the first time Debbie's spoken since Ruth came into the room, and it jolts her.

'There.' Kate gestures to an old shoebox on the kitchen table, a thick elastic band holding the lid in place.

'Did you read them?' Ruth asks. It matters to her, for some reason, that she and Debbie read them first.

'No, not once I realised what they were. They're not for me, are they?'

Ruth thinks that they're not really for her either. Or Debbie. They're addressed to her father, and now he isn't here to ask permission. Ruth reaches for the box, takes it into the living room, knowing Debbie will follow. And for the next couple of hours, they sit in silence, taking it all in.

36

When she gets on the train to London, Debbie feels ever so slightly sick. Should they have called this off, now they know what they set out to find out? She thinks of the letters. Certain lines have etched themselves onto the inside of her eyelids and there's no escaping them. Kate and Ruth look like they've been up all night, and Debbie wonders whether the makeup people will be able to hide their grief. They can work magic, she knows, but there are dark circles under Ruth's eyes that look like they'd be impossible to cover.

'Did you get any sleep?' she asks. They are sitting at a table, Debbie on one side and Ruth and Kate on the other.

'Not much,' Ruth says. 'You?'

Debbie doesn't want to tread on their grief, but yesterday was hard for her, too. 'Some,' she says.

They read all the letters together, in the end. Debbie and Ruth. It felt right that they should find things out at the same time. For Debbie, reading words she couldn't quite imagine coming from her mother, in her mother's handwriting, was like a needle pressing into her skin, over and over. But what was it like for Ruth, seeing that same handwriting that meant nothing to her, and finding out exactly why her mother gave her up?

Debbie looks out of the window on her left. She tries to focus on the fields rushing by but finds her attention drifting. Kate and Ruth's perfumes are competing for space and it's making her feel like she can't breathe properly.

'Can we just get it over and done with as quickly as possible?' Ruth asks.

Kate nods. 'We could have postponed.'

'I know. I just... wanted to show myself I could still do it.'

For a long time, it's quiet, just the low chatter from other passengers. Debbie rests her head against the window, tries to recall train journeys from her childhood. There weren't many. Her mum loved to drive, and she didn't mind city traffic or winding country roads. They had an old green Mini and they went everywhere in it. When Debbie was old enough to sit alongside her mum in the passenger seat, she found that it was easier to talk to her this way, when they weren't looking at each other and her mum's focus was partly on something else. In the car, Debbie shed her secrets, told her mum about friends who'd hurt her and boys who chose other girls over her. And her mum listened, and consoled, and gave advice.

Debbie makes a conscious effort to remember things like this, because it would be so easy to just dismiss her mum as not fit for purpose. And there were certainly times when that was the case. But she was a whole person, complex and layered, and there were good things, too. When she was driving, one hand on the wheel and the other on the gearstick, the music turned up loud and her thin but tuneful voice joining in on the chorus of Rolling Stones songs, Debbie's mum was perfect. Or near as dammit. One day, she'll tell Ruth about these things. But not now, when Ruth's just lost the only mum she's ever known.

At the magazine's offices, a young woman with a burgundy dress and matching lips gushes over them. How alike they look, how disconcerting it must have been when they first discovered one another, how wonderful it must be now. Ruth and Debbie go into a spacious room with rails of clothes and lots of people milling about, and when Kate appears with the burgundy woman, whose name is Olive, Debbie knows that Kate has filled her in. Her whole demeanour has changed.

'Listen,' she says, perching on the edge of the sofa where Debbie and Ruth are sitting, 'Kate's just told me about your... mum. I'm so sorry. We'll make all of this as quick and painless as possible and you can get back to your grieving. And if any of you want to stop or need a few minutes to get yourself together at any time, just say the word.'

For some reason, she delivers these words while looking mostly at Debbie, and Debbie wonders if she's confused about which of them is which. It's very possible. She squirms a little under Olive's focus, wants to say that she lost her mother many years ago, and she is all grieved out. But she doesn't, of course.

When Olive leaves them, telling them to help themselves to food from the buffet table and that people from hair and makeup will come and find them soon, Debbie feels like a weight has lifted.

'She seems nice,' Kate says, and Debbie and Ruth nod, because there's really no arguing with that. 'She'll be the one doing the interview, but photos are up first.'

A wardrobe assistant comes over and introduces himself. Wes. 'We thought about dressing you the same, but we decided it was too cutesy. Don't you think?'

'Definitely,' Debbie says, and then she wonders whether Ruth dressed her boys the same when they were children. It's the kind of thing she can ask but would have preferred to see.

'So we thought what about a sort of mix and match. Ruth in black trousers and a blue top, with Debbie in a blue skirt and a black top. We've got plenty of accessories and we can make it look really classy. What do you think?'

Ruth shoots Debbie a look and Debbie isn't sure what it means. Is she okay with this? Is she asking for Debbie's help getting out of it? Debbie tries to convey that she doesn't understand the message and waits for Ruth to answer the question.

'Could we steer clear of black?' Ruth asks. 'It washes me out. Otherwise that sounds fine.'

Wes gets Debbie's approval and then dashes off to see what they have in the right sizes. An hour later and they are ready, their makeup heavy but natural in tone, their hair shiny and full. Debbie is wearing an electric blue dress with a red belt and red sandals, and Ruth is wearing a top in the exact same shade as Debbie's dress, paired with wide-legged red trousers and a chunky red necklace. Debbie feels uncomfortable, sort of trussed up, her dress tighter than she would have chosen herself, but everyone keeps telling them how wonderful they look, and Debbie can see that it will look great in the photos, so she pastes on a smile and goes with it.

After the photos, Debbie feels exhausted but there's still the interview to go. They change back into their own clothes and Olive appears and sends someone out to get coffee and cakes. 'So,' she says, slapping her hands on her thighs, 'where to begin?'

'We weren't adopted,' Ruth says. 'I guess that's what people might assume. It was the first thing we thought of. But we were raised by one parent each.'

Olive nods, scribbles something down on her notepad. 'And the mother you just lost? I'm sorry to bring it up, but was she...?'

Debbie would leave her question hanging there, force her to finish it. But Ruth steps in.

'She raised me, but she wasn't my biological mother. She was married to our dad.'

Olive doesn't say anything for a moment. She's getting it straight in her head, Debbie thinks. 'So you' – she turns to Debbie – 'grew up with yours and Ruth's biological mother?'

'Yes,' Debbie says. She feels too hot, all of a sudden. Like something is going to explode, or catch fire, or just come tumbling down.

'So really' – Olive turns to Ruth, her head tilted slightly in a show of sympathy – 'you've lost two mothers in quick succession.'

'What do you mean?' Ruth asks.

'Well, you found out that your mother wasn't your biological mother, and that your biological mother was already dead. And then your other mother, for want of a better phrase, died too.'

'Joan wasn't my "other" mother,' Ruth says. 'She *was* my mother. There are things that matter more than biology. Being there day after day, for the whole of a person's childhood. Ironing the school uniform, cooking the tea, plaiting the hair. She didn't give birth to me but she was absolutely my mother.'

Debbie wants to hug Ruth, but she is sitting on the opposite sofa, and Kate has stepped in, pulled Ruth into her arms. It makes Debbie feel strange in a way she can't quite pin down.

'I didn't mean any offence,' Olive says.

'Then perhaps,' Debbie says, not knowing until the last second that she's going to do it, 'you shouldn't have been offensive. This situation is delicate, and there are strong feelings, and there's grief, not only for lost lives but for lost opportunities too, lost time.'

Olive's face reddens, and Debbie sees her for what she is. A young girl who's made her way into this world of glamour, full of false confidence. She's out of her depth, treading water, looking around for someone to rescue her.

Kate is the one to do it. She's the one in charge, after all. 'I think,' she says, 'emotions are heightened at the moment, for obvious reasons. We understand that you didn't mean to upset anyone.'

Debbie understands that Kate's trying to smooth things over, but she isn't sure she wants them smoothed. She isn't sure what they are doing here. She stands up.

'I don't want to do this,' she says.

Kate and Ruth look at her, alarmed, but Olive keeps her head down, presumably hoping to avoid another dressing down.

'I know we said we would,' Debbie says, looking at Ruth and Kate, fixing them with her eyes, 'but that was when we were trying to get to the bottom of what happened all those years ago. And we know now, don't we? There's nothing we need from these people now. Do we really want people to be reading about our lives at the hairdressers? Telling their friends about it? Being someone's great story at a dinner party? I know it's crazy, what happened, us finding each other like that, but it's ours. When we went on TV, it was like giving some of it away, and this feels like that too. And I want to keep it. I want to spend more time with you, Ruth, and discover all the things I don't know. And I want to know you better too, Kate. But I don't want to do it in public.'

Almost immediately, Ruth stands up, and Debbie sees it as a show of solidarity and knows that she could easily start to cry. 'You're right,' she says. 'Kate, I'm sorry, I know we signed up for this but is there anything you can do?'

Debbie thinks about the clothes, the photos that were taken. Everyone's time, from the makeup girl to the person who just arrived back with a tray of coffees and a box of dainty-looking cakes, to see the entire thing falling apart. She feels guilty, but not enough to go through with it. She will pay for those things, if it comes to that. She'd rather keep her integrity.

Kate looks flustered, but she gathers herself. She's a professional. She'll have been in worse situations than this one, Debbie is sure. 'Olive,' she says, 'could you and I have a word outside?'

When they have gone, Debbie finds she can't quite bring herself to look at Ruth, and when she forces herself to, they both laugh. It's nerves and the euphoria of standing up for yourself, doing the right thing. It's doing something together. It's choosing yourself, and each other.

It's all very quick after that. Debbie doesn't see Olive again, but Kate tells them it's all off and there are no hard feelings. They won't get the fee that was agreed, but that will be the end of it.

'What about you?' Ruth asks.

Kate looks confused.

'Do you mind?'

'Mind? God, no. This is your story. You've got to feel in control of it. Maybe if we hadn't done this so soon after Mum, it would have been different, but who knows? Now, let's go home, shall we?'

37

We did the right thing. I have to believe that. Because if I don't, what have I got? A broken marriage, an estranged child. I couldn't believe it the first time you turned up. No warning, nothing. Just there, on the doorstep. Debbie was three by then and I introduced you as an old friend. I saw the tears in your eyes when she reached out a hand to shake yours.

You tried to show me photos of Ruth but I couldn't look at them. When Debbie was in bed, I turned on you and asked why you'd come. I was so torn. I wanted you back. You, but not her. We'd never be a happy family again, I knew that. So I asked you to leave. I spent so much time asking people I loved to leave.

I didn't think you'd come back, but you did. Not for a couple of years. Debbie didn't remember you and we did the old friend thing again. That time, she gave you a hug. I could see in your eyes what it meant to you. And I remember thinking it was a shame that we couldn't fix it, couldn't put it all back together.

The next decade was a blur. Hospital visits, visits from you, Debbie growing and changing at an alarming rate. Once, you talked about taking her. About giving me space and time to get better. I was terrified. Debbie was all I had. We were in the kitchen, Debbie out at a friend's, and I came at you with a knife I was clutching in my hand. I was no match for you, but something ended that day. We never saw you again. And these days, I wonder: how are you? And how is Ruth?

38

Nigel wants to be at the funeral and Ruth doesn't have the energy to fight him on it. Besides, who is she to deny his attendance? He has known her mother almost as long as he has known her. Their relationship has never been close but it's always been cordial. Ruth suspects he wants to talk to her, rather than pay his respects and say goodbye, but she gives him the benefit of the doubt. She doesn't sit with him, though. She sits with her sisters and Kate's children on the front row, with Nigel and their boys behind her. It's nice, she knows, that she is surrounded by people who care for her. But it doesn't feel like care, somehow. It makes her feel trapped.

At the pub, after the service, Ruth drinks three gin and tonics way too fast and on an empty stomach. So when Nigel approaches her, she's ready to tell it like it is.

'I'm sorry for your loss,' he says, and it's what a stranger would say, and Ruth isn't sure how to respond. 'But I think you're allowing it to cloud your judgement. This Debbie, she's only been on the scene for five minutes.'

'But she's been my twin forever,' Ruth says.

Nigel makes a scoffing sort of noise, and Ruth thinks about all the things she's felt unable to talk to him about over the years. Everything is cut and dried for him. He believes in things or he doesn't. If she'd told him that she'd always felt a little rootless, a little lonely, like something had been severed, he wouldn't have believed it. And yet, here is the proof. Debbie. A sister, a twin. Here, from nowhere.

'There shouldn't be a "but" when you're telling someone you're sorry for their loss,' Ruth says.

Nigel peers at her, swills the dregs of his lager in his glass. Ruth suspects he's wondering whether he's ever really known her at all. Good. Let him wonder. He hasn't. Not inside and out, the way a partner should. There is so much she's held back from him.

'When are we going to get together to talk properly?' he asks. 'I know today's probably not the time to ask, but...'

'No, it isn't. And really, I don't know what there is to say.'

'You don't just throw away a marriage, Ruth!'

People are looking. Ruth's always hated being the centre of attention, but she finds she doesn't mind so much, now. 'Nigel, let me say goodbye to my mother. I'll call you next week or something.'

In the past, she would have waited for his response, but she knows that he will just try to argue with her, try to tell her why she is wrong about everything. So she doesn't let him. She just walks away. It's so easy, she realises, to walk away. At the bar, she orders another gin and tonic, and when Max puts a hand on her arm and asks whether she thinks she should slow down, she tells him very calmly that she doesn't. He shakes his head at her and walks away, and she feels, in that moment, so let down. She's let go of Nigel and she knows it's the right thing. But what about Max and Chris? How is it that she ploughed so much of her time and energy and her whole heart into raising these men and sometimes she feels like she barely knows them? Today is the first time she's seen Max since she left him in that Indian restaurant, and she knows she isn't quite forgiven for it.

Out of the corner of her eye, Ruth sees Debbie. Standing in a corner, sending a message on her phone. Ruth orders them both a drink and goes over.

'How are you doing?' Debbie asks, taking the glass Ruth thrusts at her.

'I'm questioning my entire life,' Ruth says, and she can hear that there's a slight slur to her words, but it's not enough to stop her from lifting her glass and drinking again.

'How so?'

'Nigel, and the boys. I gave them everything, Debbie. Everything. Every last bit of me. And what do I have to show for it?'

Debbie clears her throat, shuffles a bit on her feet. 'A family,' she says. 'I know it's not perfect, but you have something I've never had, the four of you.'

Ruth shakes her head as if trying to dislodge Debbie's words. 'Max has his own family, and it's over with Nigel. Which just leaves Chris, who's so wrapped up in himself that he's barely noticed I've left the family home.'

Debbie says nothing, and Ruth knows she's pushing things too far, that she should stop before she says something she can't take back, but there's a part of her brain that's egging her on, telling her to push and push and push and see how much strain Debbie will take before she snaps. She feels like she's full to the brim with spite, and it's dripping out through her mouth.

'And you,' Ruth says, quite unsure what she's going to say about Debbie until the words come. 'You collect people. That guy with the dog, and Jitu, and now Russell. I can't work out whether you care about any of them, or whether it's just something to do because you don't have a family of your own.'

'That's enough,' Debbie says.

But it isn't. Not quite.

'You know you can't just take people on, like projects. Like they're your children. You know that, don't you?'

It's Kate who speaks then, who tells Ruth she's said enough, had enough. Who appears from somewhere in the crowd and takes the drink from Ruth's hand and tells her she thinks she should go home. And Ruth, who hasn't cried all day, turns on her heel, thinking – mistakenly – that it's not too late to save her dignity and walks out of the pub, out of her own mother's wake, and sets off for home.

She's wearing heels and they're pinching, and when she's about halfway to Kate's house, Ruth stops and leans back against a shopfront and the tears come. Unexpected, fast. Why did she attack Debbie like that? Why is she trying to push everyone away? Is she just trying to find out who'll go, who'll come back? A man comes out of the shop and asks whether she's okay, and Ruth nods her head, though it's clear she isn't, and starts walking again.

Back at Kate's, she runs a hot bath. Too hot, the kind it's hard to step into. She catalogues her failings. Two sons who aren't always the people she'd hoped they would be. A wrecked marriage. And now, a twin she's only just become aware of, who she's shared some of the best moments of her life with, somehow, in these past few weeks, but who will almost certainly walk away from her because of the things she said. She didn't even mean them. She thinks it's amazing how Debbie can be friends with everyone, how she can just turn up somewhere and find her place. She wishes she was more like that. Who wouldn't?

When Ruth hears the door opening, she's dressed in pyjamas

and slippers, and she goes downstairs. Kate is inside, leaning against the front door. She looks exhausted. She looks like she's just buried her mother.

'What on earth was all that?' Kate asks. Her voice is soft, and Ruth is grateful. She can't face more admonishment today, and she suspects Kate knows that.

Ruth shakes her head. 'I don't know. Did Debbie...? Is Debbie...?' She doesn't know how to end the question. *Does she hate me? Will she forgive me? Is it all over as soon as it's begun?*

But Kate knows without her having to ask it fully. 'Debbie was upset, but she'll calm down. Give her a couple of days.'

Ruth wants to say that she doesn't know how to go a couple of days without Debbie now, but it seems faintly ridiculous, given that she managed to go for more than sixty years of her life that way. 'Do you want tea?' she asks. She can't quite work out whether Kate is drunk. Her lipstick has been reapplied inexpertly, but there's nothing else to suggest it. Nothing in her movements or her speech. For her part, Ruth feels completely sober, after the walk and the bath.

'Tea would be good,' Kate says.

At the kitchen table, they sit quietly, mugs and a plate of biscuits in between them.

'Sometimes I wished for it, you know,' Kate says.

'For what?'

'For Mum to die. It all just felt so bleak, at the home, when there were no clear days for ages and it felt like visiting a stranger. I used to wish it was over. And now I hate myself for that. Because I feel like I'd give pretty much anything to see her again. To have another hug or a chat or to be told my hair was too short.'

Ruth laughs. Their mother was critical sometimes, and they always went to each other with their stories. *Mum said I never really grew into my nose. Mum said she hoped I wasn't driving.* Kate's hair, cropped close to her head for the past forty years, came up a lot. How men might like it longer, how people might think she was hard.

'Do you think when she said people might think I was "hard" she really meant they might think I was a lesbian?'

Ruth laughs. 'Maybe. I think mostly she wanted to see you settled down again, and mistakenly thought your hair was the key to that.'

Kate shakes her head. 'And she went to her grave with two single daughters, in the end.'

'Although,' Ruth says, 'I never told her about me and Nigel. There was no point. It would have upset her.'

'Yes, she always liked Nigel.'

'More than us, sometimes, I used to think.'

There is a moment of silence, and Kate reaches across to place her hand over Ruth's. They sit like that until the door opens again, and it's Kate's son, James, and he's asking whether anyone fancies fish and chips for dinner. Ruth doesn't think she has any appetite, but the mention of it wakes something up in her, and she says it's on her, as long as James doesn't mind going to get them as she's in her pyjamas. They eat them with loads of salt and vinegar, and they don't talk about their mum again, but she's there, in the background. The way she always will be, probably.

39

Debbie is thinking about what she'll do if Russell tries to kiss her when he slips his hand into hers. It's casual, sweet. They are walking around the park. She has Bonnie's lead in one hand. The kissing, though. She hasn't kissed a man other than Richie since she was a teenager, and what if she's simply forgotten how? Or what if the way she did it with him isn't the way Russell does it, and he thinks she's strange?

'It feels like you're not quite here,' Russell says. 'What are you thinking about?'

And because she doesn't feel able to tell him what she was really thinking about, she says she's worried about Jitu. 'He's just staying on friends' sofas. And he desperately doesn't want to go back to his parents'. He hasn't told them, about leaving uni. He wants to have something to show them before he does. You know, so they'll see he's doing okay. He doesn't want to go home like this, with his tail between his legs. Plus he likes the charity work.'

Russell doesn't say anything and when Debbie turns to look

at him, she can see he's thinking. He's a solutions man. Richie was too. Perhaps all men are.

'So he needs somewhere to live, but not a job?' Russell asks.

'Well, he probably needs a job too, if he can find something he can fit in around the charity stuff.'

'In that case, I might be able to help.'

Bonnie stops and they wait while she looks for somewhere suitable to go to the toilet. She's very particular, and there's often a lot of stopping and starting.

'How?' Debbie asks, genuinely curious about what Russell might have come up with.

'You know my business, the property renovations?'

She nods.

'I could always do with an extra pair of hands, painting and moving furniture around, that sort of thing. If that's something he'd be interested in...'

'I'm sure it is. But what about the living situation?'

Russell scratches his stubble and Bonnie pulls at the lead, so they set off again.

'Well, it's sort of connected. It's not ideal, but I always have at least one house we're working on that's vacant. If he was happy to move from place to place, he could stay in them rent-free. Give him a chance to build up some savings, you know?'

Debbie doesn't know what to say, and Russell must assume she's not keen.

'If it's a stupid idea,' he says, holding up his hands, 'just tell me. I'm not precious. Just firing things out here.'

Debbie pictures Jitu, the way he looked the last time she saw him, when he said he wanted to stay but couldn't. She knows he will go for this, even if it's just a temporary measure. She knows he will be grateful, and work hard, and make it work.

'Thank you,' Debbie says.

'For what?'

'For helping.'

He slips his hand into hers again, and it is cool and dry, and feels different to Richie's, but that's okay. 'Anytime,' he says. 'Anything else, while I'm on a roll?'

Debbie thinks carefully before she speaks again. 'I don't need you to do anything about it, but things are strange with Ruth.'

'Did you say strange or strained?'

'I said strange, but both apply.'

Debbie wasn't sure why, but she'd felt a bit nervous when she'd first told Russell the story of her and Ruth. It sounded so far-fetched, like the kind of thing you'd read in a magazine. Like the kind of thing people almost did read in a magazine. But he'd listened and taken it all in and asked the right sort of questions.

'How so?'

'She really went for me at her mum's funeral. Said all kinds of hurtful things.'

'I think the key word there might be funeral.'

Debbie looks at him, unsure what he means.

'I've seen some otherwise perfectly rational people behave completely outrageously at funerals. They bring out the worst in everyone.'

Debbie thinks of the funerals she's been to, but stops when she gets to Richie's. It's still too painful. 'I haven't noticed that,' she says.

Russell stops walking, looks at her with wide eyes. 'Never? Never seen siblings fighting over the inheritance or a drunk widow listing her late husband's shortcomings? You haven't lived. Stick with me.'

'And you'll take me to some funerals with people behaving badly?' Debbie can't help but laugh.

Russell scratches his head. 'That's not a great offer, is it?'

'Not really.'

'Well, stick with me anyway. I'll show you some happy things, too.'

Debbie believes that he will. He makes her happy by messaging her in the morning asking how she slept and at night asking how her day has been. Sometimes he talks about his wife, and it's sweet, the way he loved her. They've both had their hearts broken, and it doesn't have to be the end.

'So do you think I should just overlook it, the stuff Ruth said? Just go on as if nothing's happened?'

'No,' Russell says. 'I don't think you should do that. I just think you should consider the pain she was probably in, when you're deciding whether you can forgive her. What did she say, anyway?'

Debbie takes a deep breath. 'That I collect people. Jitu and you and' – she nods down at Bonnie – 'Pete and Miles. That I can't pretend those people are really mine. That it's not the same as having a family.'

'Wow, that's quite the little speech. I'm sorry you had to hear that.'

'It isn't true,' Debbie says, and she feels a bit like she's trying to convince herself.

'I know that. And I'm pretty sure she knows it too. If she's anything like me, she admires you for the way you attract people, the way you take care of them.'

They both stop walking, as if by unspoken agreement, and Russell puts his hands on Debbie's waist, turns her so they're facing one another. Debbie feels like she's naked, somehow, when he looks at her like that. Exposed and vulnerable. He reaches out a hand and tucks a lock of hair behind her ear, and then he leans in and kisses her. Gently, softly. And it isn't at all like kissing Richie, but Debbie finds that that's okay, that there is time in her life for a different sort of kiss.

'I've wanted to kiss you since I saw you in that pub with Jitu,' he says.

Debbie laughs. 'Not when I was on your doorstep selling raffle tickets?'

Russell shrugs. 'Maybe then, too. But in the pub, it felt like something vital. It felt like I might die if I didn't kiss you.'

Nobody has said anything remotely like this to Debbie in her life. She has never felt like the sort of woman someone would obsess over. But here is this kind, well-dressed man, who really listens to what she's saying and cares about the things she cares about, and he's chosen her. It makes her catch her breath.

'I think this one's keen to get going,' Russell says, nodding down at Bonnie.

'Yes, it's time I got her home. I'm working in an hour. Thanks for the advice, Russell. I feel better. I can't wait to tell Jitu about your suggestion.'

'And Ruth?'

Debbie considers this. 'I think Ruth and I will be okay. We'll be fine. We're family now, aren't we?'

'And you know what they say about family,' he says.

'That you can't choose them?'

'No, that they're like a compass that always brings you home.'

Debbie has never heard anyone say this, but she doesn't tell Russell that, because it's a phrase she wants to tuck away in her heart. When they part, he kisses her again, just lightly, their lips just grazing. Debbie knows there will be more to come. That one day soon she'll feel comfortable enough to take her clothes off with this man, to let him really see her. She feels a shiver of excitement at the thought, and barely any fear.

After she's dropped Bonnie off, Debbie only has twenty

minutes at home to turn herself around before work. She eats some toast, has a cup of tea. Tries to think about Russell, but finds herself thinking about Ruth. When her shift is done, she will go to Kate's and let Ruth know that she hasn't broken things. That the damage is reversible. After all, like the woman at the magazine said, Ruth has lost two mothers in a very short space of time, and no one is prepared for that.

Jitu's waiting for her on the corner of Maple Avenue.

'Matty's sick or hungover or something,' he says. 'Just you and me.'

Debbie's glad of that, because she wasn't sure how she was going to get to say the things she needs to say to Jitu with Matty around. 'We'd better get a move on, then.'

'I'm handing in my notice at the end of the week,' Jitu says, when they've both been to a few houses and they're heading into a cul-de-sac. 'Admitting defeat. Going home.'

'Is it what you want?' Debbie asks. She feels like she's holding her breath.

'No, but it's the only option left.'

She touches his arm and he stops before turning off for the next house. 'I might have something for you. Well, Russell might.' She explains the offer and waits for Jitu's reaction. It isn't clear, at first, what he thinks. He is frowning, and Debbie thinks perhaps she's got it all wrong. That he might think this is an insult, this expectation that he will move from one house to another like a nomad.

'I don't want to give this up,' he says.

'You wouldn't have to,' Debbie says. 'You could do both. Russell's not expecting to have you full time.'

'You didn't have to do that,' Jitu says, after a pause.

Debbie feels her brow furrow. 'But I wanted to. And if it isn't right for you, Jitu, that's fine. There's no pressure. I just wanted you to have another option, if you could. Russell said you'd come in handy, that he always needs extra help. What do you think?'

He nods, his head low, and when he looks up Debbie sees that there are tears in his dark eyes. Without thinking, she reaches out to hug him, and he folds himself into her arms and they stand there for a minute or more. When Jitu pulls away, he says thank you. He says that it means the world. And Debbie thinks about that all afternoon. About how sometimes it's so easy to do something that makes a big difference to someone else.

40

'I think I'll have a burger,' Layla says.

Ruth nods. 'Have whatever you like. It's on me.'

They are in a bright, airy pub conservatory near Layla and Max's home. Grace is at nursery. She's just started, and Ruth knows that Layla worries she's too young, but she seems to have settled in fine. Things are just different now to how they were when she was raising children, Ruth thinks, and that doesn't mean they're better or worse.

When she called to ask Layla if she wanted to go for lunch, Layla sounded surprised. And it's no wonder, because the two of them have rarely spent time alone together over the years. But Ruth has found that she likes this woman her son has married, that she wants to get to know her better. And she hopes Layla feels the same way. She was quick to agree, after all.

'How's Grace?' Ruth asks.

A fleet of emotions cross Layla's face, and Ruth finds she recognises them all from the rollercoaster of early motherhood. Guilt, anguish, pride, worry. They're all still in Ruth, deep down, when she thinks of her boys.

'They say she's doing brilliantly. Eating, sleeping, all of that. Some babies refuse to do one or the other. I just hope I'm not going back too soon, but we need the money, honestly. And it's not every day.'

Ruth knows what Layla is doing. She's trying to justify it. Not to Ruth, but to herself. She wants to tell her daughter-in-law that there are no right answers, that she just has to do what she thinks is best and hope it all works out. But she doesn't have the words. Not quite. So she sticks to safer ground.

'And how's Max? I haven't seen him since the funeral.' Ruth feels sick when she thinks about the way she behaved at the funeral. She hasn't seen Debbie yet, but she knows she owes her a huge apology. She just hopes Debbie will accept it.

'He's all right,' Layla says. 'I think the news about his grandmother hit him harder than he expected. What with her being his last grandparent.'

'They were close, when the boys were small,' Ruth says. 'Mum used to have them to stay over and do all sorts of activities with them. Painting and crafting, all the things I said no to at home because I didn't want to deal with the mess. That's the joy of being a grandparent, I suppose.' She will do all those things with Grace, she decides. Anything Grace wants. She won't spoil her but she will encourage her interests, whatever they may be. Not that she thinks Max and Layla won't. But grandmother is a very specific role, and she takes it seriously.

'Can I ask you something?' Layla asks. She pours them both water from the carafe on the table.

'Of course.'

'Is it really over, with you and Nigel? I think that's hit Max quite hard too. He seemed fine at first, but since your mum, he's a bit of a mess.'

Ruth doesn't mind talking about this but she doesn't know

quite how to explain. To her, it's so clear and obvious. The marriage had been dead for a long time but it's only now that she's burying it. 'It's over. I'll talk to him, if he wants. But there's no going back.'

Layla nods, looks thoughtful. 'And what will you do?'

'What do you mean?'

'I guess I just mean, where will you live? Will you carry on with the baking business? Are you going to make other big changes?'

Ruth sits back in her chair and closes her eyes for a moment. Big changes. It doesn't feel impossible, like it once did. She will carry on baking, because she loves it. It's a way to do something creative and make money from it, a way to express herself. And she doesn't know where she'll live, not yet. She doesn't want to share a bed with her sister indefinitely, and she's sure Kate doesn't want that either. Could she go to Leicester, to be closer to Layla and Max and Grace? No, she thinks. And for a moment she's not sure what's holding her back. But it's Debbie, she realises. She wants to be able to see more of Debbie.

'I don't have all the answers yet,' she says.

And Layla seems satisfied with that. Their food arrives and Layla picks up her burger and eats it with her hands, seeming to barely notice the sauce that runs down her fingers. Ruth likes to see her like that, enjoying her food, caught in the moment.

'How is it being back at work?' Ruth asks. Layla is going back to her teaching role in September, and for now she's doing bits and pieces of supply work.

Layla puts her half-eaten burger down, eats one fry and then another. 'I love it,' she says, shrugging.

Ruth can tell she feels guilty about it. In the past, she wouldn't have said anything about this struggle. 'That's good.

Motherhood can feel so all-consuming. It's important that you don't lose yourself in it.'

Layla is quiet and Ruth wonders whether she's thinking about the baby she lost. About how life might be different now if she'd decided to have that baby, or not to. Eventually, she speaks. 'Grace is my favourite person in the world, but I can't be with her all the time.'

'And that's okay,' Ruth says. She really believes it. There were days when the twins were young that she thought she would go mad if she didn't get away from them. There were days when she put them in their cots and walked away for five minutes, ignoring their cries. A memory comes to her, from the time when they first had proper beds. Tiny ones. They shared a bedroom and she would tuck them in, making sure they had water and their favourite soft toys. And then she'd go back to check on them an hour or so later and one would have snuck into the other's bed and they'd be lying there asleep, entwined. She feels a pang that's partly about Max and Chris but mostly about what she missed, with Debbie.

'Can I have her for a sleepover soon? Give you a lie-in.' Kate won't mind, she's sure.

Layla nods enthusiastically. 'Anytime you like,' she says.

When they part, after Layla has tried to pay part of the bill and been refused, they hug. Layla is slim and Ruth has always thought of her as sort of fragile, but she is strong in Ruth's arms. Her hug is powerful. 'Give Max my love,' Ruth says. She hopes there will be more of this, seeing Layla away from Max. That it's the start of a new phase of their relationship. But she will phone Max later, too. Try to smooth over what is crumpled between them.

Ruth knows what she needs to do, but it's hard to face it, so she wanders around town for a bit first. She thinks about the way Debbie has with people, the way they are drawn to her. And not just initially, either. They stick around, and love her. Is that what's happening with her and Layla? It feels good to open the doors and really let someone into her life. It's possible that she's learned a thing or two from her twin, even at this advanced age. Ruth has a coffee, buys some flowers. Two bunches, one for Kate and one for Debbie. And then there's nothing left to do but deliver them. Standing on Debbie's doorstep, Ruth tries to prepare herself for any kind of reaction. Debbie might shut the door on her, refuse to speak. She might cry. She might be calm, but say that she doesn't want any part of this now she knows who Ruth really is. But that isn't who Ruth really is, and she hopes Debbie has seen enough to know that. The person she was at the funeral is gone. She was made of fear and grief and loneliness.

Debbie opens the door and just the sight of her is enough to make Ruth feel calmer. 'Oh,' she says. 'I didn't, I wasn't...'

'Are you free?' Ruth asks. 'Even for a few minutes. I just want to tell you how sorry I am.'

Debbie doesn't speak but she opens the door a bit wider, and Ruth accepts the invitation to go in. But then they are in the hallway and Debbie is closing the door and Ruth doesn't know where she should lead them. The kitchen? The living room? Before she can decide, Ruth becomes aware of something moving in her direction and then Bonnie is jumping up at her legs and it breaks the tension.

'Hello, Bonnie.' Ruth reaches out to let the dog sniff her hand.

'Her dads are away for a few days so she's come to stay with me.'

Ruth goes into the kitchen, because it's the first door she comes to, and Debbie flicks the kettle on without asking if Ruth wants a drink. They stand at either side of the small room while it boils.

'I'm so sorry,' Ruth says when the noise of the kettle has died away. 'I was awful. There's no excuse for it. I didn't mean any of the things I said.'

Debbie's expression is neutral, and Ruth wonders how she learned to do that. All her life, Ruth has found herself unable to hide her true emotions. Her excitement, or resentment, or sadness always clear to see on her face. Is that something Debbie learned from their mother? And if it is, what was she hiding?

'I was hurt,' Debbie says, at last. 'But I knew that wasn't you. I knew the you I'd seen all those other times was the real one.'

Ruth feels like she might cry at the relief of it. She's been thinking that she'd spoiled it, this fragile, fledgling relationship they've been building. That she'd torn down in an afternoon what had taken weeks to put together. But Debbie is forgiving; she is good. Ruth should have known.

Debbie makes tea and they pull back chairs and sit at the small kitchen table to drink it. 'What you said,' Debbie says, 'about me collecting people—'

'It was wrong,' Ruth interrupts. 'Please don't dwell on it.'

'I think there's some truth in it. I've always felt like a bit of an outsider, even as a child. It was just me and Mum, and sometimes Granny, but no siblings and not many friends, to be honest. I think when I meet people and they seem to want to be friends with me, even now in my sixties, I get a bit overexcited about that. Sometimes I smother them. I need to learn to take a step back.'

Ruth waits to be sure Debbie has finished. She can see that this wasn't an easy thing to admit. She wants to give it the space and solemnity it deserves. 'I don't think you do,' she says. 'I've seen the way Russell looks at you. I know Jitu cares about you deeply. And Pete and Miles, well, you do such a lot for them, with Bonnie. I'm sure they appreciate it. Please don't let a spiteful thing I said when I was hurting change the way you behave with people. Because really, it isn't that you collect people, more like you're a magnet. You pull people to you, and I don't, never have.'

Debbie laughs then, and it pulls Ruth up short. 'Do you know what I think is going on here?' She is stroking Bonnie, who's sitting by her chair.

'What?'

'I think it's a classic case of wanting what the other has. Or at least thinking the grass is greener, sometimes. I'm pretty sure a lot of siblings do it, but usually they've grown out of it by now.'

Ruth thinks about her and Kate when they were children. How she always wished she had Kate's bravery. How Kate once said, in the middle of an argument, that it wasn't fair how easy Ruth found school. At the time, she'd just brushed it aside. She hadn't found school easy, anyway. She'd just put more into it than Kate, worked harder. But now she sees just what Debbie is saying, and it's like puzzle pieces slotting into place.

'These past weeks, with you,' Ruth starts. 'They've meant so much to me. I had Kate, and I love her to distraction, but I think I always knew on some level that there was someone missing.'

Debbie's eyes light up. 'Yes! I wrote it off as wishing I had a brother or a sister. I used to ask Mum if it would ever happen, and she would get this lost look in her eyes and say she didn't think so. But really, I think I was feeling the loss of a sibling. Of you.'

'I think the key is to keep talking. We're going to hit these stumbling blocks, going to hurt one another. But we have to remember that we've been through something pretty unusual. We've got to help each other through it.'

'Deal,' Debbie says, holding out her hand. Ruth shakes it, and then they don't let go for a few seconds, and a rush of images flood into Ruth's memory. Long journeys in a hot car, games of Monopoly, trips to the seaside. Shopping for clothes, lazy lunches, playing with dolls. All the things she has done with Kate, that Debbie might have been a part of. All the things Debbie would have done alone.

'Thank you,' Ruth says. 'You've been more understanding than I could have hoped for.'

Debbie doesn't quite meet her eye. Is she embarrassed? She shrugs. 'It took us sixty-two years to find each other. I'm not about to let that go.'

41

'We're getting married,' Pete says. 'Will you come?'

Debbie is blindsided. 'Me? To look after Bonnie?'

Pete's brow furrows. 'No, because you're our friend.'

Debbie feels tears prick at her eyes and swallows to counter the lump in her throat. 'I would love to come,' she says.

'Great, we'll have invitations soon but it's on the fifth of September. You know those people who hate their wedding being referred to as a party? I'm like the opposite of that. It's going to be the biggest and best party I've ever thrown, and I once had a party that resulted in two pregnancies, so...'

Debbie laughs. 'It will be good to let my hair down. It's been quite the emotional few months.' Debbie has told Pete about her life in snippets. They chat for five minutes or so when she picks Bonnie up, five minutes when she drops her off. Pete knows about Richie, and about Russell. He knows about Ruth.

'And you'll bring Russell?' Pete asks. 'We'd love it if you could.'

Debbie pictures Russell dressed up for a wedding. He always looks immaculate, and she can imagine him in a suit and tie, shiny shoes. She is meeting him for lunch soon, and she will ask him. It feels like a big thing, their first event together as a couple. But that's what they are now – a couple. She knows he will say yes.

'Yes,' she says. 'Well, I mean, I'll have to check the date with him. I'll let you know.'

Pete waves a hand as if to say it isn't important. 'No rush. Oh, and before you go, can you and Russell come for dinner too? Maybe next Saturday? Miles wants to make you his famous lamb curry. It's really good but it'll blow your head off. I'll tell him to go easy if you're not a fan of spice.'

'Great,' Debbie says. 'I'll check with him about that too. I'll text you. And the spicier the better for me. I don't know about Russell. I'll let you know.'

'Thanks,' Pete says, waving. He's holding Bonnie in his arms and he holds up one of her paws in a wave too. 'See you soon, Debbie.'

On the walk into the town centre, Debbie feels light. It's partly having made up with Ruth, she knows, but it's about Pete's friendship, too. A wedding! It's been a long time since she's been to one and she loves getting dressed up and having a dance. She imagines Pete and Miles, standing at the end of the aisle facing one another. Perhaps they'll have Bonnie there, like a bridesmaid or a ring bearer. She already knows it will be a wonderful day.

Russell's waiting for her, a cold beer on the table, condensation running down the side of the glass.

'Am I late?' she asks, moving her wrist to check her watch.

'No, I was early.' He stands, helps her with her jacket, holds out her chair for her.

Debbie's still getting used to this. Richie never did that sort of thing. It wasn't that he wasn't a gentleman, more that he was absent-minded. There are a hundred ways to show someone you care, she knows now. More than a hundred. She orders a white wine spritzer and when it comes, they clink their glasses together.

'What are we drinking to?' Russell asks.

'Oh, to love!' Debbie says. And then she realises he might be startled by that. They haven't said they love each other. Not yet. 'Not us! Pete and Miles, Bonnie's owners. They're getting married and we're invited to the wedding.'

'I love a wedding,' Russell says.

Debbie is pleased. There is so much to learn, with a new person, and there's always the chance that they'll suddenly say they hate cats or dancing or chocolate and you'll have to look at them in an entirely new way. Everything she's learned so far about Russell has been good. She has her standards. She couldn't be with anyone who was quick to anger or irritable about small things. She doesn't have any time for people who are rude to waiting or retail staff. She has loved one good man and she will only make space in her life for another if he is kind and brings her more joy than worry.

'Me too,' she says. 'Will we dance?'

'Oh, we'll dance all right.'

There's nothing suggestive in it, but Debbie suddenly feels a blush creeping up her neck. One of these days, Russell will want to take her to bed. And she thinks she is ready for that. Perhaps it will be after the wedding, after they've celebrated someone else's love.

'How's Jitu getting on?' she asks.

Russell laughs. 'He's like a puppy!'

Debbie isn't sure whether that's a good or a bad thing. Surely most people wouldn't want a puppy around at their workplace. She raises her eyebrows, invites him to continue. They have placed their order and the food comes, then. Sea bass for him, steak for her. Debbie only realises how hungry she is when she sees it.

'He's full of energy,' Russell goes on. 'Enthusiastic. Works hard. I'm not sure this is the career for him, but he'll do me for now. He's a dab hand with a roller.'

Debbie tucks into her food. It sounds like it's working out okay. She will take Jitu out for lunch, get his side of things. Before Russell made his offer, she had a few sleepless nights wondering whether she should offer Jitu her spare room, but something stopped her. It wasn't that she minded sharing her space, or that she didn't feel safe or comfortable with him. She wasn't sure what it was, exactly. But she's relieved it's worked out the way it has.

'Tell me something from your day,' Russell says.

He always asks this, and he isn't looking for big news. He likes to listen to the small stories, the ones you might forget to share. His asking makes her pick over her hours to find the right anecdote for him. The one that will make him laugh or help him to understand her a bit better. But today, as it turns out, she has big news.

'Ruth came, and we sorted things out.' Debbie feels herself breaking into a big smile, and Russell mirrors it with his own.

'That's a relief. Did she apologise?'

Debbie knows why he's asked this. He doesn't want her to be treated badly, to be taken advantage of. He's told her that he thinks she is almost too good-natured, that he feels like stepping in to protect her. But she doesn't need him to. 'She did but it didn't matter, really. I knew she didn't mean any of it. Grief does funny things to all of us, like you said.'

There's a slightly faraway look in Russell's eyes for a moment, and then he smiles. It's clear, when he talks about his wife, how much he loved her. 'I smashed up someone's car,' he says.

'What?'

'It was just after Gail died. No more than a couple of weeks, I'd say. I don't think we'd had the funeral. I was parking and someone beeped at me for taking the space he thought was his and I got out of my car and gave his a good kick.'

It's so unexpected, so hard to picture, that Debbie can't quite believe it. The Russell she knows is composed, pristine. Always in control. But it's like she said, about grief. It comes out in strange ways, sometimes at strange times. It won't be contained or ignored.

'I think the first time you lose someone very close, that's when you learn how to grieve. I knew what to do when Richie died, because I'd grieved my mum.'

Russell tilts his head slightly to one side. 'But isn't it different, for every person? Different kinds of love, different emotions, all of that. Your love for your mum was complicated, from what I understand, while your love for Richie was simple.'

Debbie thinks about that. He's right, in a way. She realises that what she said, about learning how to grieve, is something she's trotted out over the years. She's not even sure she believes it any more.

'I saw a counsellor for a while,' Russell says. 'She said you have to make friends with grief. I know how it sounds. But you wouldn't feel it if you hadn't loved, so it's sort of a privilege, in a way.'

Debbie feels, as she often does with Russell, like he's held something up in front of her and then tilted it so she can see it from a different angle. She likes that, thinking of grief as a friend. She'll tell Ruth, when she seems strong enough.

'I'm going to ask Ruth to move in with me,' she says.

She hadn't known she was going to say it, but as soon as it's out there, it is so obvious. Ruth's marriage is over, and there isn't really space at Kate's, and Debbie is there, with an empty spare room that she somehow knew she needed to save for someone. The thought of seeing Ruth every day, of catching up on some of the lost time, making breakfast together and learning what Ruth likes to watch on TV, all of it seems exciting. She just hopes Ruth will agree.

'Great. Shall we have dessert?'

Russell has a sweet tooth, loves every kind of dessert from stodgy sponge puddings to light as air mousses. More often than not, when they eat out, she orders something simple like ice cream. But he always wants her to try what he's having. Wants to share the joy he finds in it. 'Yes,' she says. 'Let's have dessert.'

On the walk home, Russell takes Debbie's hand, and it sends a shiver straight to Debbie's core, while also feeling sweet and pure. 'I was thinking,' she says. 'Would you like to come back to mine?'

'Are you propositioning me?' He stops walking, and Debbie can't quite meet his eye. She is sixty-two years old, about to take a man home and let him really see her. She forces herself to look at him, and there is nothing but kindness in his eyes.

'I think I am,' she says. She imagines her embarrassment as a piece of paper, imagines screwing it up into a ball, throwing it away.

'I would like that very much,' he says. 'But listen. I know this is a big deal. It's the same for me. Only Gail for years and years. If you change your mind, just say the word.'

Debbie knows she won't change her mind, but she appreciates it anyway. They start walking again, a little faster, and Debbie can feel her heart in her chest. And it doesn't feel broken. It feels like it's mended.

42

'Was I such a bad husband?' Nigel asks.

Ruth isn't sure what to say to that. Nigel has moved on from not accepting the separation to lamenting it, which is progress. And he wasn't a bad husband by many measures. He wasn't unkind or abusive, didn't hurt her body or her feelings. It wasn't the right fit, and she's as much to blame as him for that, because she stayed. Because she never said that he wasn't giving her the things she needed. 'Don't do that,' she says. 'You don't need to do that.'

He lifts his arms out from his sides and then lets them drop. They are in their kitchen, the place where Ruth has baked and cooked and made cups of tea and talked the boys through various dramas. The light is falling through the window in the way it does in the mid-afternoon, bouncing off the worktop. She will miss this house, and in a way, she will miss this man. But not enough to stay.

'Where are you going to go? Do you expect me to sell this place so we can buy two smaller, less nice homes?'

Ruth thinks it will come to that, eventually. But for now, she is trying to keep the boat steady. She shakes her head. 'Not yet. I'll find somewhere. I'll rent. We both need a bit of time to find our feet without one another.'

Nigel steps closer, and Ruth knows exactly what he's going to say. Going to do. 'I don't want to find my feet without you,' he says, and he tries to wrap her in a hug. But Ruth feels like she won't be able to breathe in his arms, and pulls away. 'Our marriage was a good thing,' he says. 'We raised two wonderful boys. We had some happy times.'

Ruth doesn't know what to say. Suspects she doesn't need to say anything. He is telling himself, reassuring himself. Ruth has spent so long recently worrying about the boys, about the men they've become. But she has to accept that they are works in progress. Like Nigel is. Like she is, too.

'How's Chris?' she asks.

Nigel gives a little shake of his head, and Ruth recognises it. He's shaking off tears, pretending he didn't shed them. It would be better all round to acknowledge them, she thinks, but Nigel is not her project to work on. Especially not now. 'He's going back to London,' Nigel says, a hairline crack in his voice.

'Oh? Has a job come up?'

'He has a couple of interviews. He seems to be quite confident that one of them will come off. But he knows he can come back if he needs to. Unless...'

Ruth can guess what he was planning to say. Unless he's in a boxy one-bedroom flat because she's divorced him and taken all his money. 'He can come back,' she says. 'To either of us.'

She wants to know whether he's softened up at all, about Chris's sexuality. Whether it's something he and Chris will ever talk about. Not about sex, but about love. She can't ask him. Not today. All she can do is be clear with Chris that he can talk to her. That nothing is off-limits.

'Well,' Nigel says.

There's nothing else to say, and he's gearing up to end the meeting. She can hear it in the tone of his voice. Remembers hearing that 'well' when he was standing at the door talking to a neighbour. It's his escape signal. She knows him so well. Will she ever know anyone else the way she knows Nigel? She hopes so. Look at Debbie, well on her way to falling in love again after the devastation of losing her husband.

'I should get going,' Ruth says. 'But would you mind if...?'

'What?'

Ruth tries again. 'Would you mind if I just did a quick walk around the house?'

'It isn't the last time you'll be here. At least, it doesn't have to be. You don't have to say goodbye.'

'I think I do,' Ruth says, and he holds an arm out to indicate that she should go ahead.

Upstairs, alone, Ruth stands in the doorway of the room the boys shared as babies. Later, it was Max's room, and Chris moved in to the one next door, but she will always be able to see this room with a cot pushed against each side wall and a rocking chair between them. The nights she spent in here, rocking and soothing and feeding and changing. They used to set each other off, to tag team. She'd be on her way back to bed after sorting one and she'd hear the cry of the other and feel like her feet were made of lead as she dragged them back. She felt like she was drowning, at the time, and it felt endless, but from this distance it feels like such a short time. What she would give to hold one of their tiny bodies to her chest again, to hear them mispronounce 'sweetcorn', to see their chubby little legs toddling from room to room. It was hard and relentless but there was so much beauty in it.

She doesn't realise Nigel is behind her until he speaks. 'Going back over the past?'

Ruth jumps and turns slightly, and he's a little too close and she worries, for a brief moment, that he's going to try to kiss her. When did he last kiss her? It feels like it's been years.

'Something like that.'

'We did okay,' he says, placing a hand on her shoulder. She's looking into the room and he's behind her, and it would be so easy to take her own hand and cover his, but she doesn't want to give him false hope or confuse things, so she doesn't do it.

* * *

Later that same day, she is in town and she sees Chris, quite by chance. He goes from shop to shop, obviously running some personal errands. Ruth follows him from a distance, not really noticing what he buys but simply observing his interactions. He is a man, has been for many years, but somehow to her he is also still the small boy who held her hand and had to be dragged around shops. Inside his man's body, all the other versions of him nestle, like Russian dolls. And for her, the smaller ones are the ones she remembers best, most fondly. After three shops, she allows him to see her. He has just come out of Boots.

'Mum!' He's surprised to see her, just as she was surprised to see him, despite them both living, for the moment, in this same town.

'Hello, Chris.' They kiss each other's cheeks. 'Dad says you're going back to London.'

'Yes, it's about time. Enough wallowing,' he says.

Ruth shrugs lightly. 'Sometimes we need some time out. But I'm glad you feel ready to get back to your life.'

'Have you got time for a coffee?' he asks, nodding in the

direction of a chain café. It comes as a surprise to Ruth, but she has. She tells him she has.

'I'll get them,' Chris says. 'What will you have?'

'A latte, please.'

'You find us a table.'

There are lots of mums with small children dotted about. Ruth finds a table in a quiet corner. When she was at home with the boys, you just didn't take your children to cafés. There were no cafés that were child-friendly. You stayed at home, or you went to a friend's house, and you did your jobs with the children in tow. So much is geared up for children now. They are the centre of everything. It's not a bad thing, Ruth thinks. Just so very different. If it had been like this all those years ago, would she have treated the boys any differently? Would her relationship with them be altered by it? There's no way of knowing.

Chris comes over with the drinks on a tray. He's brought a few sachets of sugar, and it strikes her that perhaps he doesn't know how she takes her coffee, which feels astonishing somehow.

'Dad's learned how to use the washing machine,' he says, grinning.

'Did you teach him?'

'No, I offered to, but he got the manual out. Sat there with his reading glasses on, holding it about two centimetres from his face. Seems to have done the trick.'

Ruth will not feel guilty about these new skills Nigel is having to learn. He should know them. Even if she hadn't left him, she might have died. Everyone should know how to look after themselves.

'I saw Debbie,' Chris says, and Ruth is genuinely surprised.

'Where?'

'She came to the house, to see me and Dad.'

Ruth thinks about when she last spoke to Debbie. They sent a few messages back and forth yesterday, and there was no mention of this. 'Why?'

'I think she wanted us to understand that all this change isn't about you and her. And to tell us that she's looking out for you. That she loves you.'

Ruth is almost embarrassed at the word 'love'. Almost. 'It's been the most wonderful thing,' she says. 'Finding her. I feel like there was something missing, and I didn't know what it was, and now it's in place. You must understand, being a twin.'

Chris scratches the back of his neck. 'I can't imagine ever not having known Max.'

'No, I suppose you can't.' Ruth pauses, then speaks again. 'I didn't know, that she came over.'

'She said you didn't. It's so weird talking to her, with her being so like you and so different at the same time.'

Ruth nods. She knows how that feels. Sometimes she would decide that a particular mannerism or phrase was Max's alone, and then Chris would use it and she would be back to square one. Her boys were always separate people, just like she and Debbie are, but there was so much similarity to wade through. Ruth sips her coffee, and it is strong and slightly bitter, just how she likes it.

'I didn't get everything right,' she says. 'When you were growing up.'

Chris jumps straight in. 'Nobody does.'

But Ruth puts a hand on his arm to ask him to let her go on. 'You are what me and your dad made you, plus what you've become since. A whole mix of things. But if there's any part of you that feels shame about being gay, that's on us and I'm sorry.'

Chris looks away from her, towards the window, and she thinks perhaps he's blinking away tears. Eventually, he speaks. 'I think Dad's coming round to it, you know. I went on a date last week, and he asked me what the guy's name was. That felt like progress.'

For a few moments, they sit in silence.

'Will you come to visit me, in London? I know Dad hates the traffic but you'd come on the train, wouldn't you? You could bring Debbie.'

Ruth pictures it, the two of them on a train like on their trip to Amsterdam. Debbie's snacks. Ruth looking after the tickets, finding their seats. 'Yes,' she says. 'I'll come. We'll come.'

She feels she can answer for Debbie, because Debbie likes an adventure. Debbie says yes to things, almost without thought. And she is determined to become a little more like that herself, in these remaining years she has to play with. And then Chris stands, says he has to get on, that he has some jobs he wants to apply for, and Ruth stands too. They part at the door.

'Thanks for the coffee,' she says.

Chris looks a bit bashful. 'Thanks for all the coffees,' he says.

She isn't sure what he means at first, but then it comes to her. This is the first time he's bought one for her, but she's bought and made hundreds for him, over the years. He is thanking her for her mothering, and she could weep, because it's the hardest job she's ever done, and the most worthwhile. They hug and Chris walks away, and Ruth watches him go. Striding off at a good pace, knowing where he's going. She isn't so sure, yet. But she'll get there.

43

Matty has given up the charity job and Debbie and Jitu are meeting a new recruit. A girl, this time. Adelaide. Debbie notices Jitu noticing her as she approaches, her dark hair long with a few tiny plaits running through it, her eyes like pools.

'I'm Debbie,' she says, shaking the girl's hand.

'Jitu,' Jitu says.

'I'm Adelaide.'

She looks at Jitu for slightly longer than Debbie would expect, and Debbie wonders if she's witnessing the start of something here. That elusive spark that people talk about. They explain to Adelaide how it all works and she's a natural, charming and polite.

'Are you a student?' Debbie asks her when they take a break.

'No, I just finished my A-levels. I'm trying to work out what to do.'

'Aren't we all?' Debbie laughs.

Jitu tells a story about the house he's living in, how he thought it was being broken into one night and went downstairs wielding a plank of wood only to find a cat had come through the cat flap to get out of the rain. When Adelaide laughs, she has dimples, and it's hard not to join in. Some people are like that, silently inviting you to take part in their happiness. She and Jitu talk easily, swapping stories, and Debbie takes a back seat, listening but not saying much.

'Debbie, tell Adelaide about you and Ruth,' Jitu says, when there's a natural pause in the conversation.

'What about us?'

'About how you met, while we were doing this very job. All of it. It's still the maddest thing I've ever heard.'

They're sitting on a bench, in a row. Adelaide, then Jitu, then Debbie. Adelaide leans forward so she can see Debbie, tilts her head in readiness for the story. But Debbie hasn't worked out how to shape it yet, how to show it to strangers. She doesn't know the ending.

'I have a twin I knew nothing about until she opened the door to me one day,' she says.

'An identical twin,' Jitu adds.

Adelaide's eyes widen. 'No way. Did you see that documentary about those triplets who didn't know about each other?'

Lots of people have asked Debbie this. She has watched it, and it made her cry. Not for them, but for her, and Ruth. 'Yes. They were adopted, though, and my sister and I, we just had one of our parents each.'

'So why didn't they tell you about each other?' Adelaide asks.

Debbie has asked this question so many times. While lying in bed, staring at the ceiling. While going between houses, talking about mental health and suicide and asking for money. While sitting at home, half watching something on TV.

'Are you okay?' Jitu asks.

And Debbie puts a hand to her cheek and there are tears there.

'I'm sorry,' Adelaide says. 'I didn't mean to...'

But Debbie shakes her head, tries to reassure them. 'I'm all right, really. It just hits me sometimes. Our mother, she wasn't well. Mentally. She thought Ruth was evil. Our dad took her away to protect her.'

She hasn't said this, in such straightforward terms, to Jitu, and when she looks at him his mouth is hanging open.

'Shit,' Adelaide says. 'That's heavy stuff.'

They get back to work, and all afternoon Debbie thinks about those words. It is heavy stuff, but it's over now, and she thinks it has a happy ending. She can forgive her mum and her dad, because they both did what they thought was best at the time. They both did what they needed to do, to survive. And she has Ruth, despite it all. They have found each other without even knowing to look, in a town of thousands, a country of millions, a world of billions. They have been so lucky.

When she gets home at the end of her shift, Ruth is there. She moved in three weeks ago and it's going better than Debbie could have hoped. The kitchen smells like icing sugar and chocolate and Ruth says she's doing a stir-fry for their dinner, if that's all right with Debbie. Debbie thinks of the cooking Richie used to do, the microwave meals she's existed on since she lost him. Says that a stir-fry sounds good to her.

They eat it in the kitchen, and it is the best thing Debbie has tasted for a long time. The crunch of the vegetables and the noodles, gloopy with sauce.

'Where did you learn to cook?' she asks.

'Nowhere, really. I just picked it up. I guess a bit at school, but that was mainly baking.'

Debbie has seen the cakes Ruth creates. They are small masterpieces, some of them. 'Will you show me?' she asks. 'The basics? I just... never learned.'

'Of course,' Ruth says.

Debbie pictures them in the kitchen together, ingredients all over the counter, Ruth calling out instructions and Debbie doing her best to follow them. What can she teach Ruth, in return? She can get her car into the tightest of spaces. She can do flamenco dancing. She can play a couple of basic tunes on the piano. What does any of it add up to?

A life, she thinks.

'What are you thinking about?' Ruth asks.

'When Richie died, I felt like my good years were behind me. I knew I'd carry on, because you do, don't you, but I didn't think I had much in my future that would surprise me, or make me happy. And I was so wrong.'

Ruth smiles. 'We should go on another trip.'

'We absolutely should. Where?'

Ruth puts a finger to the side of her lips to mime thinking. 'Italy? I've always wanted to see the Cinque Terre.'

Debbie doesn't know what the Cinque Terre is, but she knows a bit about Italy. Has stood on the Spanish Steps in Rome and looked at art in Florence. 'Italy,' she repeats. 'Let's book it.'

'And if you're still keen, I was wondering about us getting a cat.'

Debbie claps her hands together in excitement. 'I wasn't sure whether it was fair, because I'm out quite a bit, but with both of us here, that won't be a problem. Let's have a look at some shelters online after dinner, see what the requirements are.'

They chink their water glasses in a sort of cheers.

'I don't want to get in the way of you and Russell,' Ruth says.

Debbie bats this away with a hand. There is plenty of time for both. Russell knows how much this means to her. Understands.

'You know, the things I said to you at my mum's funeral—'

'It's forgotten,' Debbie cuts in.

'I know that. But it's been on my mind. I think I was jealous of the way you are with people. The way you've curated your life with all these people in it that you want to spend time with. Meanwhile, I was feeling so trapped in my marriage. It just looked like you had it all worked out.'

Debbie thinks about this. Has she curated her life? She supposes she has. Choosing to move here, after Richie's death. Finding Jitu, and Pete and Bonnie. Russell. When she first met Ruth, it seemed like she had so much more than Debbie did, but now, it doesn't look like that at all. 'Thank you,' she says. 'I think I'm just where I need to be. And we'll get you there, too.'

Ruth nods. She looks content, here in Debbie's small kitchen. 'I made brownies,' she says, jumping up to get them.

Debbie thinks of Amsterdam, the way they talked there, opened up. All that happened before and all that's happened since. All that might happen, in the future.

'Thank you,' she says. And she doesn't really mean for the brownies, and she thinks Ruth understands that.

Debbie looks Ruth in the eye and recalls the shock of seeing her face for the first time. Now, she doesn't see someone who looks like a slightly better-preserved version of herself. She just sees Ruth. And she knows that Ruth sees her.

* * *

MORE FROM LAURA PEARSON

Another book from Laura Pearson, *The Many Futures of Maddy Hart*, is available to order now here:
www.mybook.to/MaddyHartBackAd

ACKNOWLEDGEMENTS

This book is dedicated to my editor, Isobel Akenhead, because she took a chance on me a couple of years ago and has been backing me ever since. It's so amazing to work with someone who's completely open to your ideas and always there when you get stuck. I hope we will publish many more novels together.

The team at Boldwood are truly incredible, and publishing a book is such a team effort. Thanks to everyone who gets involved. Huge thanks, too, to my agent, Jo Williamson, for also taking a chance on me and always being in my corner.

When I reached 30,000 followers on Twitter (when it was still Twitter), I offered to name a character after someone and the winner was Kate Mason (@munchkinmason). Ruth's sister Kate is named after her. Thank you for your name, Kate!

There are so many people who support me with this writing malarkey in different ways. Thank you to all my friends who buy/read/ask about my books. I love talking about my wild ideas everywhere from the school playground to various WhatsApp groups. Special shout out, as always, to Lauren North, Nikki Smith and Zoe Lea, who prop me up behind the scenes. And to Abi Rowson, Jodie Matthews and Lydia Howland, my very clever friends who usually read much more serious literature but sometimes make an exception for one of my books.

This is the first acknowledgements I've written since losing my mum. I'd like to thank her anyway, for just about everything. And my dad, for sometimes chatting through plots even though philosophy is more his thing. Thanks to my sister Rachel for telling everyone I'm a famous author. Thanks to my in-laws for always cheering me on.

The biggest of thanks to my little team: Paul, Joe and Elodie. None of it would mean anything without you.

ABOUT THE AUTHOR

Laura Pearson is the author of the #1 bestseller *The Last List of Mabel Beaumont*. She founded The Bookload on Facebook and has had several pieces published in *The Guardian* and *The Telegraph*.

Sign up to Laura Pearson's newsletter to read the first chapter of her upcoming novel and a free short story.

Visit Laura's website: www.laurapearsonauthor.com

Follow Laura on social media here:

- facebook.com/laurapearson22
- x.com/laurapauthor
- instagram.com/laurapauthor
- bookbub.com/authors/laura-pearson

ALSO BY LAURA PEARSON

The Last List of Mabel Beaumont
I Wanted You To Know
Missing Pieces
The Day Shelley Woodhouse Woke Up
Nobody's Wife
The Beforelife of Eliza Valentine
The Many Futures of Maddy Hart
The Woman Who Met Herself

BECOME A MEMBER OF THE SHELF CARE CLUB

The home of Boldwood's book club reads.

Find uplifting reads, sunny escapes, cosy romances, family dramas and more!

Sign up to the newsletter
https://bit.ly/theshelfcareclub

Boldwood

Boldwood Books is an award-winning fiction publishing company seeking out the best stories from around the world.

Find out more at www.boldwoodbooks.com

Join our reader community for brilliant books, competitions and offers!

Follow us

@BoldwoodBooks

@TheBoldBookClub

Sign up to our weekly deals newsletter

https://bit.ly/BoldwoodBNewsletter

Printed in Great Britain
by Amazon